KINDRED SPIRITS

cover art by George Barr

KiNDRED SPiRiTS

an anthology of gay and lesbian
science fiction stories

•

Jeffrey M. Elliot, editor

ALYSON PUBLICATIONS, Inc.

This is a paperback original from Alyson Publications, Inc., PO Box 2783, Boston, MA 02208. Distributed in England by Gay Men's Press, PO Box 247, London, N15 6RW.

First edition, May 1984   5 4 3 2 1

ISBN 0 932870 42 2

ACKNOWLEDGMENTS

"Vamp," by Mike Conner; copyright © 1977 by Damon Knight; reprinted by permission of the author.

"When It Changed," by Joanna Russ; copyright © 1972 by Harlan Ellison, for *Again, Dangerous Visions*, Doubleday & Co., Inc.; reprinted by permission of Ellen Levine Literary Agency, Inc.

"The Night Wind," by Edgar Pangborn; copyright © 1974 by Edgar Pangborn; reprinted by permission of Mary Pangborn.

"The Woman Who Loved the Moon," by Elizabeth A. Lynn; copyright © 1979 by Elizabeth A. Lynn; reprinted by permission of the author.

"Going Down," by Barry N. Malzberg; copyright © 1975 by Roger Elwood, for *Dystopian Visions*, Prentice-Hall; reprinted by permission of the author.

"Black Rose and White Rose," by Rachel Pollack; copyright © 1974 by Rachel Pollack; reprinted by permission of the author.

"Flowering Narcissus," by Thomas N. Scortia; copyright © 1973 by Auteursrechtenmaatschappij ("A.R.M.") B.V.; reprinted by permission of the author.

"Nuclear Fission," by Paul Novitski; copyright © 1979 by Terry Carr; reprinted by permission of the author.

"Passengers," by Robert Silverberg; copyright © 1968 by Damon Knight; reprinted by permission of the author and Agberg, Ltd.

"The Prodigal Daughter," by Jessica Amanda Salmonson; copyright © 1981 by Jessica Amanda Salmonson; reprinted by permission of the author.

"Broken Tool," by Theodore L. Thomas; copyright © 1959 by Street and Smith Publications, Inc.; reprinted by permission of the author.

"How We Saved the Human Race," by David Gerrold; copyright © 1972 by David Gerrold; reprinted by permission of the author.

Contents

To Rick Sanchez
For all his words, spoken and unspoken,
with love, I dedicate this book.

Introduction

Life, love, sex — possibilities — infinite in number, rich in variety. This anthology explores the subject of same-sex love, within the perimeters of the science fiction-fantasy genre. As such, this is a unique work — the first to deal *exclusively* with gay/lesbian subject matter. While similar stories have appeared in other collections, this is the first volume to focus wholly on the gay/lesbian experience.

Until the mid-1960s, science fiction–fantasy authors, by and large, portrayed same-sex love, in the words of one critic, in a manner that could be described as "offensive, repellent, and clichéd." In many ways, gays/lesbians were treated much like blacks: as non-existent. When they were, they appeared as minor characters, peripheral to the story, often as ugly stereotypes conjured up by homophobic authors. Rarely did gay/lesbian characters occupy center stage — they were, instead, part of the furniture, put there to be laughed at, pitied, or scorned.

As times changed, so did the portrayal of same-sex love. This change is directly attributable to the influence of the lesbian-feminist and gay liberation movements, which fostered a new consciousness about gays/lesbians. As people's attitudes changed, so did fictive literature and the ways in which same-sex love was presented. Science fiction–fantasy characters became more human, better rounded, less stereotypic — they became real people with real emotions — rather than the cardboard stereotypes perpetuated by the straight world. Clearly, progress has been made, though much more needs to be done. Too many gay/lesbian characters are portrayed as tragic figures: pained, flawed, depraved; cheated by nature, spurned by God, doomed to unhappiness. Fictive literature abounds with such characters: characters who are neurotic, schizoid, debauched, promiscuous. . . .

In recent years, more and more science fiction–fantasy authors have sought to debunk these stereotypes — fine writers like Ursula K. LeGuin, Samuel R. Delany, Joanna Russ, Thomas N. Scortia, Elizabeth A. Lynn, Thomas M. Disch, and scores of others. This is all to the good. Fictive literature is a mirror of the real world. As real-world attitudes change, so does literature.

The present work reflects an exhaustive reading of gay/ lesbian–related science fiction and fantasy. Hundreds of stories were scoured to identify twelve which were particularly interesting and provocative. This anthology seeks to portray same-sex love in all its richness and diversity. Some of these stories are romantic, others are not. Some have happy endings, others are quite sad. Some deal with love relationships, others with sexual experimentation. Each story, regardless of its focus, speaks to some aspect or facet of the gay/lesbian experience. They are as varied as life itself and, as such, reflect the wide range of gay/lesbian love and sex.

Keep in mind, these are fictive tales: they are not political tracts or religious sermons. Their goal is not to preach, or advocate, or incite. Rather, they were selected because each, in its own way, is a *good* story — meaning, each seeks to entertain, excite, stimulate, and move the reader. Some will make you happy, others sad; some will please you, others anger you. These are not simple tales with simple messages. In this sense, they are much like life — full of beginnings and endings, some happy, some sad.

It is hoped that this work, when viewed in its totality, will speak to you in words that are powerful, and yet plain, revealing, and yet entertaining. After all, that is what fiction is all about. And maybe, just maybe, it will stimulate a heightened awareness of what it means to be gay/lesbian — both in the real world and in the world of the imagination.

Jeffrey M. Elliot
Durham, North Carolina

Vamp
Mike Conner

Mike Conner describes himself as part of the Midwestern wave of the baby boom. Born in Chicago, he grew up in Hopkins, Minnesota during the fifties and sixties before moving to California in 1970. There, his interest in literature, particularly the stories and novels of "new wave" science fiction, prompted him to try writing. His story, "Vamp," was his first professional sale. About it, he says:

"'Vamp' was written in the fifth week of the Clarion workshop at East Lansing, Michigan, July 1974. Lots of things were happening: tornado warnings, squirtgun fights, and plots to destroy the gigantic pyramid of a summer's worth of Orange Crush cans collected by the rich kid would-be writer across the hall. Our favorite diversion was to go down to the television room on the main floor and watch Japanese exchange students record Nixon resignation speeches and periphera on tiny little cassette machines.

"I had been trying all session long to produce an 'arty' story for the workshop, without much luck. Like many young artistically inclined people, I was very paranoid about my ability to 'make it' as a writer, and as an artist. These fears brewed themselves into the story, which basically became Svengali/Trilby with a twist. The imagery was a Midwestern boy's attempt to be as weird as possible. Fortunately, the story values are strong enough to overcome such earnestness, but if I had it to do over again, I'd give my hero a female comrade/confidante and perhaps lover, just to intensify the choices involved. At any rate, much to my surprise and relief, Damon Knight bought the story right at the workshop, and published it three years later in *Orbit 19*. It holds up pretty well, and I hope you enjoy it."

Conner lives with his four children in Pleasant Hill, California, thirty miles east of San Francisco. His novel, *I Am Not the Other Houdini*, was published by Harper & Row in 1979, and his novella-length stories appear regularly in *The Magazine of Fantasy and Science Fiction*. Presently, he is working on a science fiction novel, *Five Mercies*, between forays into his overgrown yard and roundup expeditions for the kiddies.

Perhaps not all art corrupts; but
absolute art corrupts absolutely.

Sunlight reflected dully from the polarized cap of the Stockton Condo Dome that rose out of the winter-morning Tule fog. Inside, a young man peered through the gloom toward the central plaza. To him, the fog presented a paradox of arrested movement, an ethereal ocean that embraced the entire circumference of the complex. Dieter, nervously gripping his portfolio, thought how dark it was for mid-morning; it was not dark enough, however, to shroud Dwalae Workshop.

There it was, almost at the center of the low curved layerings of Condo units that radiated outward from the plaza all the way to the shimmering margin of the Dome field. It stood apart, different, tawny styroflo exterior a little more massive, sculptured just enough to set it off markedly from any other building within the Dome.

Dieter crossed the plaza, scuffing his feet cautiously on the terrazzo surface, as if the fog could somehow have made the tile slick. It wasn't, and the sharp echoes across that empty space made him a little embarrassed, made him walk a little faster to the Dwalae's front entrance. There he halted to stare at the stylized lettering on the door:

K. KINCHON'S DWALAE WORKSHOP
Fine Transfers

Galleries: Tahoe, Marin, Mendocino, Santa Cruz
DEALERS ONLY

Kinchon: Dieter read the name again. The man whose elegant scrawl had graced Dieter's letter of acceptance was one of the best — no, *the* best — transferist in all of North America. From Canada to Mexico, Kinchon's work was in demand; now he, J. Dieter, was going to work for him. "Join my little stable," the fuzzy voice had told him over the phone. And he would. It was hard for him to push through the swinging panel without a complete surrender to panic. But he did it, and opened his eyes to the cool white of a waiting room.

Dieter stared. It seemed a joke, a mocking understatement. Certainly, it was not what he had expected: ivory wool (yes, wool!) carpet, simple fluorescent panels spaced at odd intervals along the concave surface of the walls. Indeed, the only color in the whole space was the red of two painfully artificial poinsettias which stood on a rough wood dais not quite in the center of the room.

The effect was unsettling, and Dieter wandered around the pedestal attempting to locate a place to sit. Abruptly a young man leaned, penstyle in mouth, from a receptionist's window.

"May I help you?"

"What? Oh." Dieter glanced quickly at his portfolio. "Yes. I'm contracted to work here."

The man stared.

"M. Kinchon requested that I see him first thing today."

"Hm. Oh, yes. M. J. Dieter, is it not? This way, please."

He opened a door for Dieter, then indicated another, stenciled with Kinchon's familiar signature. Dieter hesitated.

"Go on in," the man said. "K's been waiting."

Dieter opened the door to a room decorated in the same manner as the lounge, except that light was provided by a staggered array of skylight bubbles. In a far corner, he noticed two large viewing consoles; on either side of these stood easels and a worktable. Directly in front of Dieter was a large freemold desk where Kinchon sat gazing at some papers. For a moment, Dieter feared that he wouldn't be noticed, but suddenly Kinchon stood up.

All the pictures Dieter had seen of the man did nothing to prepare him for his presence. He was shorter than Dieter had imagined, but powerful, with a bull's chest deeply tanned where his open-fronted velcro jumpsuit revealed a thick mat of bleached golden hair. A platinum cross with a soldered Redeemer twisting across its face hung from a heavy chain around his neck. Kinchon smiled; it was a wide smile, hung between shiny protruding cheekbones and below a drooping dark-brown moustache.

"M. Dieter, welcome!" he said, quickly glancing up the length of Dieter's thin body.

"Thank you, M. Kinchon." (Oh, the feel of that warm steel hand!) "I'm a little late, I'm afraid."

"Nonsense, forget it. We're not peasants, eh?" He gently placed his hand on the small of Dieter's back, guided him to a silk brocade styrobag in front of the shining desk. "Sit down." Kinchon returned to his own chair, then pointed to Dieter's portfolio.

"May I see that, please?" Kinchon opened the portfolio and began leafing throught the work. One by one, he glanced at the sketches and holo reproductions Dieter had selected as his best. Occasionally he grunted, and Dieter had to fight the temptation to lean closer. Finally Kinchon put the work down.

"You like to sketch, I see."

Dieter responded a trifle too eagerly. "Yes, M. Kinchon, that's what I concentrated on at Sorbonne Complex."

"Mm-hm. That's good, Dieter. Allow me to say that there are not many here so proficient as you." He smiled, eye-corners crinkling in a flattering way. "*In* this area. I see you have some transfer reproductions here also. Forgive me, I know my representatives have been over this all with you before. Ah, how much console experience have you had?"

"Three months, M. Kinchon, intensive exercise in console operation and technique. However, as I told your interviewer, these transfers were made from imagined console projections, not actual beaded images. I felt—"

Kinchon held up a hand. "No need to explain — that is simply all the more impressive." He stood up and walked over to one of the consoles. "But please, I wish to show you something." As Dieter stood up next to him, Kinchon activated the screen. "The particular advantages of beaded images."

Even before Kinchon switched to holoproject, Dieter realized that he could make no sense of the image he was looking at. It *seemed* to be a corniced blackness, scuffed with gray dust, with a stark angular shadow thrusting out of the bead field. But the angles and the depth were all wrong — or all right — or simply incomprehensible. Dieter finally looked helplessly at Kinchon, who grinned, twisting his thick silver wristband.

"You see, this is something you could not imagine,

because you can't even identify it. I'll tell you. I sent someone to San Francisco last week to bead the shoe of an aged alcoholic in the old Halladie Plaza on Market Street. The unfortunate man was subsequently arrested, and this is the view from just under the back seat of the police vehicle. With a boosted light level, of course."

Dieter whistled, amazed that the man would attempt a transfer from an image containing so little real information.

"Good, good, you see it. My point is that here at the Dwalae we deal with a certain effect, different from anything the other plastic arts can produce. Of course, this effect is determined by the technology, but the selection of materials and the craft of the transferist do play their part. At any rate, it is the final product that matters, allows appreciation by many more people than do the older forms."

"Much less subjective," Dieter offered.

"Ah, yes." Kinchon strode back to the desk and pressed a button.

"Yes, K?"

"Call everyone in for a moment." He sat down again. "Dieter. I want you to meet my other artists. They are good people, though given at times to excess, eh?" He laughed. The door opened, and five people walked in.

"Persons! This is M. J. Dieter of Sorbonne Complex. He is joining us, our good fortune, as his talents are most considerable."

Kinchon gestured toward a short man with steel-gray hair who nodded curtly but did not extend his hand. "Maximus."

"Dwight." Neither the clipped smile nor the gold brocade tunic impressed Dieter.

A gaunt creature shook his hand limply, leaving a scent of fermenting orchids. "Mm. Silva."

"Bryon you've met already." The receptionist grinned, sagging slightly with a bend of his knee.

"Finally, M. C."

"Excuse me?" Dieter felt distinctly uncomfortable.

"C," C said. "I prefer it to Carruthers, wouldn't you?" He was sullenly British.

"Back to your projects now, children," Kinchon said,

waving them away. Dieter thought he heard someone — was it C? — mumble "Good luck," but he did not count upon the sincerity of this wish. Already the names were fading away, and Dieter was not sure it was worth the effort to keep them in mind.

Kinchon smiled. "They are quite a group, are they not?" He put a heavy hand on Dieter's shoulder, kneaded his neck muscles, a massage that was at once immensely relaxing and a new source of tension. "We want you here, Dieter. Go back to Bryon and he'll show you to your console. Just tell him what materials you'll need — he's quite efficient. Make good use of them and you'll succeed, eh?"

"Yes. Yes, I will. Thank you very much, M. Kinchon."

"Please." The massage ended. "My artists call me K." Dieter nodded, mumbling thanks, then left Kinchon's room.

Just as Kinchon had promised, Bryon directed him (much more cordially) back to a small cubicle that was to be his work area. It was spartan, but complete. In a corner were his console, an older and smaller unit than Kinchon's, and his chair. Beside them stood his plotting easel, and across from that a large worktable equipped with storage bins. After Bryon left, Dieter tilted several of them open and was pleased to find the bins filled with fresh materials. Finally, satisfied with his working environment, Dieter sat in the contour chair and activated the image.

Since his first assignment was more a test than a real project, a subject had been beaded for him. A single fact sheet informed him that the subject lived in the Maintenance compound outside the Condo Dome, and that a fabric-textured bead had been placed on the right sleeve of a work jumpsuit, just above the front part of the hem. The uniform was short-sleeved, so that the bead hung just below the subject's biceps, a position almost impossible to detect, given the quality of beads used by the Workshop. This particular model was a transparent disk that had even been successfully textured to blend with bare human skin.

At any rate, the bead provided an image of exceptional clarity. Dieter sat back and watched. According to the fact sheet, the subject was a waste cycler working a four-hour afternoon shift, so his mornings would usually be spent in his room in the compound. That room, in fact, was on screen now. By making a few exploratory sketches and comparing them to the screen display, Dieter was able to determine that the subject was sitting on a mattress in the corner of the room with his back against the wall, facing a brown wooden door. The subject read a book propped against his thighs, and he periodically brought a cigarette to his mouth by a slow bending of his long forearm.

It was interesting enough, but there was not much material for a transfer. Dieter thought about the theory of art he had often expounded to friends at Sorbonne Complex: that the purpose of art was to make the unnoticed noticeable in such a way as to reveal to the viewer the defects in his own perceptions. As he tried to make *something* out of the flat screen image, Dieter wondered whether his own perceptions were defective. But the fact that he was sitting in a console chair as an employee of the Dwalae Workshop made it an easy thought to dismiss.

Shortly before noon (and an hour after he had become bored, despite his desire to perform well) the image on the screen tilted crazily and grew larger as the subject rose to open the door. Then the image resumed its former angle while a visitor, a young red-haired woman, pulled a chair away from the wall. Hoping for additional information, Dieter activated audio. The woman sat down, petted the cat she had carried in (how perfect, Dieter thought, hands through fur), and asked the subject how long his beard had been growing. She called him Coe.

The conversation was not very interesting, although Dieter was amused by Coe's blunt efforts to resist what was plainly an attempt to initiate a sexual liaison. Eventually, she gave up; then Coe put on a jacket, blacking the image out for nearly forty-five minutes. It resumed inside the metal-gray confines of the cycling plant. That was a subject Dieter had no wish to deal with, so he spent the remainder of the afternoon experimenting with the console, making occasional prints whenever a partial view of Coe's face appeared.

Next morning, Dieter decided to concentrate on details and was ready to search for them when he activated the screen.

Search was unnecessary, however. When the image popped into focus it revealed a wealth of the very particulars Dieter had hoped for. He could see a worn, fuzzy carpet scattered with cigarette butts, sections of old newspapers, balled socks, along with a few books and food wrappers. Never in his life had Dieter seen such an accumulation of refuse! Fascinated, he made several prints of the scene, and was even tempted to begin a transfer. Yet he waited, hoping for more.

Several hours later Coe stood up and walked to the closet. When he turned, Dieter saw a large window just above and to the right of the mattress, centered between it and a cheap lampstand that served as a base for a hotplate and various other pieces of cooking equipment. Despite a thick coating of grease, noon light blazed strongly through the glass, resulting in an amazing visual quality Dieter recognized at once. He wondered if Coe liked the room because of that window. He printed it a few times, but again he waited for the exact image he wanted. Soon it blanked again, however, as Coe went to work. Dieter, feeling there was nothing to gain by spending the afternoon behind the console, decided to go home early to attempt a few full-face sketches of his subject. After all, as Kinchon himself had said, he was not a peasant.

Since Dieter was a new resident of the complex, his three-room unit was at the very edge of the developed area. Still, it was an easy half-kilometer walk, most relaxing to Dieter, who enjoyed exercise. When he arrived he went immediately to the largest and farthest back of the three rooms, one designed as a living area but which Dieter had converted to a workshop. Here the white walls were unadorned, save for a few prints — Van Gogh, Rand — and some of his own landscapes sketched inside French domes. An easel stood next to a tall narrow window that revealed, when the drapes were open, wavering light that passed through the Dome field, and beyond that, the city of Stockton itself. Somehow, the view of the dusty Central Valley depressed him; consequently, he was only able to work with the drapes drawn.

Dieter tossed his portfolio onto an old stuffed chair, then prepared an early dinner. When he was finished, he sat down and began studying the prints he had made of Coe. He was pleased with the contrast between Coe's place and his own spotlessly sterile unit.

Idly he went through the prints again, pulling out several of the window views and arranging them on the floor next to his sketch of Coe's face. Imagine what that man felt when he looked through that filthy glass! The window frame was bright red enamel against the leeched pink of peeling wallpaper, and Dieter stared at the colors until his eyes grew tired and he dozed off.

After a night in the chair, Dieter was not at his best the next morning at the Dwalae. Nevertheless, he was alert enough to seize his opportunity when it arose. He was watching Coe warm some soup on the hotplate, leaning over it slightly to peek out the window. At that moment Dieter lunged at the console panel, slamming the HOLD stud with his fist. He leaned back slowly, almost afraid to see if he had succeeded, but it was there: hotplate, from above, chipped enamel with milk-red soup just boiling up around the edges; Coe's left arm, shadowed, leaning palm-down on the sill. And the window in oblique view, grease split by sun and shadow. Dieter fiddled with the gain until his cubicle was flooded with this light, then sat down, suddenly intent upon an idea.

Reaching over and pulling his easel closer, he punched out print after print of the held image in a variety of projected views. He taped these prints to the top of the easel, then swiveled around to the worktable to get a large rectangular piece of neutral backing plastic. This he placed on the easel below the prints. Carefully then he began scoring the image onto the plastic with an etching stylus. As always, he took all possible care in the crafting of proportion and relationship of objects. And only when he was completely satisfied did he bring out the rolls of shiny acrylic from another bin, along with the appropriate knives, sealing irons and adhesives.

The work went quickly. He stayed late each night for the remainder of the week, making templates and cutting acrylic of various shades of red, gray and black. When he finished, he glued the cut sheets together to create a terracing of color with the window as a focal point, built up high enough to throw an actual shadow inside itself. Dieter fancifully embellished it with a tiny red trash canister embossed upon the alley below the window amidst a riotous littering of garbage.

Dieter further altered the original image by eliminating Coe's arm from the scene. Human forms appeared too stiff in acrylic layering, and anyway, he felt that the bubbling soup (he had had great stinking fun blistering the plastic) provided enough of a human element. He thought it was good; when he had squared all the edges precisely and sprayed the piece with acrylic finisher, he *knew* it was. He decided to ask Kinchon to view the finished piece.

Kinchon answered his intercom summons quickly, bounding into the cubicle with an amazing burst of energy, then halting abruptly to stare at the easel. Dieter watched tensely as Kinchon picked it up, tilting it slightly at arm's length. Inwardly, he was quite proud at the way light reflected off the fine topographic variations.

Finally Kinchon spoke. "What are you calling it?"

"Ah—" Dieter chuckled nervously. "'Soupçon,' I think."

Scowling, Kinchon turned to face him. "No, please, don't ever fool with titles." He fingered his cross. "Hm. How about 'Red in Filtered Red'?"

The wit of his own title faded against against the glow of a Kinchon suggestion. Dieter nodded. "Yes, K, that's amazing. Thanks." Still, Dieter found it impossible to look Kinchon in the eye when the artist put the transfer back on the easel.

"This is not bad, Dieter, much better in fact than I expected. It breaks down in places, here." He pointed to the silver-gray forks and spoons near the base of the hotplate and laughed. "Yes, you do see. These are very gross." Dieter did not see, exactly, but laughed anyway.

"However, I do not think anyone can really criticize you for it, *if* they notice." He placed a hand over his mouth, then snapped his fingers. "Do you know Rudi Gersch?"

Dieter shook his head.

"No matter, you will. He is a close friend with a gallery of his own in Tahoe. This is not quite up to Dwalae standards, Dieter, but. . . let's see. There will be a large showing and party there in two weeks. I'll have him show this, and some of your things from the Sorbonne, and we can go, and you will certainly make a sale and meet some important people." His grin spread as he reached out to pat the back of Dieter's head with a cupped hand. "How does that sound?"

Dieter found it difficult to say anything.

"Do not be modest! Your success is deserved. But do not become self-satisfied, begin work on something else right away! Another medium, perhaps, with the same bead. You can set up holoprojections!"

"Yes. Sine-curve aspects of the conversion were— "

"Well, whatever you decide, work hard so that Gersch can follow up on you." Then, as quickly as he had entered, Kinchon started off.

"And don't worry," he called over the partition, "I get my commission." The workroom door shut on his laughter.

Despite Kinchon's admonitions, it was several days before a renewal of interest in Coe prompted an eager Thursday-morning reactivation of the console. On the screen was the old held image, which Dieter smugly took as an affirmation of his success. Feeling guilty about the layoff, however, he did not stare at the screen long. He punched RESUME and settled into his chair.

The new field was most puzzling. Not only were its angles very odd, but it moved too, rhythmically sweeping the walls of an unfamiliar room. The periodic appearance of Coe's right hand provided no clues and at last Dieter became exasperated enough to activate audio.

Coe was playing a guitar, and playing rather well, too, despite the inadequacy of the audio transmission system built into the bead. The music had an intriguing rhythm to it, matching the sweep of the bead field. Dieter was disappointed when it stopped.

Then the image stabilized. For the first time, Dieter was able to tell that Coe was surrounded by a group of young people dressed in various Maintenance uniforms. Their conversation seemed to concern embarrassing objects found in Condo units during cleanup. Some of the stories were amusing; nevertheless, the sarcastic attitude of the storytellers made Dieter slightly uncomfortable.

A resonant voice, distorted beyond comprehension until Dieter lowered the gain, came over the console. Dieter recognized it as Coe's.

"Yeah, old Charlie, he told me he was cleaning up after a big party in a fiver near the plaza. Got down on the floor to pick up some kind of mess and he found an open box with damn near a gross of cylanite ampules. 'Damn Condopigs,' he says, 'easy to implode when you don't have to work!'"

Some of the people in the room had a rather nasty way of laughing, Dieter decided.

"Then he looked at the nice white atrium." Coe timed his pause effectively. "Which wasn't white — stains of every color, and in the corner, one dead terrysuiter, stained the same way."

Coe laughed. "Well, you know Charley wasn't going to touch a mess like that. Fortunately, the suiter was dead, so Condo Security had to handle it." He played a few chords on the guitar. "Hm. Charlie might have killed the terry anyway, just to stay away from work."

This postscript delighted Coe's companions, but it had a strange effect on Dieter. It wasn't the drugs, or the dead man, or even the flippant attitude toward them. It was everything taken together, disturbing the spherical equilibrium Dieter had always supposed existed under the perfect, nonmaterial Domes. Off-center: like the flowers in the Workshop waiting room?

Suddenly Dieter winced as a flash of afternoon sunlight came through the windows directly opposite Coe. Dieter moved to flip some filtering into line, then froze.

Someone sitting across from his subject was pointing directly bead center.

"Coe. Hey, Coe, what's that shiny thing on your sleeve?"

"What?"

Dieter saw the top of Coe's forehead as he peered into the bead. He had to fight a physical impulse to leave the cubicle. A hand came into view, grabbing Coe's arm and twisting it until Coe's face was directly centered on the console screen for the first time. Dieter printed the image.

Coe had sandy hair cut short and a thick beard which covered his square face.

His nostrils flared slightly. "I'll be damned!"

Dieter was startled back into his chair.

"You know what this is, Morry?" Coe's hand descended, thumb and forefinger looming large, separated, ready to pinch the bead. Abruptly, the image blacked out, but audio continued. "Shit. An image bead."

"Hey, someone's been watching you?" The image resumed, first Coe at arm's length, then over to window light.

"It's not government, is it?"

"Naw. This here's for Condopig scribblers." Coe's voice was nasal enough to rattle a loose screw somewhere inside the console chassis. Fascinated, unable to deactivate the unit, Dieter simply stared.

"With this I play rat-sack man for some vamp with money enough to buy me."

Not me, not me.

"What you gonna do with it?"

"First. . ." Dieter saw Coe's face instantly enlarge so that the screen contained only his mouth and teeth, which reflected the window light in long sculptured rectangles. PRINT, Dieter punched compulsively, PRINT, PRINT while Coe yelled.

"Hey, artist—" *God, can Kinchon hear?* "You eat shit, all your people eat shit!" The image shifted wildly, stabilizing finally as Dieter realized that the bead lay on the floor with Coe and Morry standing above it, their legs thick and tapering, their predatory heads bent.

"You think he can hear this?" Morry said.

"Don't matter. He'll *see* this." Coe brought his foot down on the bead as Dieter wildly punched HOLD, just before the audio terminated in a storm of static.

Even though Dieter knew it was ridiculous, he could not rid himself of the notion that the image of the gigantic heel, with Coe's face tiny along one edge, had been aimed at him. Try as he might, Dieter could not deal with the image and the emotions it stirred in him.

By Friday afternoon, even Kinchon had noticed Dieter's lassitude. "How are you approaching it?" he asked, reaching over Dieter's lap to change console settings. The heel popping in and out of holo right in front of his face annoyed Dieter, but he was too depressed to express what he felt. Instead he complained vaguely about the light level.

Kinchon sighed, ran a hand through his straight black hair, then brought a chair over and sat.

"Ah, I understand the problem. Do you know how many times my own beads have been found in this way?"

Dieter shook his head.

"Well, there were times when the ending was not so quick and easy. I have had the misfortune to bead persons with access to courts of law."

That, Dieter thought, would have been easier to take: a formal exchange of grievances —

"It happens, Dieter, and if you desire material you must take the risk. And after all, it is only a display of beamed electrons, no?"

He smiled thoughtfully and leaned closer.

"All right, Dieter, I must be plain. The first thing you must understand is that the man there" — he jabbed toward the screen with his finger — "counts for nothing. Nothing! We are concerned with one thing only — the image. The situation which produced that image is none of our concern." Kinchon emphasized his last remark by squeezing Dieter's thigh.

"K. Would it be all right for me to rebead this man?"

Kinchon's eyebrows rose.

All right, in your terms then. "I wish to prove I can deal with this subject in an objective manner. Let me get some new material and I think I can get over this block."

Kinchon rubbed his chest hair as he considered. Then, curtly, he consented. "But it is a shame you don't work on this one," he said, leaving. "It has so many possibilities."

Dieter chose to ignore this advice. Coe's violent act had disturbed the quiet relationship Dieter had enjoyed with his subject, and that relationship had to be reestablished before Dieter could hope to deal with the material. Plainly, Dieter felt like a cheap voyeur, and he *knew* he was anything but that. Only Coe could free him.

He went quickly to Materials, obtained several beads, then went back to Bryon's office to find Coe's address. Bryon was reluctant — he insisted on confirming Kinchon's permission —

but still Dieter was able to get what he wanted and was out of the Workshop, headed for the Maintenance compound before three. To get there he had to pass through a busy service checkpoint. This was a wide portal in the Dome field crowded with Maintenance personnel and their vehicles. Condo Security examined his membership certification and held it, issuing him a chit. Then Dieter walked past, feeling a faint tingle on his face as he emerged from the field.

Dieter had spent most of his life inside domes, and the experience of standing outside in the open air always unnerved him a little. Now, with the apprehension he felt toward the task at hand, he felt nauseated. The sky was large — too large — and its clarity seemed like some amorphous weight pressing on him. But Dieter managed, with several deep breaths, to control his stomach; when the dizziness passed, he studied the map Bryon had drawn for him.

Coe lived on Av D, Number 135, easy enough to locate since the compound was laid out on a grid. As Dieter passed Av A, he was most impressed by the design and arrangement of the old buildings. It was said that the compound had been an undomed complex late in the last century, and he believed it; the wood-framed structures were covered with a patchwork of weathered pine shakes and yellowing styroflo, the result of the activities of wood scavengers during the Twenty-Year Depression. Dieter was glad of the vandalism, because the juxtaposition of natural and artificial building materials made for an interesting texture. These were narrow buildings, starkly angular, with many windows. In Dieter's opinion they had more character than any of their successors inside the Dome field.

He reached Av D and walked slowly down to 135. There, a dirty glass door led to a staircase. Hesitantly Dieter touched the buzzer. But there was no response; then Dieter remembered that Coe would probably still be on his shift. Somewhat relieved, he sat down, pulled out his sketchpad and furtively observed the activities of the Maintenance people who passed.

For almost an hour he sketched the unit facing him across the Av, inventing different proportions and elevations. When street traffic increased, he stopped to check his watch. Four-twenty: the shift had ended and people in Maintenance uniforms were entering the buildings all around him.

Coe would be coming! The thought frightened him enough to make him think of returning to the complex. But what would he say to Kinchon, who had shown trust, however reluctantly, in his judgment? Firmly, he slid the pad back into the portfolio, feeling the tiny bulge the beads made in the inside of the zippered pouch.

Then he heard a voice, *the* voice, there was no mistaking it. Dieter forced himself to be calm. He turned in the direction of the sound and saw him, shocking in his solid, vital presence. Strangely, all of it — the beard, the blue eyes, everything Dieter had so casually sketched — was less emotionally intense than on those frightening prints. But there was more, Dieter realized, a way of moving, an odd combination of the fluid and the mechanical, a pulling stride that was directed by a bent head rocking a broad yoke of shoulders. He stepped in his heavy workshoes so close to Dieter that for a' terrible instant he loomed just as he had in the heel image. Dieter drew his knees up.

Coe checked his mailbox, took a key from his jumpsuit pocket. But before he could put the key in the lock, Dieter was there behind him.

Coe turned, just as Dieter was about to tap his shoulder. "Ah, ha, excuse me. Your name is Coe, isn't it?"

"Yeah," Coe said quizzically, one hand on the doorknob. "You know me. Who're you?"

"Dieter. I'd like to talk with you" — Dieter stared at the ground between them — "about that bead you found this week."

Alarm hardened Coe's impassive features. "Hey, look, if you're Security, I know right where it gives the rules about remote surveillance—"

"No! No, I'm not Security. The farthest thing from it, in fact, I work at the Dwalae, and I was at the console when you, uh, terminated the broadcast."

Coe relaxed, looked at him, laughed softly. He stared at Dieter again and laughed very loudly while Dieter gripped his portfolio tightly.

Then the laughter ended. "I ought to waste you, pig."

"You won't even find out why I want to see you?"

Impassive once again, Coe simply shrugged and turned. "Come on," he said, starting up the narrow stairway. At the second-floor landing Dieter was startled as Coe stepped around a naked woman who was talking into a pay phone. She smiled and waved at Coe, who merely grunted, continuing to the third floor. Halfway down a dark corridor, Coe unlocked a door and suddenly they were in the room.

His room! There it was — the mattress, the closet, the littered floor. And the window, different in the evening light, of course. The door closed. Coe paced in front of it.

"All right, Condo boy, tell me why you're here."

"I want to explain."

Coe nodded, continuing to pace. *Where could I bead to catch that motion?* Dieter realized that it was the wall that should have been beaded in the first place.

"You want to explain. Since when does a screen vamp have a conscience?"

"Since me. No, please, I'd just like you to look at what I was doing." Dieter reached into his portfolio, pulled out the holo reproduction of "Red in Filtered Red," and gave it to Coe. The tall man halted to peer at it.

"I watched you for a week. I got involved, and what you did was a shock. I'm still involved. That's why I came."

"Hm. My window."

"Yes, your window. I did it hoping that people would see something there that would make a difference the next time they walked into their white bedrooms."

Anxiously he watched Coe, who tilted the transfer the way Kinchon had. Suddenly he was grateful for Coe's openmindedness; the man apparently appreciated the complexity of the situation. And Dieter smiled a little too — for the first time his theory of art had practical application, and here, in a built place, it sounded solid. More solid, in fact, than all the echoing bulk of the styroflo Condo units.

"You like the window, huh? What's your name again?"

Dieter told him. Coe's deep laughter came, genuine, its phrasing matching the rhythm of his walk. "Yeah, it's a nice view. Saw Stockton all summer long. You been to Stockton?"

"No."

"You wouldn't like it." Almost shyly, he handed the holograph back. "Let's see something else."

Dieter gave him some of the partial face sketches, and, sensing a warmth between them, took the opportunity to apologize for the beading.

"I didn't do it. You see, you were my very first subject for the Dwalae, and the staff did it for me before I even came here. It's not something I really approve of, but as I sort of said before, there's always the possibility of working change in any art form." He retrieved the sketchpad while Coe settled onto the mattress to look at the rest of the drawings.

"I really prefer to sketch, you understand, and there's absolutely nothing worth drawing at the Complex." He hesitated. "You wouldn't mind if I sketched you−?"

"That depends." Coe slid the sketches across the carpet toward Dieter. "On the deal. Young man, are you vamping me?" The blue eyes didn't waver.

"Coe, this transfer will help change this rotten system − I live in there, you live in here−"

"Don't forget Stockton," Coe said drily.

"We should all be living in the same place! Look, Coe, I think my stuff is different enough to matter. Art is a way of showing people how wrong they can be, if it's done in the right way."

"Okay, okay. I've seen beadwork before. Used to work in a component shop. Maybe you can give it to those grumbies you live with. So shit, yeah, sketch, but not now. Come back later and let me see what's happening." He stretched and stood up. "I gotta take a leak. Be right back."

Without hesitation Dieter reached for a bead. He looked at the wall for a good spot, and when he was satisfied he peeled the backing off the tiny disk. He slapped in onto the stained wallpaper, then resumed his position, as if negating what he had just done.

When Coe returned, hand on zipper, Dieter obtained a vague promise to meet sometime in the future. Then he left to reenter the windless security of the force dome.

On Monday, Kinchon surprised Dieter by visiting the cubicle to remind him of the party. When he saw the new bead field on the screen, however, he scowled.

"Why place the bead in such a position? There's not much more that you can do with such a view, is there?"

Dieter was suddenly annoyed with Kinchon. "There wasn't enough time for me to find another place. He was gone for only a moment. Besides, I've got another idea for a different approach to the window. I want to make it part of a series."

Kinchon sighed. "Fine. So long as it succeeds." Dieter was sure the transferist thought he was wasting time, and he was prepared to argue; but Kinchon abruptly changed the subject.

"We will, by the way, fly to Tahoe in my hopper."

"Thanks, K."

Kinchon nodded, looked once more at the screen image, then left the cubicle.

The centered window threw a marvelous pattern of changing light and shadow onto Coe's furnishings, and sometimes Coe himself would come, somber, to muse by the window with arms folded. Each time it happened Dieter printed the image and taped it to the easel; soon the easel was entirely covered with Coe, frozen in various postures. After Coe had gone to work, Dieter spent his time assembling power components for a linear series of holoprojection strips in ascending tones, soft yellow to murderous red. With everything fabricated in advance, he might be able to assemble another transfer in time for the weekend showing. All he needed was a suitable image.

Next morning he watched Coe dress. Slowly, with Dieter following every move, Coe sauntered to the window. "Over a little, Coe, come on," Dieter muttered, and Coe seemed to respond. Suddenly he was dead center in the field, pausing in the window light, face absolutely void. One knee was bent slightly toward the bead. Dieter jammed his finger against HOLD: He had his image.

The crafting of this transfer took only about three hours. Once again he used acrylic sheets, this time as multicolored puzzle pieces in a planar rendition of the window, with Coe a gray silhouette inside it. Then, using this figure as core, Dieter mounted a succession of the holo strips to form a concentric layering of Coes, partly transparent, all surrounding the window. The shape of the finished piece *was* Coe, reduced in size and dimension but startling all the same.

Friday afternoon Dieter took the new transfer directly to Kinchon in hopes of having it presented with the other piece. At Kinchon's door he was nearly knocked down by two grinning dealers. They left the door open; inside, Kinchon was shouting violently into his phone. When he noticed Dieter standing in the doorway, he wiped his forehead with a damp silk handkerchief, then motioned him toward the styrobag. Dieter sat patiently until Kinchon was through with his tirade.

Wearily Kinchon blanked his screen and walked around the desk. "Ah, my apologies, Dieter. A dealer has attempted to take advantage of us. So! You've finished another one. Hold it up for me, please."

Dieter held it tight between his own face and Kinchon's.

"All right."

Dieter looked at him.

"Please, enough." The transfer went back to Dieter's lap. Kinchon leaned against his desk, moved his hands back and forth along its edge.

"You have fine technique in this, Dieter." His voice rose. "But again you are fascinated with the man." He shook his head. "No, this will not sell, Dieter, do you know why?"

Though he resented this blunt rejection, Dieter tried to seem unconcerned and open to criticism. "I really didn't think about that. I just did the transfer."

"Not thinking of selling! A serious fault in a commercial artist, Dieter. But beyond that, this is not a transfer. It is a sentimental fantasy, which would not be so bad, except for the fact that it is entirely subjective. Can anyone who does not know you or the subject guess the reason for this type of presentation?"

"I would think so."

"Then you are wrong. For instance, what about this man is so gray, so small? His soul, his body, who can tell? And why this magnificent expansion? Because he had the heroism sufficient to destroy a small piece of solid-state equipment? Pure projection, fancied with Dwalae facilities." He walked behind the desk, pulled open a drawer and withdrew an enameled box, from which he took a tiny red pill. "Really, Dieter, there is no excuse for this." He swallowed the pill, sighed deeply.

"You must excuse my curtness today, there have been some business unpleasantries. My point, without attacking you personally, is that this is not commercially saleable because it ignores the boundaries of the medium. *You* see what is here, but no viewer ever will. I warned you — I felt you should have moved on to other subjects. But I was inclined to trust you. If my trust was rewarded with your mistake, well—" The phone buzzed. "That is my mistake. Yes, David, how goes it!"

Dieter turned to leave.

". . . a moment, David. Dieter, it is an exercise, so do not become discouraged. Next week we start again, eh? Oh, and meet me here tomorrow at nine?"

Numbed, Dieter nodded and returned to his cubicle. The console screen was still activated, but since Coe had left for work the room was empty, a held image without the tension generated by his presence.

Searching for that presence, for that part of Coe that appealed so powerfully to him, Dieter closed his eyes and with an act of will placed Coe in the screen image. There he was, clothed, nude, clothed again; on the floor, legs apart, leaning against the table, cigarette burning dangerously close to that dry lower lip. Finally the fantasy stabilized, oh so beautifully. There was his man, near the window, his naked body edged in a beige glow that dissolved like sugar to shadow-suggestions of limb and torso. It was vivid enough for Dieter to hit the HOLD stud; vivid enough for Dieter to be desperately confused when he confronted that empty, static image. He didn't bother punching RESUME. He cut the power and went home, taking the new transfer with him.

Dieter woke groggy from the effects of a half-liter of anisette. A hot shower clarified his mind. He was going to Tahoe, work in hand! Tahoe, the most affluent complex on the entire western coast of North America, a center of art and culture. Everyone he had ever wanted to meet, everyone who mattered — patrons, promoters, all with money enough to indulge a taste for fine art — lived there at one time of the year or another. People he wanted to change — but to change them he had to meet them and be taken into their confidence.

He spent the day gathering energy; when evening came, he put on the royal blue jumpsuit he had bought in the duty-free shop at Orly Transmat. He felt quite decorative, felt even more so outside the Dwalae when he saw Kinchon's chrome hopper resting on its three rollers, its opened bubble reflecting the low crescent moon in curved slashes. Gingerly, Dieter bent over to admire the crystal panel display, the monogrammed joystick, the upholstery of the contour seats. It was beautiful. Not something to be owned, necessarily, but something to be seen in, definitely.

Kinchon called from the doorway and urged him to get in. He did so, staring as Kinchon approached. The transferist wore a golden jumpsuit, open to the navel and bound at the waist by a sash formed of tiny linked rings of white metal shiny as the hopper. The platinum cross was gone, replaced by a choker of the same metal as the sash.

Nodding to Dieter, Kinchon dropped a briefcase behind the pilot's seat, then stepped in and turned on the panel lights. Even in their soft glow Dieter could tell that Kinchon's tan had been chemically renewed. For the first time since Dieter had known him, Kinchon looked like the old idealistic concept of K. Kinchon, Master Transferist. He was beautiful, all jeweled flash and white-toothed glint. Still, Dieter wondered whether there was any substance to the man to compare with the solidity of Coe's far different life. He found the comparison unpleasant.

"Ah, now we have a *complete* cockpit, eh?" Kinchon said as they taxied through the hopper portal. They lifted off with barely a whisper from the air induction tubes. Kinchon said nothing until they reached cruising altitude. Then he leaned back from the controls.

"You look good tonight, Dieter. You will fit in well." Dieter was flattered, but relieved when Kinchon excused himself to examine some papers from the briefcase. It was enough simply to be able to watch the Sierra foothills pass below as mottled pools of black/gray in the transparent moonlight. The newsfax forecast had been correct — it was a clear night in the mountains, and the sight of the Sierras, jagged and dusted with the season's first snowfall, obliterated any trace of the strange thoughts that had disturbed him all day.

As they traveled into the mountain range, Dieter peered ahead until he was sure of the bulbous glow he saw well up the side of a large peak. It was Tahoe Complex, just as he had seen it in holo reproductions. Four kilometers of dome blistering the side of Silver Peak, the Complex dominated the entire Tahoe Basin. The mountainside had been carefully stripped and reworked so that a terracing of subcomplexes ascended to the peak, all protected by the obliquely bulging dome. Now, in the basin, Condo light competed with moonlight, a harmonious duel which cast a pale yellow on the snow. Kinchon continued studying his papers as if they were doing nothing more than driving over a dirt road. *He's used to it — he lives here.* Still, Dieter was convinced that Coe's reaction would have been at least appreciative.

"Here already?" Kinchon crammed his papers back into the briefcase, then pressed a stud on the panel. They descended slowly.

"Do you see, Dieter, there is our party." Kinchon pointed out what appeared to be a flaw in the dome high above the rest of the subcomplexes. In it, Dieter could almost make out tiny figures, but the hopper landed before he could be sure. A valet attended to the hopper; they got out, entered a small pneumatic tube that whisked them up the mountain? through it? to the party area.

The tube ended at a round platform perhaps a hundred meters in diameter, illumined by wedge-shaped floor panels. Along the perimeter was the exhibition — various works of art interspersed with large potted plants and pieces of furniture which stood unused, possibly because they provided no good view of either art or people. Most of the guests were crowded about the bar and buffet in the middle of the platform, where the gray noise of conversation drowned out the electronic efforts of the music generators.

Such scenery! Of course, the pale mountains surrounded everything here, but they were pale indeed in comparison to the people — hundreds of them, arrayed in a dazzle of color. There were several faces Dieter recognized immediately, but when he turned to Kinchon to ask about them, he discovered that his companion had been led away by an eager group.

Left to himself, he scanned the display area for his own work, and spotted it on the opposite side of the platform. He circled toward it, avoiding the knots of guests in the center.

There it was. Not near the best mountain scenery, of course, but nicely mounted on a slab covered with black velvet. His pleasure faded, however, when he discovered that his name had been misspelled "Deiter" on the small white card below the transfer. Glumly he stood back a little to watch the guests as they drifted by.

"*Tsk.* My God, Jorma, look at this! How absolutely depressing!"

"Oh, I don't know, Edith, it's—"

"It's not something I should have to look at. This Deiter person ought to have known better. Or at least Rudi should have, I'm going to talk to him. To even *think* of living this way!" She pulled her escort away.

"Condopigs," he muttered. People like her knew nothing, could learn nothing. In his frustration he walked blindly into a crowd that had collected in front of the piece to the right of his. He pushed his way through until he could see the object of their interest.

He stared, horrified. Here was a mixed-medium oil-and-holo competently executed, but of a completely degenerate character. Two stallions were fighting in a field; the mouths of both animals were open, hideously grinning, teeth smeared with holo-projected blood.

Turning away in anger, he found himself facing Kinchon. Something was wrong with the man. His mouth was like a gaping wound; his eyes were glazed, he blinked continually. "Dieter," he said, almost in a whisper, caressing the back of Dieter's neck. "Here." His other hand came around under Dieter's nose, popped a tiny ampule, releasing a puff of lime-green dust.

Instantly Dieter's eyes filmed over. He tried to blink the tears away, but could not. It was as if his visual field had expanded horizontally, narrowed vertically, while thoughts sped through his brain like a plaza faxstrip display. All of it was helplessly observed by a tiny bubble — for that was how it seemed — of fascinated objectivity. The discrepancy between the two thought-forms was immediately, sickeningly funny. Dieter giggled, awash in the moist warmth of Kinchon's hand.

"You do like cylanite, yes?"

"Oh, yes. Never, thank you, K, never had it be—"

"Good, good." Then the touching stopped and Dieter, coasting on the dwindling sensation, realized that Kinchon was gone again. He turned, vaguely searching, until he lost his balance and fell upon a providential couch to watch the distorted movement of color and form around him. He longed, achingly, for Kinchon. But the small part of Dieter untouched by the drug picked out only one face — was it Carruthers'? — from the muddle before it.

Then, gradually, the ocean cleared, the bar and the music generators rolled silently away from the platform center, leaving a space adorned only by the inlaid shield of the complex, an ambiguous heraldry of crystal and rosewood placed (deviously placed, the bubble insisted) just off center, a nagging, incorrectable deviation from the perfect. Dieter licked his lips.

"Entertainment!" someone called; from the tube exit spilled a running stream of black-clad attendants bearing armfuls of small objects which they piled in the middle of the platform. Dizzily Dieter got up and circled the ring of spectators, his wide-band perception noting that the objects were stuffed animals of some sort, the bubble determining that they were either lemurs or tarsiers. A smaller group of attendants clad in scarlet moved to the pile, each one holding an instrument resembling a large gilded garlic press. Dieter blinked; the yellow sparkle from the animals' eyes was almost too much.

Back to back, the attendants put their animals into the presses, then gently closed the handles until only the soft furry-brown heads were visible.

How orderly. A jarring screech startled him. Whizzing lemur eyes separated from exploded heads, saucering high overhead: screaming guests retreated from a heavy spray of red liquid which rolled, like mercury, on the floor. The bubble protested weakly, while the rest of Dieter watched the last few eyes caroming off the dome. He was jostled in the scramble for lemur souvenirs, and he wanted very badly to see Kinchon again.

A servant with a squeegee touched his arm impatiently, then when Dieter failed to respond, pushed him aside to continue moving the remaining drops of fluid to a small glistening pool near the bar. Light from the floor panels began to fade. Suddenly Carruthers was there, frowning.

"C! Oh, ha! You've got some of that stuff on you." Dieter tried, clumsily, to brush the glistening droplets off his sleeves.

"Leave it, Dieter. God, K's done it again."

"K. Yes, K, I must see him. C, all in gold—"

"*Shh.*" Around them, the party noise dwindled. Carruthers whispered: "You'll see him soon enough." Then he was gone. Unsteadily, Dieter leaned forward to see that only the shield remained illuminated, silhouetting the ruins of the exploded toys. No one spoke.

Suddenly someone ran past Dieter, a lithe androgynous figure dressed in a pale body stocking. As it flashed into the open space, Dieter saw, blearily, that a softly pointed cap of the same material covered its head and shoulders. A young Amanita mushroom, the bubble noted.

"M. Kinchon to do the honors!"

And there he was, Kinchon, jumpsuit shimmering in the interrupted light, a long knife held in both hands above his head. Dieter reached out in the darkness toward the devastating radiance.

Slowly Kinchon walked an eccentric route about the figure, which held its position, trembling. The knife was put to use; Kinchon cut the costume around the circumference of the cap. Then, winking, he reached up and grasped its point.

"Now—"

The lights came on full as he pulled the cap away.

Galvanized, Dieter stared at a face obliterated by glossy

flesh putty that concealed eyes, nose and ears. Only a slick and vivid red mouth remained to open and close slowly below the word "head" stenciled on the forehead. Spasmodically the figure arched its back to applause that began softly, then rose to a laughter-filled crescendo.

"Circumcision!" Kinchon screamed, both hands high again. The figure (a dancer, the bubble told Dieter) settled into graceful repose at Kinchon's feet.

Kinchon! The drug ravaged Dieter's stomach, but oh, how he wanted Kinchon. Even so, the bubble still had a voice of its own: Coe, Dieter seemed to hear, Coe, Coe, but it wasn't right. Kinchon was there and he wanted to leave with him now.

He drifted into the circle, where Kinchon was talking to the dancer and two women. Touching K's shoulder, he waited for him to turn and then stared with everything he felt into quizzical, then decidedly satisfied eyes.

Dieter began perspiring. "K, please. Could we go now?"

Kinchon laughed a little nervously in the direction of the women, who regarded Dieter suspiciously. "You do not like this? Dieter, you haven't yet met Rudi—"

"Another time. Now, please." He closed his eyes until the new drug-waves passed.

Kinchon shrugged. "Camella, excuse me please. The young man has had his first sniff of cylanite, so-o-o... Perhaps I will be back."

"I doubt it." The dancer laughed as her two companions helped her move off into the crowd.

They returned to the hopper pad in silence, Dieter unable to express his confused thoughts and emotions. Finally, when they were well away from the complex, he put his hand on Kinchon's shoulder.

"I'm sorry, K," he said blurrily. "The entertainment — I just couldn't—"

"No need, no need, it's just as well, Dieter. The party was a bore. This is just fine." He opened a compartment between their seats. There was a rattling — like the rattling of beads, said the bubble — then Kinchon busied himself with his sash for a moment. "More cylanite, Dieter?"

No. He shook his head. There was enough drug in him,

more than enough desire for contact, the flowing contact toward which he knew he was moving. The pale blister of the Stockton Dome was below suddenly, and as they landed and taxied toward Dieter's unit, he knew that something of this great artist would come to him. Shyly, Dieter leaned his head against Kinchon's powerful shoulder. He was rewarded with a smile; then Kinchon pushed him gently away.

"Dieter, up now. Yes, move slowly, that's it." Dieter managed to get his other leg out of the cockpit. "Now. Let's see where you live."

"My doorway's too wide, K." He giggled helplessly as Kinchon pushed him toward it. Somehow Dieter managed to get the door open and his hall lights switched on.

And there K. Kinchon stood, fingering his choker in a way that excited Dieter intensely. Apparently Kinchon had been feeling the effects of the drug too; shiny rivulets of sweat ran down the open V of his jumpsuit. Trembling, Dieter approached, hand extended, his intention to run a single finger slowly down that slick brown chest. But Kinchon grabbed his wrist suddenly, twisting it enough to hurt as his smile flowed smoothly. His eyes shone.

"What do we say, my young friend?"

"Wha—" Very softly: "Please?"

"Ah-ha. I could not hear you."

"Please," Dieter said, pulling his wrist away, melting.

"Much better. You learn quickly. Here" — he pulled Dieter onto the bed beside him — "we must sit together."

They faced each other, Dieter's thought bubble noting with resigned amusement the extent to which sweat stains had spread under both golden arms of Kinchon's jumpsuit.

Love, for this man! Attempting to express it, Dieter's lips only met Kinchon's salt palm. The man laughed and stood up, staring thoughtfully at his hand.

"Truly an eloquent invitation, J." Wide-eyed, Dieter looked up; Kinchon had never used this diminutive before. "However, reality intrudes upon the vapors of love. I have not been near a rest room all evening. Please, Dieter, may I use yours?"

"Uh, through here." Dieter switched on the light to the

workroom and pointed to the bathroom door. As he brushed the hair on Kinchon's forearm, the man suddenly stiffened.

Kinchon was staring at a wall covered with the sketches Dieter had made at Coe's room. His brown face went livid.

"What is *this!* You bring me here to mock me! Perhaps you love me, eh, just as you love that man there!"

Coe? Not now, oh God— Dieter's voice broke. "Please, K."

The smile hardened, as if encased in lucite. "Please," Kinchon mimicked. His hand fumbled with the sash for a moment, then cupped Dieter's neck gently.

"Is this what you like, eh?" The grip tightened cruelly; suddenly Dieter was pushed back onto the bed. "Yes, moan, you idiot. You take me for a fool! Making overtures to me when you are so obviously fascinated with that lowlife who never should have been beaded in the first place." Again he mimicked: "'I wish to deal with this subject in an objective manner.' Faugh!"

The door slammed and Dieter was alone.

In bed, alone between cold sheets, he realized what was wrong. He had wanted contact, yes. But he had gone to the wrong person.

Dieter's mind was clear and determined when he awoke. For the first time in weeks, his situation was plain. The job at the Dwalae had ended, he knew. But that was good; console spying would have destroyed him eventually, made him into another Kinchon, insulated, callous. All his life he too had been insulated, but only because he had known nothing else. Now he would leave the condos to travel with Coe, perhaps to the city, to gather material no other transferist could ever hope to capture. Together, they could change everything.

Outside the Dome it was cool and clear, strangely silent, with little traffic between complex and compound. At 135 Av D Dieter found the stairway door unlocked. He ran eagerly up to the third floor. There was no response to his rap on Coe's door. He knocked again. "Yeah, come in," came low and muffled from behind the door. Dieter opened it.

Coe stood by the window, silhouetted by the indirect early morning light. Dieter greeted him; Coe said nothing.

Dieter put down his rucksack. "I've got to tell you about

what happened last night."

"Enjoyed it, huh?"

"Enjoyed what? Whoa, I found out everything you said was right!"

"Not what I hear, terrysuiter."

"What?"

"Your fellow snotsucker came by last night, pig. Showed me where this was." Coe held out the bead on an extended fingertip. "You like to sketch. You want to change things. You, an artist. Ha!" Coe reached into his jumpsuit pocket, took out a knife.

"Coe, I, I — listen!"

"No, you don't like working on no console, no sir. You want to break up the whole act through your own little cylanite haze!" He flipped the blade out, holding it point upward in his fist.

"I — hey, I'm not afraid of your fucking knife, Coe — I didn't use the console, but I had to be sure. Kinchon was—"

Coe came forward. "You are dead on the world, fool, I'm no stunt man for the likes of you."

Seized with a desperate thought, Dieter didn't move. "Don't you see? Don't you really see? I love you. I *love* you, I won't resist, I care." His voice was hoarse.

The blue eyes softened, but only for an instant. "You eat shit. Vamp! Finger puppet!" Then the knife hand arced upward, the blade touched Dieter's waist, he pulled back violently, screaming his love.

With a calm born of years of experience, Kinchon lightly touched HOLD. He was tired, having sat up all night, but the wait had been worth it. Quite right to bead the neck, even if the image was slightly off-center. That could be corrected, for the essence was there, on the screen: the intensity of the bearded face, the flailing arm of that young fool, the first glint of blood, red as the window behind them. Dieter had been quite right about that window.

He was planning it in flat black and mylar cilia. He already had his title: "For My Vamp in Party Red."

When It Changed
Joanna Russ

"When It Changed" is not the first lesbian story Joanna Russ has written. "That dubious honor," she notes, "belongs to a story I wrote in high school (the manuscript is now lost, unfortunately) about a tall, dark, woman (me) who falls in love with a short, blond one (my friend Madeleine, whom I was crazy about in summer camp) and the story ends — can you doubt it? — with a suicide." At fifteen Russ decided that she had made the whole thing up; it didn't exist except in a few books and in her imagination. So she tucked *it* away along with her daydreams of being a famous writer, riding the whirlwind like a character out of Romantic poetry, and her hopes of having some woman fall in love with her.

"When It Changed" was written in the late winter of 1970, seventeen years after she had given up on *it*, but something had occurred in the meantime. "Feminism," reflects Russ, "had burst like a thundercloud over the university where I taught, in the form of a three-day symposium on women (hosted by the College of Home Economics, because no other college would touch it). Marriages broke up, hitherto pleasant social contacts became the places for fury and screaming. Shortly thereafter, I heard a voice in my mind whisper, 'Katy drives like a maniac' — hence this story — and six months later I went (for some odd reason I don't recall) to a Gay Liberation Front meeting — and walked out into the soft June twilight floating a good three feet above the ground. *It* was real! People really did it! What a marvelous discovery! (Writers are quite often less conscious than they seem; anybody with half a brain could've seen what I was writing about in 'When It Changed' — except me, of course.)"

The story came out in the second volume of Harlan Ellison's ground-breaking science fiction anthology, *Again, Dangerous Visions.* (The first is called simply *Dangerous Visions.*) Russ had written two books prior to the publication of "When It Changed": *Picnic On Paradise* (1968) and *And Chaos Died* (1970). Neither of these works has significant gay content. "When It Changed" was followed by the furiously feminist *The Female Man* (1975), *Alyx* (1976), *We Who Are About To* (1977), *Kittatinny: A Tale of Magic* (fantasy with a lesbian theme, 1978), *The Two of Them* (feminist, but not gay, 1978), and *On Strike Against God* (lesbian theme, 1980). Forthcoming are *The Lesson for Today Is, How To Suppress Women's Writing* (non-fiction), *The Zanzibar Cat* (story collection), *The Adventures of Alyx* (collection of stories), and a volume of essays.

From Russ, this "reassuring" note: "Yes, *it* exists and it is lovely. As I once wrote a paper on Willa Cather and was told (by four readers out of six) that I hadn't 'proved' she was a you-know-what, I had better append here for future students of twentieth-century culture: I am a lesbian. Got it? I hope you enjoy the story."

Katy drives like a maniac; we must have been doing over 120 kilometers per hour on those turns. She's good, though, extremely good, and I've seen her take the whole car apart and put it together again in a day. My birthplace on Whileaway was largely given to farm machinery and I refuse to wrestle with a five-gear shift at unholy speeds, not having been brought up to it, but even on those turns in the middle of the night, on a country road as bad as only our district can make them, Katy's driving didn't scare me. The funny thing about my wife, though: she will not handle guns. She has even gone hiking in the forests above the forty-eighth parallel without firearms, for days at a time. And that *does* scare me.

Katy and I have three children between us, one of hers and two of mine. Yuriko, my eldest, was asleep in the back seat, dreaming twelve-year-old dreams of love and war: running away to sea, hunting in the North, dreams of strangely beautiful people in strangely beautiful places, all the wonderful guff you think up when you're turning twelve and the glands start going. Some day soon, like all of them, she will disappear for weeks on end to come back grimy and proud, having knifed her first cougar or shot her first bear, dragging some abominably dangerous dead beastie behind her, which I will never forgive for what it might have done to my daughter. Yuriko says Katy's driving puts her to sleep.

For someone who has fought three duels, I am afraid of far, far too much. I'm getting old. I told this to my wife.

"You're thirty-four," she said. Laconic to the point of silence, that one. She flipped the lights on, on the dash — three kilometers to go and the road getting worse all the time. Far out in the country. Electric-green trees rushed into our headlights and around the car. I reached down next to me where we bolt the carrier panel to the door and eased my rifle into my lap.

Yuriko stirred in the back. My height but Katy's eyes, Katy's face. The car engine is so quiet, Katy says, that you can hear breathing in the back seat. Yuki had been alone in the car when the message came, enthusiastically decoding her dot-dashes (silly to mount a wide-frequency transceiver near an I.C. engine, but most of Whileaway is on steam). She had thrown herself out of the car, my gangly and gaudy offspring, shouting at the top of her lungs, so of course she had had to come along. We've been intellectually prepared for this ever since the Colony was founded, ever since it was abandoned, but this is different. This is awful.

"Men!" Yuki had screamed, leaping over the car door. "They've come back! Real Earth men!"

We met them in the kitchen of the farmhouse near the place where they had landed; the windows were open, the night air very mild. We had passed all sorts of transportation when we parked outside — steam tractors, trucks, an I. C. flatbed, even a bicycle. Lydia, the district biologist, had come out of her Northern taciturnity long enough to take blood and urine samples and was sitting in a corner of the kitchen shaking her head in astonishment over the results; she even forced herself (very big, very fair, very shy, always painfully blushing) to dig up the old language manuals — though I can talk the old tongues in my sleep. And do. Lydia is uneasy with us; we're Southerners and too flamboyant. I counted twenty people in that kitchen, all the brains of North Continent. Phyllis Spet, I think, had come in by glider. Yuki was the only child there.

Then I saw the four of them.

They are bigger than we are. They are bigger and broader. Two were taller than I, and I am extremely tall, one meter eighty centimeters in my bare feet. They are obviously of our species but *off*, indescribably off, and as my eyes could not and still cannot quite comprehend the lines of those alien bodies, I could not, then, bring myself to touch them, though the one who spoke Russian — what voices they have — wanted to "shake hands," a custom from the past, I imagine. I can only say they were apes with human faces. He seemed to mean well, but I found myself shuddering back almost the length of the kitchen — and then to set a good example (*interstellar amity*, I thought) did "shake hands" finally. A hard, hard hand. They are heavy as draft horses. Blurred, deep voices. Yuriko had sneaked in between the adults and was gazing at *the men* with her mouth open.

He turned *his* head — those words have not been in our language for six hundred years — and said, in bad Russian, "Who's that?"

"My daughter," I said, and added (with that irrational attention to good manners we sometimes employ in moments of insanity), "My daughter, Yuriko Janetson. We use the patronymic. You would say matronymic."

He laughed, involuntarily. Yuki exclaimed, "I thought they would be *good-looking*!" greatly disappointed at this reception of herself. Phyllis Helgason Spet, whom someday I shall kill, gave me across the room a cold, level, venomous look, as if to say: *Watch what you say. You know what I can do.* It's true that I have little formal status, but Madam President will get herself in serious trouble with both me and her own staff if she continues to consider industrial espionage good clean fun. Wars and rumors of wars, as it says in one of our ancestors' books. I translated Yuki's words into *the man's* dog-Russian, once our lingua franca, and *the man* laughed again.

"Where are all your people?" he said conversationally.

I translated again and watched the faces around the room; Lydia embarrassed (as usual), Spet narrowing her eyes with some damned scheme, Katy very pale.

"This is Whileaway," I said.

He continued to look unenlightened.

"Whileaway," I said. "Do you remember? Do you have records? There was a plague on Whileaway."

He looked moderately interested. Heads turned in the back of the room, and I caught a glimpse of the local professions-parliament delegate; by morning every town meeting, every district caucus, would be in full session.

"Plague?" he said. "That's most unfortunate."

"Yes," I said. "Most unfortunate. We lost half our population in one generation."

He looked properly impressed.

"Whileaway was lucky," I said. "We had a big initial gene pool, we had been chosen for extreme intelligence, we had a high technology and a large remaining population in which every adult was two-or-three experts in one. The soil is good. The climate is blessedly easy. There are thirty millions of us now. Things are beginning to snowball in industry — do you understand? — give us seventy years and we'll have more than one real city, more than a few industrial centers, full-time professions, full-time radio operators, full-time machinists, give us seventy years and not everyone will have to spend three-quarters a lifetime on the farm." And I tried to explain how hard it is when artists can practice full-time only in old age, when there are so few, so very few who can be free, like Katy and myself. I tried also to outline our government, the two houses, the one by professions and the geographic one; I told him the district caucuses handled problems too big for the individual towns. And that population control was not a political issue, not yet, though give us time and it would be. This was a delicate point in our history; give us time. There was no need to sacrifice the quality of our life for an insane rush into industrialization. Let us go our own pace. Give us time.

"Where are all the people?" said that monomaniac.

I realized then that he did not mean people, he meant *men*, and he was giving the word the meaning it had not had on Whileaway for six centuries.

"They died," I said. "Thirty generations ago."

I thought we had poleaxed him. He caught his breath. He made as if to get out of the chair he was sitting in; he put his hand to his chest; he looked around at us with the strangest blend of awe and sentimental tenderness. Then he said, solemnly and earnestly:

"A great tragedy."

I waited, not quite understanding.

"Yes," he said, catching his breath again with that queer smile, that adult-to-child smile that tells you something is being hidden and will be presently produced with cries of encouragement and joy, "a great tragedy. But it's over." And again he looked around at all of us with the strangest deference. As if we were invalids.

"You've adapted amazingly," he said.

"To what?" I said. He looked embarrassed. He looked inane. Finally he said, "Where I come from, the women don't dress so plainly."

"Like you?" I said. "Like a bride?" for the men were wearing silver from head to foot. I had never seen anything so gaudy. He made as if to answer and then apparently thought better of it; he laughed at me again. With an odd exhilaration — as if we were something childish and something wonderful, as if he were doing us an enormous favor — he took one shaky breath and said, "Well, we're here."

I looked at Spet, Spet looked at Lydia, Lydia looked at Amalia, who is the head of the local town meeting, Amalia looked at I don't know whom. My throat was raw. I cannot stand local beer, which the farmers swill as if their stomachs had iridium linings but I took it anyway, from Amalia (it was her bicycle we had seen outside as we parked), and swallowed it all. This was going to take a long time. I said, "Yes, here you are," and smiled (feeling like a fool), and wondered seriously if male-Earth-people's minds worked so very differently from female-Earth-people's minds, but that couldn't be so or the race would have died out long ago. The radio network had got the news around planet by now and we had another Russian speaker, flown in from Varna; I decided to cut out when *the man* passed around pictures of his wife, who looked like the priestess of some arcane cult. He proposed to question Yuki, so I barreled her into a back room in spite of her furious protests, and went out on the front porch. As I left, Lydia was explaining the difference between parthenogenesis (which is so easy that anyone can practice it) and what we do, which is the merging of ova. That is why Katy's baby looks like me. Lydia went on to the Ansky Process and Katy Ansky, our one full-polymath genius and the great-great-I don't know how many times great-grandmother of my own Katharina.

A dot-dash transmitter in one of the outbuildings chattered faintly to itself: operators flirting and passing jokes down the line.

There was a man on the porch. The other tall man. I watched him for a few minutes — I can move very quietly when

I want to — and when I allowed him to see me, he stopped talking into the little machine hung around his neck. Then he said calmly, in excellent Russian, "Did you know that sexual equality has been reestablished on Earth?"

"You're the real one," I said, "aren't you? The other one's for show." It was a great relief to get things cleared up. He nodded affably.

"As a people, we are not very bright," he said. "There's been too much genetic damage in the last few centuries. Radiation. Drugs. We can use Whileaway's genes, Janet." Strangers do not call strangers by the first name.

"You can have cells enough to drown in," I said. "Breed your own."

He smiled. "That's not the way we do it." Behind him I saw Katy come into the square of light that was the screened-in door. He went on, low and urbane, not mocking me, I think, but with the self-confidence of someone who has always had money and strength to spare, who doesn't know what it is to be second-class or provincial. Which is very odd, because the day before, I would have said that was an exact description of me.

"I'm talking to you, Janet," he said, "because I suspect you have more popular influence than anyone else here. You know as well as I do that parthenogenetic culture has all sorts of inherent defects, and we do not — if we can help it — mean to use you for anything of the sort. Pardon me; I should not have said 'use.' But surely you can see that this kind of society is unnatural."

"Humanity is unnatural," said Katy. She had my rifle under her left arm. The top of that silky head does not quite come up to my collarbone, but she is as tough as steel; he began to move, again with that queer smiling deference (which his fellow had showed to me but he had not), and the gun slid into Katy's grip as if she had shot with it all her life.

"I agree," said the man. "Humanity is unnatural. I should know. I have metal in my teeth and metal pins here." He touched his shoulder. "Seals are harem animals," he added, "and so are men; apes are promiscuous and so are men; doves are monogamous and so are men; there are even celibate men and homosexual men. There are homosexual cows, I believe. But Whileaway is still missing something." He gave a dry chuckle. I will give him the credit of believing that it had something to do with nerves.

"I miss nothing," said Katy, "except that life isn't endless."

"You are—?" said the man, nodding from me to her.

"Wives," said Katy. "We're married." Again the dry chuckle.

"A good economic arrangement," he said, "for working and taking care of the children. And as good an arrangement as any for randomizing heredity, if your reproduction were made to follow the same pattern. But think, Katharina Michaelason, if there isn't something better that you might secure for your daughters. I believe in instincts, even in Man, and I can't think that the two of you — a machinist, are you? and I gather you are some sort of chief of police — don't feel somehow what even you must miss. You know intellectually, of course. There is only half a species here. Men must come back to Whileaway."

Katy said nothing.

"I should think, Katharina Michaelason," said the man gently, "that you, of all people, would benefit most from such a change," and he walked past Katy's rifle into the square of light coming from the door. I think it was then that he noticed my scar, which really does not show unless the light is from the side: a fine line that runs from temple to chin. Most people don't even know about it.

"Where did you get that?" he said, and I answered with an involuntary grin. "In my last duel." We stood there bristling at each other for several seconds (this is absurd but true) until he went inside and shut the screen door behind him. Katy said in a brittle voice, "You damned fool, don't you know when we've been insulted?" and swung up the rifle to shoot him through the screen, but I got to her before she could fire and knocked the rifle out of aim; it burned a hole through the porch floor. Katy was shaking. She kept whispering over and over, "That's why I never touched it, because I knew I'd kill someone. I knew I'd kill someone." The first man — the one I'd spoken with first — was still talking inside the house, something about the grand movement to recolonize and rediscover all that Earth had lost.

He stressed the advantages to Whileaway: trade, exchange of ideas, education. He, too, said that sexual equality had been reestablished on Earth.

Katy was right, of course; we should have burned them down where they stood. Men are coming to Whileaway. When one culture has the big guns and the other has none, there is a certain predictability about the outcome. Maybe men would have come eventually in any case. I like to think that a hundred years from now my great-grandchildren could have stood them off or fought them to a standstill, but even that's no odds; I will remember all my life those four people I first met who were muscled like bulls and who made me — if only for a moment — feel small. A neurotic reaction, Katy says. I remember everything that happened that night; I remember Yuki's excitement in the car, I remember Katy's sobbing when we got home as if her heart would break, I remember her lovemaking, a little peremptory as always, but wonderfully soothing and comforting. I remember prowling restlessly around the house after Katy fell asleep with one bare arm flung into a patch of light from the hall. The muscles of her forearms are like metal bars from all that driving and testing of her machines. Sometimes I dream about Katy's arms. I remember wandering into the nursery and picking up my wife's baby, dozing for a while with the poignant, amazing warmth of an infant in my lap, and finally returning to the kitchen to find Yuriko fixing herself a late snack. My daughter eats like a Great Dane.

"Yuki," I said, "do you think you could fall in love with a man?" and she whooped derisively. "With a ten-foot toad!" said my tactful child.

But men are coming to Whileaway. Lately I sit up nights and worry about the men who will come to this planet, about my two daughters and Betta Katharinason, about what will happen to Katy, to me, to my life. Our ancestors' journals are one long cry of pain and I suppose I ought to be glad now, but one can't throw away six centuries, or even (as I have lately discovered) thirty-four years. Sometimes I laugh at the question those four men hedged about all evening and never quite dared to ask, looking at the lot of us, hicks in overalls, farmers in canvas pants and plain shirts: *Which of you plays the role of the man?* As if we had to produce a carbon copy of their mistakes! I doubt very much that sexual equality has been reestablished on Earth. I do not like to think of myself mocked, of Katy deferred to as if she were weak, of Yuki made to feel unimportant or silly, of my other children cheated of their full humanity or turned into strangers. And I'm afraid that my own achievements will dwindle from what they were — or what I thought they were — to the not-very-interesting curiosa of the human race, the oddities you read about in the back of the book, things to laugh at sometimes because they are so exotic, quaint but not impressive, charming but not useful. I find this more painful than I can say. You will agree that for a woman who has fought three duels, all of them kills, indulging in such fears is ludicrous. But what's around the corner now is a duel so big that I don't think I have the guts for it; in Faust's words: *Verweile doch, du bist so schön!* Keep it as it is. Don't change.

Sometimes at night I remember the original name of this planet, changed by the first generation of our ancestors, those curious women for whom, I suppose, the real name was too painful a reminder after the men died. I find it amusing, in a grim way, to see it all so completely turned around. This, too, shall pass. All good things must come to an end.

Take my life but don't take away the meaning of my life.

For-A-While.

The Night Wind
Edgar Pangborn

Edgar Pangborn, born in New York City on February 25, 1909, was the son of Harry and Georgia (Wood) Pangborn: a family with printer's ink in the veins. Now deceased (he died February 1, 1976), Pangborn once described his writing career as beginning at the age of seven with a five-act play. His sister, Mary, doesn't remember the play, but she does clearly remember the enormous bound notebooks they filled with literary scribbles; even then, these works dealt with imaginary countries, complete with maps. Education before high school consisted of grabbing any and all books from the family library and swallowing them whole; this process became a lifelong pattern. In the formal sense, Pangborn was educated at Brooklyn Friends School, briefly at Harvard, and at the New England Conservatory of Music. Music was a consuming love, though never a profession. His life was writing, which he summed up once by saying: "You learn to write by doing it."

Just prior to World War II, Pangborn went to Maine to have a try at what is sometimes called "subsistence farming." The war put an end to that; he served in the Army of the Pacific from 1942 through 1945. After his return, he lived in Voorheesville, near Albany, New York, gardening and writing. In 1967, he moved to Woodstock, New York where he took up the study of painting. And always, of course, writing. He never called his stories "science fiction"; he much preferred the term "projective fantasy."

Pangborn began writing in 1930, publishing that year a novel entitled, *A-100*, under the pseudonym "Bruce Harrison." He marks his own arrival as a writer with the appearance of "Angel's Egg," a novelette published in *Galaxy* in 1951. A multi-genre talent (science fiction, fantasy, mystery, historical novels...), he went on to write a number of popular works, including: *West of the Sun*, *A Mirror for Observers*, *A Wilderness of Spring*, *The Trial of Callista Blake*, *Davy*, *The Judgment of Eve*, and *The Company of Glory*. Some of his best short stories have been gathered in two collections: *Good Neighbors and Other Strangers*, and *Still I Persist in Wondering*. Of his work, critic Damon Knight observes: "It reflects the regretful, ironic, sorrowful, deeply joyous — and purblind — love of the world and all in it." His writing is characterized by two salient themes: love and human insensitivity. Pangborn was long fascinated by same-sex love, and his work is rich in variant content. Indeed, many of his stories embody gay and lesbian content.

At Mam Miriam's house beyond
Trempa, Ottoba 20, 402

I *will* do it somewhere down this road, not yet but after dark; it will be when the night wind is blowing.

Always I have welcomed the sound of the night wind moving, as the leaves are passing on their secrets and sometimes falling, but falling lightly, easily, because their time to fall is come. Dressed in high colors, they fall to the day winds too this time of year, this autumn season. The smell of earth mold is spice on the tongue. I catch scent of apples ripening, windfalls rich-rotten pleasuring the yellow hornets. Rams and he-goats are mounting and crazy for it — O this time of year! They fall to the day winds echoing the sunlight, the good bright leaves, and that's no bad way to fall.

I know the dark of autumn too. The night wind hurts. Even now writing of it, only to think of it. Ottoba was in me when I said to my heart: I will do it somewhere down this road, I will end it, my life, for they believe it should never have begun. (I think there may be good spirits down that road. Perhaps the people I met were spirits, or they were human beings and spirits too, or we all are.) And I remembered how Father Horan also believes I ought never to have been born. I saw that in him; he believes it as the town folk do, and what we believe is most of what we are.

For three days I felt their sidelong stares, their anger that I would dare to pass near their houses. They called in their children to safety from me, who never hurt anyone. Passing one of those gray-eyed houses, I heard a woman say, "He ought to be stoned, that Benvenuto." I will not write her name.

Another said, "Only a mue would do what he did."

They call me that; they place me among the sad distorted things — armless or mindless or eyeless, somehow inhuman and corrupted — that so many mothers bear, or have borne, folk say, since the end of Old Time. How could a mue be called beautiful?

When I confessed to Father Horan, he shoved his hands behind his back, afraid he might touch me. "Poor Benvenuto!" But he said it acidly, staring down as if he had tasted poison in his food.

So I will end it (I told the hidden self that is me) — I will end it now in my fifteenth year before the Eternal Corruption that Father Horan spoke of can altogether destroy my soul; and so the hidden self that is me, if that is my soul, may win God's forgiveness for being born a monster.

But why did Father Horan love me once, taking something like a father's place, or seem to love me? Why did he teach me the reading of words and writing too, first showing me how the great words flow in the Book of Abraham, and on to the spelling book and so to all the mystery? Why did he let me see the other books, some of them, the books of Old Time forbidden to common people, even the poets? He would run his fingers through my hair, saying I must never cut it, or rest his arm on my shoulder; and I felt a need, I thought it was loneliness or love, in the curving of his fingers. Why did he say I might rise in the Holy Amran Church, becoming greater than himself, a bishop — Bishop Benvenuto! — an archbishop!

If I am a monster now, was I not a monster then?

I could ask him no such questions when he was angry. I ran out of the church though I heard him calling after me, commanding me to return in God's name. I will not return.

I ran through the graveyard, past the dead hollow oak where I saw and heard bees swarming in the hot autumn light, and I think he stood among the headstones lamenting for me, but I would not look back, no, I plowed through a thicket and ran down a long golden aisle of maple trees and into Wayland's field (where it happened) — Wayland's field all standing alive with bound shocks of corn, and into the woods again on the far side, only to be away from him.

It was there in Wayland's field that I first thought, I will do this to myself, I will end it, maybe in that wood I know of; but I was afraid of my knife. How can I cut and tear the body someone called beautiful? And so I looked at the thought of hiding in a shock of corn, the same one where I found Eden idle that day, and staying in it till I starved. But they say starving is a terrible death, and I might not have the courage or the patience to wait for it. I thought too, They will look for me when they know I'm gone, because they want to punish me, stone me, even my mother will want to punish me, and they would think of the cornfield where it happened and come searching like the flail of God.

How bright they stand, the bound stalks in the sun, like little wigwams for the field spirits, like people too, like old women with rustling skirts of yellow-gray; their hair is blowing! Now I know I will remember this when I go on — for I am going on without death, never doubt it, I promise you I shall not die by my own hand.

I saw two hawks circling and circling in the upper wind above Wayland's field. I thought up to them: You are like me, but you have all the world's air to fly away in.

The hawks are bound to earth as I am, they must hunt food in the grass and branches, men shoot arrows from the earth to tear their hearts. Still they enter regions unknown to us, and maybe they and the wild geese have found an easy way to heaven.

Into the woods again on the far side of Wayland's field I hurried, and down and up the ravine that borders it, shadowed ground with alder and gray birch and a cool place of ferns I know of where sunlight comes late in the morning and mild. The brook in the ravine bottom was running scant from the dry weather, leaves collecting on the bodies of smooth shining stones. I did not go downstream to the pool but climbed the other side of the ravine and took the path — hardly that, merely a known place where my feet have passed before — to the break in the trees that lets you out on this road, and I thought: Here I will do it, somewhere farther on in the shadows.

It is wider than a wood-road and better kept, for wagons use it now and then, and it is supposed to wind through back ways southeast as far as Nupal, ten miles they say or even more — I never believed much of what I hear about Nupal. The trading of our village has always been with Maplestock, and surely nobody goes to Nupal except those tinkers and gyppos and ramblers with their freaky wagons, squirrel-eyed children, scrawny dogs. A sad place it must be, Nupal, more than seven hundred crammed into the one village, as I hear it. I don't understand how human beings can live like that — the houses may not be standing as horridly close together as folk tell. Maybe I'll see the place in passing. I've noticed a dozen times, the same souls who sniggle about with ugly fact until it looks like fancy will turn right-about and ask you to believe that ugly fancy is fact.

I went down the road not running any more, nor thinking more about Father Horan. I thought of Eden.

Then I thought about my mother, who is going to marry Blind Hamlin the candlemaker, I'm told. She wouldn't tell me herself, the winds told me. (Toby Omstrong told me, because he doesn't like me.) Let's hope the jolly wedding isn't delayed by concern over my absence — I am not coming back, Mother. Think of me kindly while tumbling with your waxy man, or better, think of me not at all, the cord is cut, and anyhow didn't you pick me up somewhere as a changeling?

Hoy, there I was on your doorstep all red and nasty, wrapped up in a cabbage leaf! Likely story. But we can't have it thought that *you* gave birth to a monster, even one begotten by a little shoemaker whose image you did your best to destroy for me. (But I saved some pieces, I try to put them together now and then. I wish I could remember him; the memories of others are not much more help than wind under the door, for people don't understand what I want to know — small blame to them, they can't hear the questions I don't know how to ask — and I think your memories of him are mostly lies, Mother, though you may not know it.) "He was a poor sad soul, Benvenuto." Was he, Mother? "He broke my heart with his unfaithfulness, Benvenuto." But Blind Hamlin is going to stick it back together with mutton-fat, remember? "He drank, you know, Benvenuto, that was why he could never make a decent living." Why, I will drink to you, Mother, I will drink to the wedding in Mam Miriam's best apple brandy before I leave this poor empty house where I am writing.

Don't destroy Blind Hamlin, Mother. I don't like him, he's a crosspatch bag of guts, but don't destroy him, don't whittle him down as you must have scraped my father down with the rasp of words — but I forget, I am a changeling. Poor Blind Hamlin! — there may be witchcraft in it, Mother. It troubles me that a man who can't see makes candles for those who will not. Don't destroy him. Make another monster with him. I'd like a monster for a half-brother — but there, never mind, I'm not coming back to Trempa, make all the monsters you wish. The world's already full of them.

I am not writing this for my mother. She will not be the one to find it here. Whoever does — I pray you, read this page if you like and the one before it that begins "She wouldn't tell me herself" — read and then throw away, in God's name. For I would like the truth to be somewhere in the world, maybe in your head, whoever you are, but I don't wish to slap my mother in the face with it, nor Blind Hamlin either. Blind Hamlin was never unkind to me. I am all soreness, the tenderest touch smarts on a burned skin. I will mend. I don't hate my mother — do I hate anyone? — is it a sign of my monsterhood that I don't hate anyone? — or if I do, I will *mend*, I'll cease hating wherever I am going, and even forget. Especially forget. Read those pages and throw away and then, you too, forget. But save the rest, if you will. I don't want to die altogether in your mind, whoever you are.

Down that road I came. I think I left behind me most of what had appeared certain in the world; the new uncertainties are still to find. Where did I encounter you ? Who are you? — oh, merely the one supposed to find this letter. So then you are not the new person I need to find — someone not Eden, not Andrea whom I loved, but some other. But with Andrea I understood that heaven would open whenever he looked on me.

In that road through the woods beyond Wayland's field the trees stand close on either side, oak and pine and enormous tulip trees where the white parrots like to gather and squabble with the bluejays, and thickets that swell with a passion of growth wherever an opening like that road lets through the sun. Oaks had shifted into the bronze along with the clear gold of maple trees when I passed by, yet I saw few leaves fallen. You remember some of the wise prophets in Trempa have been saying it'll be a hard winter, with snow in January for sure. The

Lord must save a special kind of forgiveness for the weather prophets — other kinds of liars have some chance of learning better. As I looked along the slender channel of the road, I saw the stirring of distant treetops under the wind, but here that wind was hushed, cut to a modest breeze or to no motion at all. And suddenly the stillness was charged with the fishy loathsome reek of black wolf.

It is a poison in the air and we live with it. I remember how it has always happened in the village: days, weeks, with no hint of the evil, and when we have forgotten and grown careless, then without warning the sour stench of them comes on the air, and we hear their rasping howl in the night — nothing like the musical uproar of the common wolves who seldom do worse than pick up a sheep now and then — and people will die, ambushed, throat-torn, stripped of flesh and bones cracked for the marrow. Some tell of seeing the Devil walk with them. He teaches them tricks that only human beings ought to know. He leads them to the trail of late travelers, to lonely houses where a door may be unlatched, or someone seized on the way to shed or outhouse. And yet they do say that black wolf will not attack by day; if a man comes at him then, even if he is at his carrion, he may slink off; now I know this is true. At night black wolf is invincible, I suppose. The smell hung dense on that woodland road, coming from all around me, so that I could not run away from it.

I had my thin strength, and a knife; my knife is from the hand of Wise Wayland the Smith, and there is a spell on it. For look you, no harm comes to me if I am wearing it. I was not wearing it when Andrea's family moved away and took him with them — all the way to Penn, God help me. I was not wearing it when they came on me with Eden in Wayland's field and called me monster.

In fear I went ahead, not trying for quiet because no one ever surprises black wolf. I came on the beast on the far side of a boulder that jutted into the road, but before that I heard the sounds of tearing. It had ripped the liver from the body. Blood still oozed from all the wounds. Enough remained from the face so that I knew the man was old Kobler. His back-pack was not with him, nor any gear, so he had not been on his way to the village. Perhaps he had been taken with some sickness, and so the wolf dared to bring him down in broad day.

By this time Kobler will be expected in the village. They'll wonder why he doesn't come marching to the General Store with his stack of reed baskets and Mam Miriam's beautiful embroideries and such-like, and slap down his one silver coin, and fill his back-pack with the provisions for Mam Miriam and himself. True, he was never regular in the timing of his visits; another week or two might go by before anyone turns curious. People don't think much unless their convenience is joggled, and old Kobler was so silent a man, never granting anyone a word that could be held back — and Mam Miriam herself hardly more than a legend to the town folk — no, I suppose they won't stir themselves unduly. All the same I must leave, I must not be caught here by those who would stone me for their souls' benefit. Nothing keeps me in this house now except a wish to write these words for you, whoever you are. Then I will go when the night wind is blowing.

It was an old dog wolf, and foul, alone, his fangs yellowed. He held his ground hardly a moment when I walked down on him with the knife of Wayland flashing sunlight on his eyes. I did not understand immediately that Kobler was past help — then the wolf moved, I saw the liver, I knew the look on the old man's mask was no-way meant for me. Jon Kobler, a good fellow I think, Mam Miriam's servant, companion, and more. He shrank from the world as she did, nor do I see how you could hold it against either of them, for often the world stinks so that even a fool like me must hold his nose. It will not harm them now if I tell you they were lovers.

The wolf slunk off through the brush into a ravine. It must have been the power of Wayland's knife — or is it possible that black wolf is not so terrible as folk say? Well, mine is a knife that Wayland made long since, when he was young; he told me so.

He gave it to me on the morning of the best day of my life. Andrea had come to me the day before, had chosen me out of all the others in the training yard — although I seldom shone there, my arm is not heavy enough for the axe or the spear-throwing, and in archery I am only fair, undistinguished. He challenged me to wrestle, I put forth my best, almost I had his shoulders down and he laughing up at me, and then presto! somehow I am flung over on my back and my heart close to cracking with happiness because he has won. And he invited me to go on the morrow with him and some of his older friends for a stag hunt through Bindiaan Wood, and I had to say, "I have no knife, no gear."

"Oh," says Andrea, and April is no kinder, "we'll find extra gear for you at my father's house, and as for a knife of your own, maybe Wayland the Smith has one for you."

I knew that Wayland Smith did sometimes make such gifts to boys just turning men, but had never imagined he would trouble with one so slight-built as I am and supposed to be simple-minded from the hours with the books. "You do hide your light," says Andrea, whom I had already loved for a year, scarcely daring to speak to him. He laughed and pressed my shoulder. "Go to ancient Wayland, do him some little favor — there's no harm in him — and maybe he'll have a knife for you. I would give you mine, Benvenuto," he said, "only that's bad magic between friends, but come to me with a knife of your own and we'll make a blood brotherhood."

So the next morning I went to Wayland the Smith with all my thoughts afire, and I found the old man about to draw a bucket of water from his well, but looking ill and drooping, and he said, "O Benvenuto, I have a crick in my arm — would you, in kindness?" So I drew the water for him, and we drank together. I saw the smithy was untidy with cobwebs, and swept it out for him, he watching me and rambling on with his tales and sayings and memories that some call wanton blasphemies — I paid little heed to them, thinking of Andrea, until he asked me, "Are you a good boy, Benvenuto?" His tone made me know he would like to hear me laugh, or anyway not mind it, indeed I could hardly help laughing at a thousand silly notions, and for the pleasure of it, and the joy of the day; and that was when he gave me this knife I always carry. I don't think I answered his question, or at least only to say, "I try to be," or some such nonsense. He gave me the knife, kissed me, told me not to be too unhappy in my life; but I don't know what one must do to follow that counsel, unless it is to live the way all others do, like baa-sheep who come and go at the will of the shepherd and his dog and must never stray from the tinkle of the wether's bell.

Oh, yes, that day I went on the hunt with Andrea, armed with the knife that was given me by Wayland Smith. We killed a stag together, he marked my forehead, with our own blood then we made brotherhood; but he is gone away.

There was nothing anyone could have done for old Kobler except pray for him. I did that — if there's anything to hear our prayers, if the prayers of a monster can be noticed. But who is God? Who is this cloud-thing that has nothing better to do than stare on human pain and now and then poke it with his finger? Is he not bored? Will he not presently wipe it all away, or go away and forget? Or has he already gone away, forgotten?

You will not have me burnt for these words because you will not find me. Besides, I must remember you are simply the unknown who will happen on this letter in Mam Miriam's house, and you may even be a friend. I must remember there are friends.

When I rose from kneeling beside the poor mess that was what remained of Kobler, I heard rustling in the brush. That wolf had no companions or they would have been with him tearing at the meat, but perhaps he was rallying from his fright, hungry for something young and fresh. I understood too that the sun was lowering, night scarcely more than an hour away. Night's arrival would be sudden in the manner of autumn, which has a cruelty in it, as if we did not know that winter is near but must be reminded with a slap and a scolding. Only then did I think of Mam Miriam, who would expect Kobler's return.

When was the last time any of you in Trempa saw Mam Miriam Coletta? I had not even known she was daughter to Roy Coletta, who was governor of Ulsta in his time. Or was this only something she dreamed for me, something to tell me when perhaps her wits were wandering? It doesn't matter: I will think her a princess if I choose.

She was twenty-five and yet unmarried, hostess of the governor's mansion at Sortees after her mother's death, and she fell in love with a common archer, one of the Governor's

Guard, and ran away with him, escaping from her locked bedroom on a rope made from a torn blanket. O the dear romantic tale! I've heard none better from the gyppos — their stories are too much alike, but this was like some of the poems of Old Time, especially as she told it me, and never mind if her wits wandered; I have ceased speculating whether it was true.

You think the archer was this same man who became Poor Old Kobler, marching into town fortnightly with his back-pack and his baskets, and the embroideries by a crazy old bedridden dame who lived off in the Haunted Stone House and wouldn't give anyone the time of day?

He was not. That archer abandoned her in a brothel at Nuber. Kobler was an aging soldier, a deserter. He took her out of the old stone house in the woods so long abandoned — for he was a Trempa man in his beginnings, Jon Kobler, but you may not find any bones to bury — and he took her there. He repaired the solid old ruin; you would not believe what good work he did there, mostly with wood cut and shaped out of the forest with his own hands. He cared for her there, servant and lover; they seem not to have had much need of the world. They grew old there, like that.

Rather, he did, I suppose. When I saw her she did not seem very old. Why, I first heard talk and speculation about them (most of it malicious) when I was six years old; I think they must have been new-come then, and that's only nine years ago. Yesterday or perhaps the day before, nine years would have seemed like a long time to me. Now I wonder if a thousand years is a long time, and I can't answer my own question. I am not clever at guessing ages, but I would think Mam Miriam was hardly past forty; and certainly she spoke like a lady, and told me of the past glories as surely no one could have done who had not known them — the governor's mansion, the dances all night long and great people coming on horseback or in fine carriages from all over the county; she made me see the sweaty faces of the musicians in the balcony, and didn't she herself go up one night (the dance at her tenth birthday party) to share a box of candy with them? She spoke of the gardens, the lilac and wisteria and many-colored roses, the like you never saw in Trempa, and there were odd musky red grapes from some incredible land far south of Penn, and from there also, limes, and oranges, and spices she could not describe for me. Telling me all this simply and truly, she did seem like a young woman, even a girl — oh, see for yourself, how should I know? There she lies, poor sweet thing, in the bed Jon Kobler must have made. I have done what I could for her, and it is not much.

I am wandering. I must tell of all this as I should, and then go. Perhaps you will never come; it may be best if you do not.

I prayed for Kobler, and then I went on down the road — despising the wolf but not forgetting him, for I wish to live — as far as its joining with the small path that I knew would take me to Mam Miriam's. There I hesitated a long while, though I think I knew from the start that I would go to her. I don't know what it is in us that (sometimes) will make us do a thing against our wishes because we know it to be good. "Conscience" is too thin a word, and "God" too misty, too spoiled by the many who mouth it constantly without any care for what they say, or as if they alone were able to inform you of God's will — and please, how came they to be so favored? But something drives, I think from within, and I must even obey it without knowing a name for it.

You see, I had never followed that path. No one does. The road like the old stone house itself is haunted. Anyone who ventures there goes in peril of destruction or bewitchment. So far, I am not destroyed.

Once on the path — why, I began to run. Maybe I ran so as to yield no room in my thought to the fear that is always, like black wolf, waiting. I ran down the path through a wilderness of peace. There were the beeches, gray and kind — I like to imagine something of a peace in their nearness. I know that violence might be done in their presence, in the very shadow of the beech trees, as in any other place where the human creature goes; a little corner of my mind is a garden where I lie in the sun not believing it. In their presence on that path I ran without shortness of breath, without remembering fear, and I came to the green clearing, and the house of red-gray stone. It was growing late, the sun too low to penetrate this hidden place. In shadow therefore I came to Mam Miriam's door and pounded on the oak panel. But gossip had always said that the old woman (if she existed at all outside of Jon Kobler's head, if he didn't create those dazzling embroideries himself out of his own craziness and witchcraft) was bedridden and helpless. So my knocking was foolish. I turned the latch and pushed the heavy sluggish thing inward, closing it behind me, staring about half-blind in the gray light.

The house is trifling-small, as you will see if you dare come here. Only that big lower room with the fireplace where Jon cooked, the bench where he worked at his baskets, clogs, wooden beads, and this other room up here with the smaller hearth. There's this one chair up here where I sit now (Kobler used to sit beside his love's bed, you know) and the little table I write on, which I am sure they used drawn up beside the bed for their meals together, for the night pitcher of water she no longer needs. You will be aware now that she did exist. There's the roll of linen cloth — Kobler must have gone all the way to Maplestock to buy that — and some half-finished table mats, pillow slips, dresser covers. There's her embroidery hoop, the needles, the rolls of bright yarns, and thread — I never knew there were so many sizes and colors. And there she too is lying. She was; she lived; I closed her eyes.

I looked about me in that failing evening, and she called from upstairs, "Jon, what's wrong? Why did you make such a noise at the door? You've been long, Jon. I'm thirsty."

The tone of her voice was delicate, a music. I cannot tell you how it frightened me, that the voice of a crazy old woman should sound so mild and sweet. Desperately I wanted to run away, much more than I had wanted it when I stood out there at the beginning of the path. But the thing that I will not call Conscience or God (somewhere in the Old-Time books I think it was called Virtue, but doubtless few read them) — the thing that would never let me strike a child, or stone a criminal or a mue on the green as we are expected to do in Trempa — this mad cruel-sweet thing that may be a part of love commanded me to answer her, and I called up the stairway, "Don't be afraid. It's not Jon, but I came to help you." I followed my words, climbing the stairs slowly so that she could forbid me if she chose. She said no more until I had come to her.

The house was turning chill. I had hardly noticed it downstairs; up here the air was already cold, and I saw — preferring not to stare at her directly till she spoke to me — that she was holding the bedcovers high to her throat, and shivering. "I must build you a fire," I said, and went to the hearth. Fresh wood and kindling were laid ready, a tinderbox stood on the mantel. She watched me struggle with the clumsy tool until I won my flame and set it to the twigs and scraps of waste cloth. That ancient chimney is clean — the fire caught well without smoking into the room. I warmed my hands.

"What has happened? Where is Jon?"

"He can't come. I'm sorry." I asked her if she was hungry, and she shook her head. "I'm Benvenuto of Trempa," I told her. "I'm running away. I must get you some fresh water." I hurried out with the pitcher, obliged to retreat for that moment for my own sake, because meeting her gaze, as I had briefly done, had been a glancing through midnight windows into a country where I could never go and yet might have loved to go.

Why, even with gray-eyed Andrea this had been true, and did he not once say to me, "O Benvenuto, how I would admire to walk in the country behind your eyes!"

I know: it is always true.

(But Andrea brought me amazing gifts from his secret country, and nothing in mine was withheld from him through any wish of mine. I suppose all the folk have a word for it: we knew each other's hearts.)

I filled the pitcher at the well-pump downstairs and carried it up to her with a fresh clean cup. She drank gratefully, watching me, I think with some kind of wonder, over the rim of the cup, and she said, "You are a good boy, Benvenuto. Sit down by me now, Benvenuto." She set the cup away on the table and patted the edge of the bed, and I sat there maybe no longer afraid of her, for her plump sad little face was kind. Her soft too-white hands, the fingers short and tapered, showed me none of that threat of grasping, clinging, snatching I have many times seen in the hands of my own breed. "So tell me, where is Jon?" When I could not get words out, I felt her trembling. "Something has happened."

"He is dead, Mam Miriam." She only stared. "I found him on the road, Mam Miriam, too late for me to do anything. It was a wolf." Her hands flew up over her face. "I'm sorry — I couldn't think of any easier way to tell it." She was not weeping as I have heard a woman needs to do after such a blow.

At last her hands came down. One dropped on mine kindly, like the hand of an old friend. "Thus God intended it, perhaps," she said. "I was already thinking, I may die tonight."

"No," I said. "No."

"Why should I not, my dear?"

"Can't you walk at all?"

She looked startled, even shocked, as if that question had been laid away at the back of her mind a long time since, not to be brought forth again. "One night after we came here, Jon and I, I went downstairs — Jon had gone to Trempa and was late returning — I had a candle, but a draft caught it at the head of the stairs — oh, it was a sad night, Benvenuto, and the night wind blowing. I stumbled, fell all the way. There was a miscarriage, but I could not move my legs. An hour later Jon got back and found me like that, all blood and misery. Since then I have not been able to walk. Nor to die, Benvenuto."

"Have you prayed?" I asked her. "Have you besought God to let you walk again? Father Horan would say that you should. Father Horan says God's grace is infinite, through the intercession of Abraham. But then — other times — he appears to deny it. Have you prayed, Mam Miriam?"

"Father Horan — that will be your village priest." She was considering what I said, not laughing at me. "I believe he came here once some years ago, and Jon told him to go away, and he did — but no charge of witchcraft was ever brought against us." She smiled at me, a smile of strangeness, but it warmed me. "Yes, I have prayed, Benvenuto. . . . You said you were running away. Why that, my dear? And from what?"

"They would stone me. I've heard it muttered behind windows when I passed. The only reason they haven't yet is that Father Horan was my friend — I thought he was, I'm sure he wanted to be, once. But I have learned he is not, he also believes me sinful."

"Sinful?" She stroked the back of my hand, and her look was wondering. "Perhaps any sin you might have done has been atoned for by coming out of your way to help an old witch."

"You're not a witch!" I said. "Don't call yourself that!"

"Why, Benvenuto! Then you do believe in witches!"

"Oh, I don't know." For the first time in my life I was wondering whether I did, if she in all her trouble could be so amused at the thought of them. "I don't know," I said, "but you're not one. You're good, Mam Miriam. You're beautiful."

"Well, Benvenuto, when I am busy with my embroideries, I sometimes feel like a good person. And in Jon's embraces I've thought so, after the pleasure, in the time when there can be quiet and a bit of thinking. Other times I've just lain here wondering what goodness is, and whether anyone really knows. Bless you, am I beautiful? I'm too fat, from lying here doing nothing. The wrinkles spread over my puffy flesh just the same, like frost lines coming on a windowpane, only dark, dark." She closed her eyes and asked me, "What sin could you have done to make them after stoning you?"

"The one I most loved went away last spring — all the way to Penn, God help me, and I don't even know what town. I was lonely, and full of desire too, for we had been lovers, and I've learned I have a great need of that, a fire in me that flares up at a breath. In Wayland's field a few days ago, where the corn shocks are standing like golden women, I came on someone else, Eden — we had been loving friends, though not in that way. We were both lonely and hungry for loving, and so we comforted each other — and still, in spite of Father Horan, I can see no harm in it — but Eden's people found us. Eden is younger than me — was only driven home and whipped, and will suffer no worse, I hope. Me they call monster. I ran away from Eden's father and brother, but now all the village is muttering."

"But surely, surely, boy and girl playing the old sweet game in an autumn cornfield—"

"Eden is a boy, Mam Miriam. The one I love, who went away, is Andrea Benedict, the eldest son of a patrician."

She put her hand behind my neck. "Come here awhile," she said, and drew me down to her.

"Father Horan says such passion is the Eternal Corruption. He says the people of Old Time sinned in this way, so God struck them with fire and plague until their numbers were as nothing. Then he sent Abraham to redeem us, taking away the sin of the world, so—"

"Hush," she said, "hush. Nay — go on if you will, but I care nothing for your Father Horan."

"And so God placed upon us, he says, the command to be fruitful and multiply until our numbers are again the millions they were in Old Time, destroying only the mues. And those who sin as I did, he says, are no better than mues, are a *kind* of mue, and are to be stoned in a public place and their bodies burned. After telling me that, he spoke of God's infinite mercy, but I did not want to hear about it. I ran from him. But I know that in the earlier days of Old Time people like me were tied up in the marketplaces and burned alive, I know this from the books — it was Father Horan who taught me the books, the reading — isn't that strange?"

"Yes," she said. She was stroking my hair, and I loved her. "Lying here is useless, I've thought about a thousand things, Benvenuto. Most of them idle. But I do tell you that any manner of love is good if there's kindness in it. Does anyone know you came here, Benvenuto?" She made my name so loving a sound!

"No, Mam Miriam."

"Then you can safely stay the night. I'm frightened when the night wind blows around the eaves, if I'm alone. You can keep the fright away. It sounds like children crying, some terror pursues them or some grief is on them and there's nothing I can do."

"Why, to me the night wind sounds like children laughing, or the wood gods running and shouting across the top of the world."

"Are there wood gods?"

"I don't know. The forest's a living place. I never feel alone there, even if I lose my way awhile."

"Benvenuto, I think I'm hungry now. See what you can find downstairs — there's cheese, maybe sausage, some of the little red Snow Apples, and Jon made bread—" Her face crumpled and she caught at my hand. "Was it very bad — about Jon?"

"I think he was dead before the wolf came," I told her. "Maybe his heart failed, or — a stroke? I've heard black wolf won't attack in broad day. He must have died first in some

•72•

quick way, without pain."

"Oh, if we all could!" That cry was forced from her because her courage had gone, and I think it was only then that she really knew Jon Kobler was dead. "How could he go before me? I have been dying for ten years."

"I won't leave you, Mam Miriam."

"Why, you must. I won't allow you to stay. I saw a stoning once in Sortees when I was a girl — or maybe that was when my girlhood ended. You must be gone by first light. Now, find us some little supper, Benvenuto. Before you go downstairs — that ugly thing over there, the bedpan — if you would reach it to me. God, I hate it so! — the body of this death."

There's nothing offensive in such services, certainly not if you love the one who needs them: we're all bound to the flesh — even Father Horan said it. I wished to tell her so, and found no words; likely she read my thought.

Downstairs everything had been left in order. Jon Kobler must have been a careful, sober man. While I was busy building a fire to cook the sausage, arranging this and that on the tray Jon must have used, I felt him all around us in the work of his hands — the baskets, the beads, the furniture, the very shutters at the windows. Those were all part of a man.

In some way my own works shall live after me. This letter I am finishing is part of a man. Read it so.

When I took up the tray, Mam Miriam smiled at it, and at me. She would not talk during our meal about our troubles. She spoke of her young years at Sortees, and that is when I came to learn those things I wrote down for you about the governor's mansion, the strange people she used to see who came from far off, even two or three hundred miles away; about the archer, the elopement, all that. And I learned much else that I have not written down, about the world that I shall presently go and look upon in my own time.

We had two candles at our supper table. Afterward, and the night wind was rising, she asked me to blow out one and set the other behind a screen; so all night long we had the dark, but it was not so dark we could not see each other's faces. We talked on awhile; I told her more about Andrea. She slept some hours. The night wind calling and crying through the trees and over the rooftop did not waken her, but she woke when for a moment I took my hand away from hers. I returned it, and she slept again.

And once I think she felt some pain, or maybe it was grief that made her stir and moan. The wind had hushed, speaking only of trifling illusions; no other sound except some dog barking in Trempa village, and an owl. I said, "I'll stay with you, Mam Miriam."

"You cannot."

"Then I'll take you with me."

"How could that be?"

"I'll carry you. I'll steal a horse and carriage."

"Dear fool!"

"No, I mean it. There must be a way."

"Yes," she said, "and I'll dream of it awhile." And I think she did sleep again. I did, I know; then morning was touching the silence of our windows.

The daylight was on her face, and I blew out the candle, and I told her, "Mam Miriam, I'll make you walk. I believe you can, and you know it too." She stared up at me, not answering, not angry. "You are good. I think you've made me believe in God again, and so I've been praying that God should help you walk."

"Have I not prayed?"

"Come!" I said, and took her hands and lifted her in bed. "Come now, and I'll make you walk."

"I will do what I can," she said. "Set my feet on the floor, Benvenuto, and I will try to lift myself."

This I did. She was breathing hard. She said I was not to lift her, she must do it herself. "There's money in the drawer of that table," she said, and I was puzzled that she should speak of it now when she ought to be summoning all her forces to rise and walk. "And a few jewels brought from Sortees, we never sold them. Put them in your pocket, Benvenuto. I want to see you do that, to be sure you have them." I did as she said — never mind what I found in the drawer, since you have only my word for it that I did not rob her.

When I turned back to her, she was truly struggling to rise. I could see her legs tensing with life, and I believed we had won, even that God had answered a prayer, a thing I had never known to happen. A blood vessel was throbbing fiercely at her temple, her face had gone red, her eyes were wild with anger at her weakness.

"Now let me help," I said, and put my hands under her armpits, and with that small aid she did rise, she did stand on her own legs and smile at me with sweat on her face.

"I thank you, Benvenuto," she said, and her face was not red any more but white, her lips bluish. She was collapsing. I got her back on the bed Jon Kobler made, and that was the end of it.

I will go into the world and find my way, I will not die by my own hand, I will regret no act of love. If it may be, I will find Andrea, and if he wishes, we may travel into new places, the greater oceans, the wilderness where the sun goes down. Wherever I go I shall be free and shameless; take heed of me. I care nothing for your envy, your anger, your fear that simulates contempt. The God you invented has nothing to say to me; but I hear my friend say that any manner of love is good if there's kindness in it. Take heed of me. I am the night wind and the quiet morning light: take heed of me.

The Woman Who Loved the Moon
Elizabeth A. Lynn

Elizabeth A. Lynn was born in New York City, and lived in and near it for eighteen years. She began reading science fiction when she was nine. In 1964, she moved to the Midwest, living first in Cleveland, and next in Chicago, where she earned a master's degree in English Literature from the University of Chicago, taught grade school, and discovered feminism, aikido, and radical politics. In 1972, she moved to San Francisco. Two years later she ceased fulltime work to write. Lynn did the odd things most writers have to do to make a living: she taught aikido, waited tables in a nightclub, and did temporary office work until 1977, when she sold *A Different Light*, her first science fiction novel.

Since then Lynn has published three fantasy novels: *Watchtower*, *The Dancers of Arun*, and *The Northern Girl*, a second science fiction novel, *The Sardonyz Net*, and *The Woman Who Loved the Moon and Other Stories*, a short story collection. In 1980, *Watchtower* won the World Fantasy Award for Best Novel, and "The Woman Who Loved the Moon" tied for the same award for Best Short Fiction.

Lynn lives in San Francisco with a roommate, two cats, a

dog, and an IBM personal computer. She is the science fiction/fantasy editor for *The San Francisco Chronicle*. Occasionally, she teaches a course in feminist science fiction at San Francisco State University; she has also taught science fiction workshops for the University of California–San Francisco, at the Haystack (Portland State University) Summer Program, and at (Michigan State University) Clarion. In 1981, Lynn earned a first-degree black belt in aikido. She currently trains, teaches beginners' classes, and has begun to study the art of sword-drawing, iaido.

*T*hey tell this story in the Middle Counties of Ryoka, and especially in the county of Issho, the home of the Talvela family. In Issho they know that the name of the woman who loved the Moon was Kai Talvela, one of the three warrior sisters of Issho. Though the trees round the Talvela house grow taller now than they did in Kai Talvela's time, her people have not forgotten her. But outside of Issho and in the cities they know her only as the Mirror Ghost.

Kai Talvela was the daughter of Roko Talvela, at a time when the domain of the Talvelai was smaller than it is now. Certainly it was smaller than Roko Talvela liked. He rode out often to skirmish at the borders of his land, and the men of the Talvelai went with him. The hills of Issho county resounded to their shouts. While he was gone the folk of the household went about their business, for the Talvela lands were famous then as they are now for their fine orchards and the fine dappled horses they breed. They were well protected, despite the dearth of soldiery, for Lia Talvela was a sorcerer, and Kai and her sisters Tei and Alin guarded the house. The sisters were a formidable enemy, for they had learned to ride and to fight. The Talvela armorer had fashioned for them fine light mail that glittered as if carved from gems. At dawn and dusk the three sisters rode across the estate. Alin wore a blue-dyed plume on her peaked helmet, and Tei wore a gold one on hers. Kai wore a feather dyed red as blood. In the dusk their armor gleamed, and when it caught the starlight it glittered like the rising Moon.

Kai was the oldest of the sisters; Alin the youngest. In looks and in affection the three were very close. They were — as Talvela women are even in our day — tall and slim, with coal-black hair. Tei was the proudest of the three, and Alin was the most laughing and gay. Kai, the oldest, was quietest, and while Tei frowned often and Alin laughed, Kai's look was grave, direct, and serene. They were all of an age to be wed, and Roko Talvela had tried to find husbands for them. But Kai, Tei, and Alin had agreed that they would take no lover and wed no man who could not match their skills in combat. Few men wished to meet the warrior sisters. Even the bravest found themselves oddly unnerved when they faced Tei's long barbed spear and grim smile, or Alin's laughing eyes as she spun her oaken horn-tipped cudgel. It whirled like a live thing in her palms. And none desired to meet Kai's great curved blade. It sang when she swung it, a thin clear sound, purer than the note of the winter thrush. Because of that sound Kai named her blade *Song*. She kept it sharp, sharp as a shadow in the full Moon's light. She had a jeweled scabbard made to hold it, and to honor it. She caused a great ruby to be fixed in the hilt of the sword.

One day in the late afternoon the sisters rode, as was their custom, to inspect the fences and guardposts of the estate, making sure that the men Roko Talvela had left under their command were vigilant in their job. Their page went with them. He was a boy from Nakasé county, and like many of the folk of Nakasé he was a musician. He carried a horn which, when sounded, would summon the small company of guards, and his stringed lute from Ujo. He also carried a long-necked pipe, which he was just learning how to play. It was autumn. The leaves were rusty on the trees. In the dry sad air they rattled in the breeze as if they had been made of brass. A red sun sat on the horizon, and overhead swung the great silver face of the full Moon.

The page had been playing a children's song on the pipe. He took his lips from it and spoke. The storytellers of Ujo, in Nakasé county, when they tell this tale, insist that he was in love with one of the sisters, or perhaps with all three. There is no way to know, of course, if that is true. Certainly they had all, even proud Tei, been very kind to him. But he gazed upon the sisters in the rising moonlight, and his eyes worshipped. Stammering, he said, "O my ladies, each of you is beautiful, and together you rival even the Moon!"

Alin laughed, and swung her hair. Like water against diamond it brushed her armor. Even Tei smiled. But Kai was troubled. "Don't say that," she said gently. "It's not lucky, and it isn't true."

"But everyone says it, Lady," said the page.

Suddenly Tei exclaimed. "Look!" Kai and Alin wheeled their horses. A warrior was riding slowly toward them, across the bluehills. His steed was black, black as obsidian, black as a starless night, and the feather on his helmet was blacker than a raven's wing. His bridle and saddle and reins and his armor were silver as the mail of the Talvela women. He bore across his lap a blackthorn cudgel, tipped with ivory, and beside it lay a great barbed spear. At his side bobbed a black sheath and the protruding hilt of a silver sword. Silently he rode up the hill, and the darkness thickened at his back. The hooves of the black horse made no sound on the pebbly road.

As the rider came closer, he lifted his head and gazed at the Talvelai, and they could all see that the person they had thought a man was in fact a woman. Her hair was as white as snow, and her eyes gray as ash. The page lifted the horn to his lips to sound a warning. But Alin caught his wrist in her warm strong fingers. "Wait," she said. "I think she is alone, let us see what she wants." Behind the oncoming rider darkness thickened. A night bird called *Whooo*.

Tei said, "I did not know there was another woman warrior in the Middle Counties."

The warrior halted below the summit of the hill. Her voice was clear and cold as the winter wind blowing off the northern moors. "It is as they sing; you are indeed fair. Yet not so fair, I think, as the shining Moon."

Uneasily the women of Issho gazed at this enigmatic stranger. Finally Kai said, "You seem to know who we are. But we do not know you. Who are you, and from where do you come? Your armor bears no device. Are you from the Middle Counties?"

"No," said the stranger, "my home is far away." A smile like light flickered on her lips. "My name is — Sedi."

Kai's dark brows drew together, and Tei frowned, for Sedi's armor was unmarred by dirt or stain, and her horse looked fresh and unwearied. Kai thought, what if she is an illusion, sent by Roko Talvela's enemies? She said, "You are chary of your answers."

But Alin laughed. "O my sister, you are too suspicious," she said. She pointed to the staff across the stranger's knees. "Can you use that pretty stick?"

"In my land," Sedi said, "I am matchless." She ran her hand down the black cudgel's grain.

"Then I shall challenge you!" said Alin promptly. She smiled at her sisters. "Do not look so sour. It has been so long since there has been anyone who could fight with me!" Faced with her teasing smile, even Tei smiled in return, for neither of the two older sisters could refuse Alin anything.

"I accept," said Sedi sweetly. Kai thought, *An illusion cannot fight. Surely this woman is real.* Alin and Sedi dismounted their steeds. Sedi wore silks with silver and black markings beneath her shining mail. Kai looked at them and thought, I have seen those marks before. Yet as she stared at them she saw no discernible pattern. Under her armor Alin wore blue silk. She had woven it herself, and it was the color of a summer sky at dawn when the crickets are singing. She took her white cudgel in her hands, and made it spin in two great circles, so swiftly that it blurred in the air. Then she walked to the top of the hill, where the red sunlight and the pale moonlight lingered.

"Let us begin," she said.

Sedi moved opposite her. Her boots were black kid, and they made no sound as she stepped through the stubby grass. Kai felt a flower of fear wake in her heart. She almost turned to tell the page to wind his horn. But Alin set her staff to whirling, and it was too late. It spun and then with dizzying speed thrust toward Sedi's belly. Sedi parried the thrust, moving with flowing grace. Back and forth they struck and circled on the rise. Alin was laughing.

"This one is indeed a master, O my sisters," she called. "I have not been so tested in months!"

Suddenly the hard horn tip of Sedi's staff thrust toward Alin's face. She lifted her staff to deflect the blow. Quick as light, the black staff struck at her belly. Kai cried out. The head blow had been a feint. Alin gasped and fell, her arms folding over her stomach. Her lovely face was twisted with pain and white as moonlight on a lake. Blood bubbled from the corner of her mouth. Daintily, Sedi stepped away from her. Kai and Tei leaped from their horses. Kai unlaced her breastplate and lifted her helmet from her face.

"Oh," said Alin softly. "It hurts."

Tei whirled, reaching for her spear.

But Alin caught her arm with surprising strength. "No!" she said. "It was a fair fight, and I am fairly beaten."

Lightly Sedi mounted her horse. "Thy beauty is less than it was, women of Issho," she said. Noiselessly she guided her steed into the white mist coiling up the hill, and disappeared in its thick folds.

"Ride to the house," Kai said to the frightened page. "Bring aid and a litter. Hurry." She laid a palm on Alin's cheek. It was icy. Gently she began to chafe her sister's hands. The page raced away. Soon the men came from the house. They carried Alin Talvela to her bed, where her mother the sorcerer and healer waited to tend her.

But despite her mother's skills, Alin grew slowly more weak and wan. Lia Talvela said, "She bleeds within. I cannot stanch the wound." As Kai and Tei sat by the bed, Alin sank into a chill silence from which nothing, not even their loving touch, roused her. She died with the dawn. The folk of the household covered her with azure silk and laid her oaken staff at her hand. They coaxed Kai and Tei to their beds and gave them each a poppy potion, that they might sleep a dreamless sleep, undisturbed even by grief.

Word went to Roko Talvela to tell him of his daughter's death. Calling truce to his wars, he returned at once to Issho. All Issho county, and lords from the neighboring counties of Chuyo, Ippa, and Nakasé, came to the funeral. Kai and Tei Talvela rode at the head of the sad procession that brought the body of their sister to burial. The folk who lined the road pointed them out to each other, marveling at their beauty. But the more discerning saw that their faces were cold as if they had been frost-touched, like flowers in spring caught by a sudden wayward chill.

Autumn passed to winter. Snow fell, covering the hills and valleys of Issho. Issho households put away their silks and linens and wrapped themselves in wool. Fires blazed in the manor of the Talvelai. The warrior sisters of Issho put aside their armor and busied themselves in women's work. And it seemed to all who knew them that Kai had grown more silent and serious, and that proud Tei had grown more grim. The page tried to cheer them with his music. He played war songs, and drinking songs, and bawdy songs. But none of these tunes pleased the sisters. One day in desperation he said, "O my ladies, what would you hear?"

Frowning, Tei shook her head. "Nothing," she said.

But Kai said, "Do you know 'The Riddle Song?'" naming a children's tune. The page nodded. "Play it." He played it. After it he played "Dancing Bear" and "The Happy Hunter" and all the songs of childhood he could think of. And it seemed to him that Tei's hard mouth softened as she listened.

In spring Roko Talvela returned to his wars. Kai and Tei re-donned their armor. At dawn and at dusk they rode the perimeter of the domain, keeping up their custom, accompanied by the page. Spring gave way to summer, and summer to autumn. The farmers burned leaves in the dusk, covering the hills with a blue haze.

And one soft afternoon a figure in silver on a coal-black horse came out of the haze.

The pale face of the full Moon gleamed at her back. "It's she!" cried the page. He reached for his horn.

Tei said, "Wait." Her voice was harsh with pain. She touched the long spear across her knees, and her eyes glittered.

"O my sister, let us not wait," said Kai softly. But Tei seemed not to hear. Sedi approached in silence. Kai lifted her voice. "Stay, traveler. There is no welcome for you in Issho."

The white-haired woman smiled a crooked smile. "I did not come for welcome, O daughters of the Talvelai."

"What brought you here, then?" said Kai.

The warrior woman made no answer. But her gray eyes beneath her pale brows looked at Kai with startling eloquence. They seemed to say, patience. You will see.

Tei said, "She comes to gloat. O my sister, that we are two, and lonely, who once were three."

"I do not think—" Kai began.

Tei interrupted her. "Evil woman," she said, with passion. "Alin was all that is trusting and fair, and you struck her without warning." Dismounting from her dappled mare, she took in hand her long barbed spear. "Come, Sedi. Come and fight *me*."

"As you will," said Sedi. She leaped from her horse, spear in hand, and strode to the spot where Tei waited for her, spear ready. They fought. They thrust and parried and lunged. Slowly the autumn chill settled over the countryside. The spears flashed in the moonlight. Kai sat her horse, fingering the worked setting of the ruby on her sword. Sometimes it seemed to her that Sedi was stronger than Tei, and at other times Tei seemed stronger than Sedi. The polish on their silver armor shone like flame in the darkness.

At last, Tei tired. She breathed heavily, and her feet slipped in the nubby grass.

Kai had been waiting for this moment. She drew *Song* from the sheath and made ready to step between them. "Cease this!" she called. Sedi glanced at her.

"No!" cried Tei. She lunged. The tip of her spear sliced Sedi's arm. "I shall win!" she said.

Sedi grimaced. A cloud passed across the Moon. In the dimness, Sedi lunged forward. Her thrust slid under Tei's guard. The black-haired woman crumpled into the grass. Kai sprang to her sister's side. Blood poured from Tei's breast. "Tei!" Kai cried. Tei's eyes closed. Kai groaned. She knew death when she saw it. Raging, she called the page, "Sound the horn!"

The sweet sound echoed over the valley. In the distance came the answering calls from the Talvela men. Kai looked at Sedi, seated on her black steed. "Do you hear those horns, O murderous stranger? The Talvela soldiers come. You will not escape."

Sedi smiled. "I am not caught so easily," she said. At that moment Tei shook in Kai's arms, and life passed from her. The ground thrummed with the passage of horses. "Do you wish me caught, you must come seek me, Kai Talvela." Light flashed on her armor. Then the night rang with voices shouting.

The captain of the guard bent over Kai. "O my lady, who has done this thing?"

Kai started to point to the white-haired warrior. But among the dappled horses there was no black steed, and no sign of Sedi.

In vain the men of the Talvelai searched for her. In great sadness they brought the body of Tei Talvela home, and readied her for burial. Once more a procession rode the highway to the burial ground of the Talvelai. All Issho mourned.

But Kai Talvela did not weep. After the burial she went to her mother's chambers, and knelt at the sorcerer's knee. "O my mother, listen to me." And she told her mother everything she could remember of her sisters' meetings with the warrior who called herself Sedi.

Lia Talvela stroked her daughter's fine black hair. She listened, and her face grew pale. At last Kai ended. She waited for her mother to speak. "O my daughter," Lia Talvela said sadly, "I wish you had come to me when this Sedi first appeared. I could have told you then that she was no ordinary warrior. *Sedi* in the enchanter's tongue means Moon, and the woman you describe is one of the shades of that Lady. Her armor is impervious as the moonlight, and her steed is not a horse at all but Night itself taking animal shape. I fear that she heard the songs men sang praising the beauty of the women warriors of the Talvelai, and they made her angry. She came to earth to punish you."

"It was cruel," said Kai. "Are we responsible for what fools say and sing?"

"The elementals are often cruel," said Lia Talvela.

That night, Kai Talvela lay in her bed, unable to rest. Her bed seemed cold and strange to her. She reached to the left and then to the right, feeling the depressions in the great quilts where Alin and Tei had been used to sleeping. She pictured herself growing older and older until she was old, the warrior woman of Issho, alone and lonely until the day she died and they buried her beside her sisters. The Talvelai are long-lived folk. And it seemed to her that she would have preferred her sisters' fate.

The following spring travelers on the highways of Ryoka were treated to a strange apparition — a black-haired woman on a dappled horse riding slowly east.

She wore silver armor and carried a great curved sword, fashioned in the manner of the smiths of the Middle Counties. She moved from town to town. At the inns she would ask, "Where is the home of the nearest witch or wizard?" And when shown the way to the appropriate cottage or house or hollow or cave, she would go that way.

Of the wisefolk she asked always the same thing: "I look for the Lady who is sometimes known as Sedi." And the great among them gravely shook their heads, while the small grew frightened, and shrank away without response. Courteously she thanked them and returned to the road. When she came to the border of the Middle Counties, she did not hesitate, but continued into the Eastern Counties, where folk carry straight, double-edged blades, and the language they speak is strange.

At last she came to the hills that rise on the eastern edge of Ryoka. She was very weary. Her armor was encrusted with the grime of her journey. She drew her horse up the slope of a hill. It was twilight. The darkness out of the east seemed to sap the dappled stallion's strength, so that it plodded like a plowhorse. She was discouraged as well as weary, for in all her months of traveling she had heard no word of Sedi. I shall go home, she thought, and live in the Talvela manor, and wither. She gained the summit of the hill. There she halted. She looked down across the land, bones and heart aching. Beyond the dark shadows lay a line of silver like a silken ribbon in the dusk. And she knew that she could go no further. That silver line marked the edge of the world. She lifted her head and smelled the heavy salt scent of the open sea.

The silver sea grew brighter. Kai Talvela watched. Slowly the full Moon rose dripping out of the water.

So this is where the Moon lives, thought the woman warrior. She leaned on her horse. She was no fish, to chase the Moon into the ocean. But the thought of returning to Issho made her shiver. She raised her arms to the violet night. "O Moon, see me," she cried. "My armor is filth-covered. My horse is worn to a skeleton. I am no longer beautiful. O jealous one, cease your anger. Out of your pity, let me join my sisters. Release me!"

She waited for an answer. None came. Suddenly she grew very sleepy. She turned the horse about and led it back down the slope to a hollow where she had seen the feathery shape of a willow silhouetted against the dusk, and heard the music of a stream. Taking off her armor, she wrapped herself in her red woolen cloak. Then she curled into the long soft grass and fell instantly asleep.

She woke to warmth and the smell of food. Rubbing her eyes, she lifted on an elbow. It was dawn. White-haired, cloaked in black, Sedi knelt beside a fire, turning a spit on which broiled three small fish. She looked across the wispy flames and smiled, eyes gray as ash. Her voice was clear and soft as the summer wind. "Come and eat."

It was chilly by the sea. Kai stretched her hands to the fire, rubbing her fingers. Sedi gave her the spit. She nibbled the fish. They were real, no shadow or illusion. Little bones crunched beneath her teeth. She sat up and ate all three fish. Sedi watched her and did not speak.

When she had done, Kai Talvela laid the spit in the fire. Kneeling by the stream, she drank and washed her face. She returned to the place where she had slept, and lifted from the sheath her great curved blade. She saluted Sedi. "O Moon," she said, "or shade of the Moon, or whatever you may be, long have I searched for you, by whose hand perished the two people most dear to me. Without them I no longer wish to live. Yet I am a daughter of the Talvelai, and a warrior, and I would die in battle. O Sedi, will you fight?"

"I will," said the white-haired woman. She drew her own sword from its sheath.

They circled and cut and parried and cut again, while light deepened in the eastern sky. Neither was wearing armor, and so each stroke was double-deadly. Sedi's face was serene as the lambent Moon as she cut and thrust, weaving the tip of her blade in a deadly tapestry. I have only to drop my guard, Kai Talvela thought, and she will kill me. Yet something held her back. Sweat rolled down her sides. The blood pounded in her temples. The salty wind kissed her cheeks. In the swaying willow a bird was singing. She heard the song over the clash of the meeting blades. It came to her that life was sweet. I do not want to die, she thought. I am Kai Talvela, the warrior woman of Issho. I am strong. I will live.

Aloud she panted, "Sedi, I will kill you." The white-haired woman's face did not change, but the speed of her attack increased. She is strong, Kai Talvela thought, but I am stronger. Her palms grew slippery with sweat. Her lungs ached. Still she did not weaken. It was Sedi who slowed, tiring. Kai Talvela shouted with triumph. She swept Sedi's blade to one side and thrust in.

Song's sharp tip came to rest a finger's breadth from Sedi's naked throat. Kai Talvela said, "Now, sister-killer, I have you."

Across the shining sword, Sedi smiled. Kai waited for her to beg for life. She said nothing, only smiled like flickering moonlight. Her hair shone like pearl, and her eyes seemed depthless as the sea. Kai's hands trembled. She let her sword fall. "You are too beautiful, O Sedi."

With cool, white fingers Sedi took *Song* from Kai's hands. She brought her to the fire, and gave her water to drink in her cupped palms. She stroked Kai's black hair and laid her cool lips on Kai's flushed cheek. Then she took Kai's hand in her own, and pointed at the hillside. The skin of the earth shivered, like a horse shaking off a fly. A great rent appeared in the hill. Straight as a shaft of moonlight, a path cut through earth to the water's smooth edge. Sedi said, "Come with me."

And so Kai Talvela followed the Moon to her cave beneath the ocean. Time is different there than it is beneath the light of the sun, and it seemed to her that no time passed at all. She slept by day, and rose at night to ride with the Moon across the dark sky's face, to race the wolves across the plains and watch the dolphins playing in the burnished sea. She drank cool water from beneath the earth. She did not seem to need to eat. Whenever she grew sad or thoughtful Sedi would laugh and shake her long bright hair, and say, "O my love, why so somber?" And the touch of her fingers drove all complaint from Kai's mind and lips.

But one sleep she dreamed of an old woman standing by a window, calling her name. There was something familiar and beloved in the crone's wrinkled face. Three times she dreamed that dream. The old voice woke in her a longing to see sunlight and shadow, green grass and the flowers on the trees. The longing grew strong. She thought, Something has happened to me.

Returning to the cave at dawn, she said to Sedi, "O my friend and lover, let us sit awhile on land. I would watch the sunrise." Sedi consented. They sat at the foot of an immense willow beside a broad stream. A bird sang in the willow. Kai watched the grass color with the sunrise, turning from gray to rose, and from rose to green. And her memories awoke.

She said, "O my love, dear to me is the time I have spent with you beneath the sea. Yet I yearn for the country of my birth, for the smell of bread and meat. Sedi, let me go to my place."

Sedi rose from the grass. She stretched out both hands. "Truly, do you wish to leave me?" she said. There were tears in her gray eyes. Kai trembled. She almost stepped forward to take the white-haired woman in her arms and kiss the tears away.

"I do."

The form of Sedi shuddered, and changed. It grew until it towered in silver majesty above Kai's head, terrible, draped in light, eyes dark as night, a blazing giantess. Soft and awful as death, the Moon said, "Dare you say so, child of earth?"

Kai swallowed. Her voice remained steady. "I do."

The giantess dissolved into the form of Sedi. She regarded Kai. Her eyes were both sad and amused. "I cannot keep you. For in compelling you to love me I have learned to love you. I can no more coerce you than I can myself. But you must know, Kai Talvela, that much human time has passed since you entered the cave of the Moon. Roko Talvela is dead. Your cousin, Edan, is chief of the Talvelai. Your mother is alive, but very old. The very steed that brought you here has long since turned to dust."

"I will walk home," said Kai. And she knew that the old woman of her dream had been her mother, the sorcerer Lia.

Sedi sighed. "You do not have to do that. I love you so well that I will even help you leave me. Clothes I will give you, and armor, and a sword." She gestured. Silk and steel rose up from the earth and wrapped themselves about Kai's waist. The weight of a sword dragged at her belt. A horse trotted to her. It was black, and its eyes were pale. "This steed will bring you to Issho in less than a day."

Kai fingered the hilt of the sword, feeling there the faceted lump of a gem. She pulled it upward to look at it and saw a ruby embedded within it. She lifted off her helmet. A red plume nodded in the wind. She lifted her hands to the smooth skin of her face.

"You have not aged," said Sedi. "Do you wish to see?" A silver mirror appeared in her hands. Kai stared at the image of the warrior woman. She looked the same as the day she left Issho.

She looked at the Moon, feeling within her heart for the compulsion that had made her follow Sedi under the sea. She could not feel it. She held out her hands. "Sedi, I love you," she said. They embraced. Kai felt the Moon's cold tears on her cheek.

Sedi pressed the mirror into Kai's hands. "Take this. And on the nights when the Moon is full, do this." She whispered in Kai's ears.

Kai put the mirror between her breasts and mounted the black horse. "Farewell," she called. Sedi waved. The black horse bugled, and shook its ebony mane, and leaped. When Kai looked back she could not see the willow. She bowed her head. Her hair whipped her face. Beneath the silent hooves of Night the earth unrolled like a great brown mat. Kai sighed, remembering the laughter and the loving, and the nightly rides. Never would she race wolves across the plains, or watch the dolphins playing in the moonlit sea.

The black horse traveled so fast that Kai had no chance to observe the ways in which the world beneath her had changed. But when it halted she stared in puzzlement at the place it had brought her. Surely this was not her home. The trees were different. The house was too big. Yet the token of the Talvelai family gleamed on the tall front gate.

Seeing this lone warrior, the Talvelai guards came from the gatehouse. "Who are you?" they demanded. "What is your business here?"

"I am Kai Talvela," she said.

They scowled at her. "That is impossible. Kai Talvela disappeared fifty years ago!" And they barred her way to the house.

But she laughed at them; she who had fought and loved the Moon. She ripped her sword from its sheath and it sang in the air with a deadly note. "I am Kai Talvela, and I want to see my mother. I would not suggest that any of you try to stop me." She dismounted. Patting the horse, she said, "Thank you, O swift one. Now return to Sedi." The horse blew in her ear and vanished like smoke. The soldiers of the Talvelai froze in fear.

Kai Talvela found her mother in her bedroom, sitting by the window. She was ancient, tiny, a white-haired wrinkled woman dressed in lavender silk. Kai crossed the room and knelt by her mother's chair. "Mother," she said.

An elderly man, standing at the foot of the bed, opened his mouth to gape. He held a polished wooden flute. "Lady!"

Lia Talvela caressed her daughter's unaged cheek. "I have missed you," she said. "I called and called. Strong was the spell that held you. Where have you been?"

"In the cave of the Moon," Kai Talvela said. She put off her helmet, sword, and mail. Curled like a child against her mother's knee, she told the sorcerer everything. The old flute player started to leave the room. A gesture of Lia Talvela's stopped him. When she finished, Kai Talvela lifted her mother's hands to her lips. "I will never leave Issho again," she said.

Lia Talvela stroked her child's hair and said no more. Her hands stilled. When Kai looked up, her mother's eyes had closed. She was dead.

It took a long time before the Talvelai believed that this strange woman was truly Kai Talvela, returned from her journey, no older than the day she left Issho. Edan Talvela was especially loath to believe it. Truthfully, he was somewhat nervous of this fierce young woman. He could not understand why she would not tell them all where she had been for fifty years. "Who is to say she is not enchanted?" he said. But the flute master, who had been the sisters' page, recognized her, and said so steadfastly. Edan Talvela grew less nervous when Kai told him that she had no quarrel with his lordship of the

Talvelai. She wished merely to live at peace on the Issho estate. He had a house built for her behind the orchard, near the place of her sisters' and her mother's graves. During the day she sewed and spun, and walked through the orchard. It gave her great pleasure to be able to walk beneath the sun and smell the growing things of earth. In the evening she sat beside her doorway, watching night descend. Sometimes the old musician came to visit with her. He alone knew where she had been for fifty years. His knowledge did not trouble her, for she knew that her mother had trusted him. He played the songs that once she had asked him to play; "The Riddle Song" and other songs of childhood. He had grown to be both courtly and wise, and she liked to talk with him. She grew to be quite fond of him, and she blessed her mother's wisdom.

In the autumn after her return the old musician caught a cold, and died. The night after his funeral Kai Talvela wept into her pillow. She loved Issho. But now there was no one to talk to, no one who knew her. The other Talvelai avoided her, and their children scurried from her path as if she were a ghost. Her proper life had been taken away.

For the first time she thought, *I should not have come home. I should have stayed with Sedi.* The full Moon shining through her window seemed to mock her pain.

Suddenly she recalled Sedi's hands cupped around a mirror, and her whispered instructions. Kai ran to her chest and dug beneath the silks. The mirror was still there. Holding it carefully, she took it to the window and positioned it till the moonlight filled its silver face. She said the words Sedi had told her to say. The mirror grew. The moon swelled within it. It grew till it was tall as Kai. Then it trembled, like still water when a pebble strikes it. Out from the ripples of light stepped Sedi. The Moon smiled, and held out her arms. "Have you missed me?" she said. They embraced.

That night Kai's bed was warm. But at dawn Sedi left. "Will you come back?" Kai said.

"I will come when you call me," promised the elemental. Every month on the night of the full Moon Kai held the mirror to the light, and said the words. And every month Sedi returned.

But elementals are fickle, and they are not human, though they may take human shape. One night Sedi did not come. Kai Talvela waited long hours by the window. Years had passed since her return to Issho. She was no longer the woman of twenty who had emerged like a butterfly from the Moon's cave. Yet she was still beautiful, and her spirit was strong as it had ever been. When at last the sunlight came, she rose from her chair. Picking up the mirror from its place, she broke it over her knee.

It seemed to the Talvelai then that she grew old swiftly, aging a year in the space of a day. But her back did not bend, nor did her hair whiten. It remained as black as it had been in her youth. The storytellers say that she never spoke to anyone of her journey. But she must have broken silence one time, or else we would not know this story. Perhaps she spoke as she lay dying. She died on the night of the full Moon, in spring. At dawn some of her vigor returned, and she insisted that her attendants carry her to the window, and dress her in red silk, and lay her sword across her lap. She wore around her neck a piece of broken mirror on a silver chain. And the tale goes on to say that as she died her face brightened to near youthful beauty, and she lifted her arms to the light and cried, "Sedi!"

They buried Kai Talvela beside her mother and her sisters, and then forgot her. Fickleness is also a human trait. But some years later there was war in Issho county. The soldiers of the Talvelai were outnumbered. Doggedly they struggled, as the orchards burned around them. Their enemies backed them as far as the manor gate. It was dusk. They were losing. Suddenly a horn blew, and a woman in bright armor rode from out of nowhere, her mount a black stallion. She swung a shining sword in one fist. "Talvela soldiers, follow me!" she called. At her indomitable manner, the enemy was struck with terror. They dropped their swords and fled into the night. Those soldiers who were closest to the apparition swore that the woman was tall and raven-haired, as the women of the Talvelai are still. They swore also that the sword, as it cut the air, hummed a note so pure that you could almost say it sang.

That was the first appearance of Kai Talvela's shade. Sometimes she comes unarmored, dressed in red silk, gliding through the halls of the Issho estate. When she comes in this guise, she wears a pendant: a broken mirror on a silver chain. When she appears she brings courage to the Talvelai, and fear to their enemies. In the farms and the cities they call her the Mirror Ghost, because of the mirror pendant and because of her brilliant armor. But the folks of the estate know her by name. She is Kai Talvela, the warrior woman of Issho, who loved and fought the Moon, and was loved by her in return.

The daughters of the Talvelai never tire of the story. They ask for it again and again.

Going Down
Barry N. Malzberg

Between 1967 and 1975 Barry N. Malzberg published about
twenty science fiction novels, six collections, and somewhere
in excess of 200 short stories. While there were other writers in
this field's history who wrote more or with greater intensity of
ambition, probably none did both within this relatively small
compass of time. Since 1975, he has slowed production to a
trickle and indeed, he anticipates no further novels after the
1982 *Cross of Fire* (which was his first science fiction novel in
half a decade and itself based upon a 1977 novella).

Why a writer who did so much is now doing so little is not
a paradox but a confluency; the strained and intense production
would, at least in his case, have inevitably led to silence and ex-
ile (if not precisely "cunning"). All of these issues have been
much discussed in his collection of essays, *The Engines of the
Night* (Doubleday, 1982), in which all of the interstices of the
writer and the field are plumbed to the limits of his ability. "It
is worth saying only," opines Malzberg, "that my favorite
science fiction novels of my own, at this time, are *Beyond
Apollo, The Men Inside, The Last Transaction,* and *Scop,* and
my least favorite *The Empty People* (which was my first novel).
But my favorite novel altogether is *Underlay,* which was
published invisibly by Avon in 1974, enjoyed a sales life of

about five minutes, and is now completely unknown outside of my desultory efforts to propitiate it."

"Going Down," an intense and intensely bleak novelette, was written in the summer of 1972 for an original anthology of stories about futuristic sex (as opposed, he points out, to anachronistic sex); that anthology never appeared but the same editor eventually published the story in a volume entitled *Dystopian Visions*, which appeared in 1975 and, in his words, "enjoyed a commercial success to make *Underlay's* look like Stephen King." Malzberg recollects little of this novelette and even less — "happily, happily, oh so happily — of the stricken postpubescent who wrote it."

I

The subject will, through the devices of the Institute and the services offered, be enabled to explore all avenues of sexual release that tantalize him, but which, for one reason or another, he cannot enact in the "real world." Included for instance, might be such practices as homosexuality, bestiality, pedophilia, generalized sodomy, specialized sodomy, necrophilia or rape. These processes will also enable the subject to "unblock" buried or unconscious fetishes which, once discovered, will be similarly gratified. Since all of the experiences are inducted, (needless to say!) through hypno-therapy and do not impinge upon "reality," the subject will be shielded at all times from the very serious consequences that he might incur if he were to perform such acts in the public domain. The hypno-therapeutically induced experiences will be no less vivid or satisfying, however, than their actual counterparts, and the guidance of experienced and specially-trained Institute personnel will be available at all times to lead the subject through these diverse avenues in order to bring him to a fuller understanding of his drives and their fulfillment.

It is understood that such processes are guaranteed by the Institute under the mandates of the congress. It is further understood that those who psychologically desire entrance for prurient reasons alone will be summarily rejected. It is also a condition of entrance that a full release shall be signed by the patient — that is, the Institute assumes no specific liability for behavioral syndromes evidencing themselves subsequent to treatment — although all reasonable efforts will be made to avoid post-hypnotic shock. The possibility of adverse reaction is certainly low. Every subject who completes the course successfully will be granted a certificate available for display.

Unsuccessful candidates rejected by psychological profile may reapply after a waiting period of six months, during which time psychotherapy or meditation may be desirable.

II

"I want to be President," I said to the girl. "I want to design cities. I want to change the face of our time. I want to effect a change of consciousness so vast that no one will ever again look at the world in the same way. I want to survive death. Isn't that a perfectly normal set of ambitions? What do you think?"

"No," the girl said, a gentle, submissive girl whose name I do not recall; she must have been one of that succession of gentle, submissive girls I knew in those summers. "No, there shouldn't be anything wrong with it. What's the matter with ambition?" She leaned down to touch me again, and I felt the brush of her breasts at my knees, her hands on my back, the heat coming from her body in slow waves. "Let's just fuck now," she said, but there was nothing left of me even for this persuasion; we had fucked away the enormous afternoon of August, and now, slow changes inside and out, I looked at the fading light of her bedroom and tried to make order of what was building. "Come here," she said, but I rolled from her then, knees to chin, rolling and rolling to the far side of the bed where I reared to an elbow and spoke against the wall. "But I cannot do it," I said, "because I am trapped within myself, small obsessions, small desires, wracked by fantasies of the impossible. Everything the brochure says is true; I can never be free of them, nor with them can I design cities."

"I don't understand you. I know you're not crazy, but what are you talking about?"

"No one understands," I said. "Everybody's crazy, but you must believe that I have tested limitations of which you yourself would never be aware."

I talked that way that summer. It was a very long time ago and I thought that elevation of language was elevation of thought, pity me, but then, again, I had excuses. "I want to capture the world. I want my name to be world-famous. I want women who do not know me to feel desire, but this will never happen."

"Why should it?"

"I am going to enter the Institute," I advised the wall with some real decision, "and see if they can do the job for me. I have read the brochures and they make a good deal of sense, although, of course," I added gently, showing that I had a subtle grasp of reality, "you can never be entirely sure of everything from public relations copy."

"No," she said, "don't do that. Don't go into the Institute. What do you want to go into the Institute for? They're a bunch of crazy people there; it's very dangerous. Let me help you," she said, touching me again, shadow's touch on the buttocks, easing within, praying for some lever of excitement to unlock me. "Can't I help you?" A nice girl; of course, I may be sentimentalizing her a bit, and this conversation did not exactly take place, at least not in this way, but it would be nice to think that it did, and from the standpoint of a finished (or even unfinished) work of art, it *should* have happened.

"I don't think so," I said. "I just wanted to tell you this, really. I've already applied and been accepted. I'll be starting next week and retreat begins tomorrow, so this is really the last time for us. But you were entitled to know why," I added, then pivoted from her, stood up, began to search for my clothing. "I wouldn't want you to think that I had just rejected you," I pointed out.

"No!" she said. "No!" And she sprang from the bed, the eaves and ledges of her body wobbling away, reached toward me with insistence and cunning. To the end I did not retreat further but leaped upon her, took her by instinct if without lust for the last time, moving my body in the old way, making the familiar gestures of penetration, my mind tight, hard, bound at some great distance, and finally, like a tree breaking from age, she came around me in little strings and lay quietly as I pierced here, poked there, stroked her cheek. Her chest heaved. Her eyes closed. She slept.

I came away from her and went quietly from the bed, dressed quickly, buttocks hoisted to the wall for balance, and then I left her quickly. Her breath was even and regular, with a slight gasping intake when I closed the door. I knew then that she had not been sleeping, but out of some understanding I could not touch . . . she had released me.

Well, it makes a pretty scene. Whether it happened or not, I have no idea.

III

"It's 2020 now," the assistance case said, sweat breaking from the ledge of her forehead and coming into her eyes, not entirely unlike this girl of many years ago (I leak associations like a foundering ship spews water). "It's 2020 and a new era; I don't have to take this from you. I know my demands and rights; you give me what I need," she said, then leaned forward against the desk, shook her head in an effortful pause and then spat in my face.

I felt the spittle curve like blood off the chin, dripping then to the papers scattered on the desk. "Policies and procedures," I pointed out, using my training. "We must have policies and procedures. If you want larger quarters you'll have to explain—"

"Explain nothing, you old son-of-a-bitch!" the assistance case pointed out. "I demand!" Old I was to her, indeed — old at forty-five, hunched over my clerk's forms in clerk's posture (I tend to objectify myself nowadays; depersonalization is one of the signs of oncoming schizoid reaction, I calmly note), the sounds of the loft going on to the right and left of us, but locked into this booth one bare fan above putting out gusts of exhausted air. "Put it through for me," she said, "or I'll have you beaten out of the Government. Old fucker, we have rights!"

Rights. All of them have rights. Looking at her through the one necessary moment of flat confrontation, the drugs making her assume a somewhat sentimentalized posture (after all, she could have been a madonna, I reminded myself — a madonna in trouble), those sweeping, soaring hands which, if they were knives, would have cut me open, the garments parted drably here and there to give out whiffs of her body — looking at her in this way it occurred to me that I should stand, close down the investigation and leave this area. Just *leave*, prowl the streets, have some more drugs, consider the convolutions and difficulties of a public assistance program that in eighty-seven years had not changed from its original assumptions that themselves were wrong. This really occurred to me despite the fact that I would risk loss of pension rights and the Ever Horizons Program offered by the agency. But, of course, I would not do this, attractive as it seemed, because I had accepted my fate, much as it had accommodated me, and what would be worked out would only occur within these spaces. Sound of fans, low murmurs in the center, isolation. Cases like this might have attracted attention (in the era of low confrontation, confrontation should in itself be interesting), but since the four murders committed in the center last month, staff tends to keep to itself. Any shriek here might be semaphore to more blood; certainly, I would not go near an agitated recipient. "I don't think that this is getting us anywhere," I said. "Maybe you should simply leave now and come back another time when you're somewhat calmer." Disassociative reaction; not interested now in my own identity, I can hardly be expected to pay much attention to theirs.

"I'm terminating this interview," I said. "I am terminating this interview," he said as well. He and I both said it.

Halfway through the corridor, however, she caught up with me. Clinging, grabbing, gnawing. Her earlier aggression had been tenuous; the drug had misled me into seeing menace where there was only despair. The usual error. "Please," she said, hanging on, "please, now, you've got to help me, sir. I'm really sorry that I cursed you before, but I'm so worried, worried about everything, don't you understand, understand, understand that? Got to help me, got to help me get a place." No, I do not. "Yes, you must. You've got to." No, I am afraid that I do not. Get away from me, cunt.

Away from her, leaving her sprawled on the floor, I strode the corridor like a demon, strong and calm, brave and free, in control for that instant of my destiny and the world's. Only, however, for a moment. These flashes will not carry anymore; increasing amounts of drugs must be taken just for little shy twitches of the way it used to be almost always.

Alone, alone at last, I found myself a booth on the next level and was able to sit before the spasms began. The spasms brought out tears that made him very sick; let me tell you that.

IV

The subject is a white, Anglo-Saxon male. Birthdate: 11/22/63. He states that the fact of his birthday has "always had a profound effect," since the incidence of that birthday with the assassination of Kennedy Number One has given him a feeling of "unique destiny and obligation." Subject is five feet, eight inches tall; one hundred and forty-three pounds; blood pressure one-forty over seventy-five; reflexes and motor responses within the gross normal range. Health may be considered acceptable at the present time; the shocks of therapy involve no mortal risk.

Subject states that he "wants to be President, wants to design cities, be loved by women who do not know me," et cetera, but he does not feel capable of realizing his drives at the present time. "I am trapped within myself, small obsessions, small desires, wracked by fantasies of the impossible. That is why I am seeking treatment. I need and deserve treatment." The preceding has some air of rehearsal. It is indicated that the subject has planned out his approach. Spontaneity is lacking. Subject says that he "teems with sexual repression" and hopes that the Institute will provide the opportunity to "explore" said repression so that at last he will be "free."

In summary, although the subject seems to be reasonably intelligent and aware of the nature of the treatments, he is *not* aware of the intentions of the Institute.

Subject's questionnaire indicates interest in the following acts: pederasty, homosexuality, anal intercourse and bestiality. Under preliminary hypnosis it was discovered that the subject's obsessions verge upon an extreme sadomasochistic syndrome with possible fantasies of murder. Such drives are sublimated. Subject lacks insight into these drives. He has had a number of relationships of a heterosexual nature, all of them superficial. Most have been of short duration. He states, however, that he has never had much trouble in "meeting girls or getting laid," and judging from internal and external evidence, interviewer can agree with this!

Under hypnosis, subject disclosed a strong identification with John F. Kennedy, thirty-fifth President of the United

States: 5/30/17–11/22/63. John F. Kennedy, the subject stated, "had none of the repressions that I have. Why, here was a man able to accomplish every conceivable act he dreamed of doing, desire equaling achievement. I want to be strong and successful just like him, and because I was born on the day of his death I'm entitled to that, the transmigration of souls and so on. . . but how can I get things done if I am constantly over-whelmed by terrible, unspeakable desires? Oh, my, I teem with urges, urges I can barely express, and if I cannot pass beyond them I know that I will always fail."

Subject also revealed a number of extraneous details that are excluded from the report since they are not relevant.

Subject disclosed accounts of $19,321 in conventional savings and stock-transfer holdings, assets that were the result of a recent inheritance from his father, who had died on 4/11/87, willing his entire estate to his son. It was the receipt of this inheritance, the subject stated, that made it possible for him to think for the first time of the Institute as the solution to his difficulties. "What is $19,000 now?" subject stated. "I couldn't live on it; I could barely die on it, but it would finance my way into the Institute, and then I might be found an interesting case, worthy of further treatment." Assignment of said assets has, of course, already been effected.

It is recommended, accordingly, that the subject be admitted. Only as much of the purpose and processes of the Institute have been explained to him as the interviewer felt minimally necessary at the present time. Subject should be an excellent candidate. He expresses resistance to treatment at no conscious or preconscious level. He can be expected to cooperate throughout. He is, therefore, an ideal candidate.

V

Later at night, merged with Antonio, sliding and blending with him, rising above him, I felt on the verge of a breakthrough, some reciprocity of feeling not known before, and then, with orgasm, the same grief and futility. Nothing, nothing: at the last moment I have been betrayed, as has happened time and time again (notice the self-pity, but I am entitled to it, friends), and I do not know if the fault is within Antonio (homosexuality is, after all, still a perversion, I feel) or in myself. I cannot tell; he cannot tell. Leaving Antonio then spent on the bed, not a word between us, because he understands my failure as I understood his (coming into him I knew that he, too, had felt nothing), and so I left the apartment, then, throwing on an overcoat, nothing else, naked under the wool, a perverse excitement reaching at me again, and I took the elevator to the bottom level, then went out on the path to an open space and looked out upon the city.

The wind tore at my body through the coat, tore at the man's body, stirring the ruined blood. At length I realized that there was someone on the overhang beside me, and I thought for a moment that it was Antonio, come to speak with me again... for at the end of all failures comes, in Antonio, anyway, the inexhaustible need to converse, whereas I desire only silence... but, turning, I could see that it was not. It was a little man from the second level, a clerk in the assistance center in which I work whose name I had never known and did not want to know... but in a terrified way this clerk has been pursuing me for weeks, scuttling through and around the trap of our mutual lives, happening on elevators as I did, joining me on the overhang, thrusting a frozen hip cruelly into mine when I had been wandering, alone I would have thought, on the grounds surrounding the complex.

"Beautiful night," he said, "isn't it? Even for the city it's a beautiful night."

I said nothing; gathered my coat more tightly around me. Surely if he sensed that I was naked underneath he would take it as an invitation. The man was naked underneath, I said; the feel of the wool against him gave him a perverse sense of excitement. I control no situations anymore.

"It's just like the two of us are here alone in this wonderful city," the man said. "Haven't you ever felt that — that you're with someone you hardly know in an isolated spot and all of a sudden it could be only the two of you in the world, for all that that world cares? Feel the wind," he said, granted lunatic inspiration by my silence, or, then again, maybe he simply liked to talk that way. "Aren't you cold?" He reached forward to touch me.

"No," I said, stepping brutally from him. "I am not cold. Please leave me alone. I don't want to talk."

"Come to my room," he said, his voice thin and fragrant in the night. How I must have incited his desire! Well, this is only natural, I being a most attractive man. "Only for an hour. Why not? I've wanted you for weeks; don't you know that? I can make you happy." Something had opened up within the madman; he was no longer shy. I could feel the pressure of him more insistently now, digging in waves below the surfaces, lightening and deadening in alteration. It might have reminded the naked man in the overcoat of the girl he had once known, although I do not want to seek such easy cohesion. Quickly the man in the overcoat moved from him, leaned tightly against the balcony, then turned at last for a fuller confrontation.

Oh, my! He was old, old, disorder had eaten away, desire had shriveled, his mouth opened and he showed me his tongue. "Please," he said, "surely you know I won't hurt you. I know that you want to come with me. You don't care for the other at all; I know that. I've researched your life," he said. "You can't hide anything from me, not ever. The other will not work out. Come with me."

"No," the naked man in the overcoat said finally. After a pause, he then said, "You feel; do you think that it would make any difference if I did? How can I give you identity? I have none of my own."

"I don't want identity; I want to fuck you," the stranger said hopelessly, "and, besides, I'll make you happy. . . ."

"There are no promises," the disassociative naked man in the overcoat said. "There are no possibilities; there is simply the infinite trap of self, the one refracting instant when that frozen self is known again and forever." He gestured floridly, perhaps repelled by his rhetoric. Then he moved quickly away from the stranger, miming a violent gesture. "Find someone else," he said. "There are a million others in the city who spend hours in the rooms of others, and any one of them would give you more than I. I have nothing; do you understand that?" And then he added, after an instant, "I'm sorry," and he did not know if he was extending mercy or a taunt as he went inside, the wool sticky with perverse sweat, beating at him with insect wings as he closed the door and headed toward the elevator.

He thought that he might have seen the stranger bend on the balcony in a posture of tears; he thought that he might have seen no such things — his perceptions are muddled, he is fifty-seven years old and rarely sees what he used to, although in the best of health, of course, the overcoat swaddling him as he trotted back to his rooms carrying, as always, that eternal burden: the body.

VI

Under hypno-therapeutic block, the subject was given the usual tapes and promptings. He was permitted to enact the fetishes and practices disclosed at the conscious level. Subject was led through homosexuality, pederasty, bestiality and other practices. This stage of treatment lasted one week, at the end of which the subject appeared for standard, checking interview. He was not articulate about his reactions; had to be coached into response.

Under strong questioning the subject finally disclosed that "It was all right, everything I could have expected. I mean, I'm not quibbling with the reality of it; it certainly seemed real enough. But I have the feeling that I'm missing something, haven't put it together yet." This response well within the normal range.

Subject hesitated and continued under prodding: "It's hard to tell what I'm missing exactly, because I did do everything I wanted to do, but there was a feeling of incompletion. Knowing through all of it in the back of my head that it was just a dream. That can hold you back and make you feel silly, and then, too, I wonder if I was telling the truth; I mean, I thought it was the truth, but evidently I was holding something back. There must be another level of desire, if you follow what I'm saying — things that I've wanted to do that I can't even admit to myself."

Subject, it can thus be said, showed an initial level of insight. The prediction of this interviewer that he would be an excellent candidate was therefore completely verified. I call the attention of the board to this.

"I'm ready," the subject stated. "I feel that I'm ready now, that the rest of it was just a preparation. Show me now. Show me what I *really* want to do. I'm ready for it; I'll never be what I can until I see where I've been, and I know this. Show me the dark heart of my desire, at least until the $19,000 is used up."

Subject's rhetoric has persistent flashes of this nature. He tends to become melodramatic at key moments and shows some lability of effect, manifested primarily in abstruse speech and florid, rhetorical devices. These may be discounted as potent defense mechanisms.

It is recommended that we proceed.

VII

Disassociative reaction much better, much better — I know exactly who I am, gentlefolk, thank you very much — and so onward, into the dark. Kennedy ceremonies at the center, a day off although attendance at the center is itself compulsory. Government employees must pay minimal homage, et cetera. My clerkly forms folded for the holiday, my clerkish frame bent to an appropriate shuffle, I proceed past the gate and to the great adjoining lane where the ceremonies take place. It is necessary and just that employees show affinity with their history by attendance at the ceremony... but if it were all the same to me I would rather be elsewhere, even in a small room with Antonio... and this morning, incidentally, I told the man that all was finished. In my head. Extrinsically, not quite yet. But soon, soon. Will he cry? There are still, I believe, reservoirs of feeling here or there.

Kennedy Day? John F. would have been 103 if he had survived, the other merely ninety-six, the third ninety, but I never saw powers of survival in the two younger. It was that elder who interested me, not only because of the coincidence of birthdate — and sometimes I must smile, remembering what that meant to me long years ago — but because it is possible to tell by those old photographs, bedazzling in the light outside, that he was a man who had passed all barriers of expression. He had literally every experience that the simple accesses of the body might accommodate, and it was this knowledge — every orifice satisfied, that is to say — that had given him the power of command.

In youth, tantalized by this collision of his death, my birth, I had scurried through the libraries and museums seeking information on Kennedy Number One so that I would be able somehow, somehow to emulate, and even thirty years later (thirty years!) something within that lordly memory must call to me yet... for I stand upon the street during the ceremonies, transfixed once again by their simple elegance. Their meaning.

Opening their masks, the dancers come for the ritual, then the speeches and finally re-enactment of the assassination itself, a re-enactment that is simply a renewal of that martyrdom that sent us on our simple way. In this dense crowd, jammed comically among the bodies of other clerks, I feel surges — for just a moment — of the old desire. I feel that I could rise above and by the power of my rage alone seek control... but this emotion, too, passes, and as the assassins crawl from their high places to kill the dancers I feel the energy dwindle. It collapses within me. In place, drained, I remain.

"What's wrong?" Antonio says. We work close together in the center; it is impossible to avoid him, ever. There are no partitions in our relationship, then, which is one of the reasons why I have decided that it must end. "You look terrible." He laughs at this, touches me on the back. Winks. "Tonight," he says, reconstituting an old joke, "I will make a man out of you." His humor.

I retreat from his touch, stumbling into other bodies. I wave my arms to establish between us a small, neutral area as the dancers crumple. And then, not entirely to my surprise, I find that I am screaming.

"Leave me alone!" I scream. "You have got to leave me alone now!"

"What's wrong with you?" Antonio says, looking keenly in the old way, then turning to some of the others as if to seek the approval he deserves. "You look crazy. What's happened to you?"

"Nothing happened. Nothing will ever happen." The gun, amplified, booms over the dancers and the great mask, sixteen feet high and five feet wide, is hoisted slowly into the air, dominating us, flapping by rotors in the still, dead little currents. Disassociation begins once more. "Nothing's happened," he says. "It's just that you must leave me alone."

The man of whom we are speaking — the clerkly protagonist of this narration — wants to run, is seized throughout his fifty-seven-year-old frame by an idiot wish for flight... but attendance at Kennedy Day is compulsory, and what would happen to him if he dived into the center, whimpering? What would they make of this man and what has happened to his control: he feels that he has become translucent.

Translucent, he is attacked by color: little red and gray fibers of fright coming alive under the skin, giving him the feeling, or should we say *impression* of phosphorescence. He reaches to the crowd. "Oh, my God!" the fifty-seven-year-old clerk cries. "Oh, my God!" A definite sense of inadequacy seizes him. "This isn't right."

The mask is hoisted, the solemn and dead eyes of that long-ago murdered chief of state peering at and through the clerk with distance as he huddles before that mask. "What is going on?" the clerk avers. "What is happening here?" He turns to pelt from the area, then, despite the rules and regulations of the service, he staggers through bodies and up against the implacable doors of the center, beating, beating like a heart for entrance. "I identified with him," he mentions, expostulating in a cold, mad, furious little voice, expostulatory and tearful by turns as he tries to make this vital point. "I thought that I could be like him if the Institute had done its dreadful work." And now Antonio comes behind him.

Antonio's hands rush up and down his back as a matter of fact, excess of connection, but it is not lust, not this; it is inspection that drives him through his gestures and, mumbling, the clerk submits to his grasp. What else could he have done? The doors of the center, gentlefolk, are locked.

"You thought you could be like him?" Antonio says. He cackles in an unseemly way, but his laughter is no less offensive than the clerk's; it streams and bubbles, rivulets of laughter running like blood. "You like him?" And he is all around the hapless clerk, pity him, and bodies are all over. He must be having an attack of some sort, first heart attack at fifty-seven, and events become magnified, events become removed, dwindled and enormous, beating like a heart around him... like ancient film — Zapruder, I may say — near and far, far and near, the very best of it picking up in rhythm with the clerkly pulse, the pulse ragged and frantic, and it must only be then, mercifully, that the clerk faints, or at least this episode of his memoirs concludes: the ceremonies of memory, the mask dancing above him, he thinks in his faint, and locked into position he dies on the stones, a bullet in his neck, in his head, that second bullet penetrating the shoulder. An Anglo-Saxon white male. Think of that.

VIII

In the Institute, under the block, I fucked an old man. As I fucked I murdered him. Oh, my God, the ecstasy of it! To say nothing of the cunning of the Institute to give me such sweeping rejoinder to possibilities. Leaning over him on the bed, penetrating fully, opening like a flower inside him, and so I fucked him and struck, using the knife to make a swift cross-stroke from back to ribs that opened him like a vegetable. Nevertheless, those strokes would not kill him for a long, long time. He would suffer. Indubitably, in or out of dreams, he would suffer.

Who would have thought that I had it in me?

Who would have thought that this be my mean desire? But I believed them. I believed the Institute, for I had come there to be fulfilled... and, also, under the drugs, anything — *anything* — I believe would have been an ecstasy and a release, or so the technicians whispered as they shot me full. "Remember, remember that this isn't real," they counseled as I went under, every single time, "this isn't actually happening, no matter how concrete the interior reality, or, at least if it's happening, it isn't happening very often." How comforting! Did they think, then, that I would take all of this and disappear underneath in a conviction of actuality? Well, there must have been policies and procedures established.

"It isn't real, it isn't real," they pointed out as the drugs seized me, and then I was astride the old man, beating and flailing, screaming at him as I cut and pumped, and I could see life running out of him in small, bright pulses as I worked the incisions with the tenderness of a lover, biting away at his body.

I never saw his face.

His face lay buried in the pillows, and, try as I did to taunt and strike him into confrontation, he never would, the old fucker. All of his expression was in the line and heave of his body, that and in the small grunts he made as he took me in. The pumping and the knife. He never pleaded; he never protested. And he never resisted me at all.

"Take that, you old son-of-a-bitch!" I mentioned, driving at him. "That and that and that!" I cut and jabbed and the full darkness of my deed overtook then with a singing vault and I felt myself beginning to emerge within him. "And that!" I commented, putting the knife between his shoulder blades with all force.

And came within him then, colors of the blood intermingling. That queer orgasm was intense. I closed my eyes and in that enclosure had a view of his face: it was burned within the tormented eyelids, that face woeful and turned toward me at last in shades of red and green, and I looked at that face in the fluorescence for a long time, all the rivers running away, away: the face was that of my father.

I recall wondering at just that moment whether this treatment was quite necessary, after all. Or whether I had been misled.

Meanwhile, quite excited, I fucked my father.

IX

The next day, lying in that apartment, quite alone, stunned by the heat coming through the grillwork and the aftermath of the Kennedy ceremonies, the clerk was visited by the man who he met on the overhang, that man who had been pursuing him, that man who he had begun to think of (he has a very ordinary mind) as the Traveler.

The Traveler came in quietly through the open door, swept through the archway and into the bed nook where the clerk had been sitting propped up, reading memorabilia while dozing intermittently on the pillows Antonio had heaped for him. Too weak to battle, the clerk has agreed that it would be best for him to stay away from the center until strength was fully restored. He had feared the uselessness and boredom of idleness, but the apprehensions had been all wrong; that day had been pleasant and easy, restful and pleasant and filled with images of Antonio, who had proved once again how well he understood and knew how to take care... of the clerk. If for no other reason, the clerk thought, the relationship with Antonio must continue.

"Hi, there," the Traveler said, coming to the bedside, leaning over, with great compassion. "I missed you there today and heard that you were home. I wanted to come and see you." He lays a hand on the bed clothes. The clerk can feel the warmth trembling through the various layers, but he lies there quietly, giving no indications of his true response, which is still in the process of preparation. He lies quietly underneath him then, that touch.

"Are you feeling better?" the Traveler asks. "That's the important thing, of course."

"There is nothing to be done for you," the clerk says. The weakness has led to a fusion of purpose, an impatience of gesture that guides him through dialogue. "You must understand this now. I have nothing inside. All of that disappeared a long time ago."

"There is much I can do for you," the Traveler says blandly, sensuality darting in and out of that masking face on bird's wing. The pressure of his hand increases. "I want to do much for you."

"I can no longer feel," the clerk contributes. "I live by convenience and endure life because it is too much trouble to resist." He is rather a self-pitying clerk, as has been noted previously. "I have nothing for you. I have nothing for anyone."

"You have not lost feeling," the Traveler says. "You abandoned it."

"Not so."

"Yes, you did. It was the price." The Traveler's face is deep and filled with knowledge; it hovers over the clerk. "The other means nothing," he says, "so come with me. Live with me and be my love," he says huskily. The clerk smiles at the archaicism. He has little enough at which to exercise his keen and highly developed sense of humor; he can at least enjoy a sentimental archaicism when it makes itself present. Grant him this. Have pity. Be reasonable.

"I am fifty-seven years old," the clerk notes. "I am an obscure man; I am deadened. There is nothing left." Memorabilia slide to the floor from his diminished grasp, portraits of the dull, elder Kennedy mingling with photostats of ancient newspaper pages. "You are wrong if you think there is anything. Please go," the clerk concludes, "and you would have made all much easier."

"You don't realize," the Traveler says. He lowers himself against the clerk on the bed and with an easy gesture holds him. The clerk snaffles and sighs. Why not? "You misunderstand even yourself."

The clerk feels arms gathering around him, the hot, uneven whisk of brow against brow as the faces meet, and in that instant the clerk's control breaks to dependence and he begins — consider this, gentlefolk! — to cry. "Oh, my!" he says. "Oh, my God!" And he utters other similar reactions as his body begins to move in the ancient winding motions. He brings down the sheet under which the clerk lies naked, seeks with his hand. "Please let me," the Traveler suggests, "please let me do this. There is nothing wrong with desire; it is only the warping that leads to destruction."

The clerk closes his eyes. He drifts at once into a far space divorced of sensation. In this space it is easy to allow the Traveler to proceed. His touch of insistence is like a wandering fly's crawl to the clerk. The Traveler's hands clamber over the body; the clerk allows them that majesty. After all, he is not personally culpable. We are now talking of someone else.

The Traveler heaves and groans; he penetrates as quickly and insistently as that fly might invade an ear, and the clerk permits this, too. No fissure at the entrance as is so often the case with Antonio. He does not split me — I mean the clerk — open; the Traveler (we are talking about someone else; I have nothing to do with this), instead, he closes up. The clerk regards this with detached interest. He feels to be at a great remove. The energy of the motions heightens; the Traveler groans and bucks behind. Rear entry. Invisible that way, he begins to whisper words of love, meanwhile twisting hair. The clerk closes his eyes once again and sees him radiant, an arc of light shrouding.

The Traveler comes. I hear — I mean the clerk hears; I have nothing to do with this — the faint whine and sputter of release. Otherwise, no sensation. No sensation. He falls away. The clerk digs his little heels into parting and stares at the ceiling as he rolls. Now, in the aftermath of emission, the face of the Traveler is cold, hard, driven to stone. Only the faint beating of those eyelids indicates that only months ago, moments ago, he reared over as if he felt that I, inert receptacle, could share his life.

The clerk knows that it is finished, and to the degree that he knows this the Traveler and he have become one.

One.

X

At the final interview it was determined that the sexual fantasies of the subject were not granted, but the deeper sexual fantasies *were* granted, and the condition of the subject as a result of this may indicate that the Institute has no business going beyond its position as stated in the mandates.

The interviewer would also like to take this occasion — this report, that is to say — to resign from the Institute. This is an irrevocable decision, I believe.

XI

All is spiritless with the clerk the next morning when however spiritless he wends himself into the offices. On the access staircase, an assistance case who may or may not have been the woman the clerk remembers as threatening him some days ago looks at him profoundly and then with a giggle hurls him into the wall.

"I knew," she says, "I knew that you folks meant nothing; we can do anything to you, beat the shit out of you," and then she departs, leaving the clerk severely disturbed and agitated, although he does not, does not retaliate. Indeed, the woman may be right, although the clerk has not investigated the issue to sufficient death.

On the balcony, signals of the ceremony still remain. Posters and flyers and reproductions that the custodial staff have neglected to remove dot the walls. They mean nothing to the clerk. They have lost the power to touch.

He now hangs up his jacket in the staff area and then walks to a window where he looks out upon the city for a long, quiet time, meditating all of the events of the week and where they will take him. He tries to induce some feeling by tearing out scenes from those recollections and making posters of them himself — the Traveler panting, Antonio weeping, the assistance case shouting. Circuitry is dead and disassembled, however. Nothing happens. He should have expected nothing else, of course; it has been this way for many years.

At length, the clerk senses a presence behind him. He turns and sees Antonio and the Traveler together, their hands clutched, looking at him with expectation. In the joining of those hands he sees all that he needs and turns back from them, faces the window, looks out past the rim of the city to the brown fields of the enclosure. He feels a tap on his shoulder, however. So much for disassociation.

Antonio says, "We wanted to tell you. . . "

"I know."

"I tried," the Traveler says encouragingly, "but. . ."

"I understand that, too," the clerk says. He moves from them, gracefully opening up space between them and the window. "It does not matter. Nothing matters."

"Do you give permission, then?" Antonio says. His face is like a young boy.

"I have no permission to give."

"Leave him," the Traveler says, "just leave him alone."

"Do that."

"I know how you feel."

"I do not feel. I feel nothing."

"I know that," the Traveler says, this small shapeless man showing an authority never before suspected. Insistently, he leads Antonio away. It must be love that has given him this strength, the clerk sentimentally concludes.

He watches them disappear together. Perhaps he is envious. More likely not. Moment by moment, he will connect the devices of his life and resume the day: he knows this, but it is not without reluctance that he leaves the small ground that has been staked out and moves away from the colors of the city beneath.

Antonio will have left, he concludes, by the time he returns.

He should not feel pain at this.

He does not.

He feels nothing.

XII

"I want to build cities. I want to love women. I want to enter the Institute and become a part of myself."

XIII

The clerk lies like a bloodstain in the bed, sopping. He lets the night overtake him.

XIV

He hurled himself into the girl of that summer — he moved into her so deeply that he could not tell if it was flight or discovery. He fucked. He came. He felt.

XV

In these months that pass he sees Antonio and the Traveler together and they seem happy. They looked at him with the careful, measuring eyes of strangers and he does not speak to them. If he spoke, it would be in a language that they did not understand. He does not want to hurt them. He can salvage that much.

XVI

"I will enter the Institute and become a part of myself."

XVII

In March, at the first brush of spring, death whisks at him with a groan in the heart and as he falls to the stones, breaking, what spills from him is the first that he has felt in over thirty years... and the explosion is so great that he seizes the lover death with a roar of need and mounting, mounting, rides him like a stallion through all the mad halls of forever.

Black Rose and White Rose
Rachel Pollack

Rachel Pollack was born in Brooklyn in 1956 and moved at the age of nine to Poughkeepsie, New York. After earning an M.A. in English, she worked at IBM, taught at the State University of New York, then moved to Europe. For a year she lived in London, then in Amsterdam, where she has lived for the last ten years.

Pollack's writing spans several genres, an approach difficult in our categorized time. Her science fiction includes a novel, *Golden Vanity*, published by Berkley, with a second, *The Country of the Dead*, due out shortly from the same publisher at the end of the year. Pollack has written a two-part study of Tarot cards, *Seventy-Eight Degrees of Wisdom*, the result of several years as a professional reader and a course she taught at a meditation center in Amsterdam. Stories and poems of hers have appeared in literary magazines in Holland, England, and America. Several series of a form she calls "Fake Dreams" have appeared or will appear in various journals, including *Dreamworks*, a university quarterly on dream studies. As a founder-member of the Amsterdam poetry group, Cooperative Intuition, she has performed her work in centers in

Holland, as well as reading on a poetry program on television in Woodstock, New York.

"Black Rose and White Rose" was composed almost whole as a kind of adult bedtime story told to Edith Katz after a day of walking the chill windy beach at Zandvoort near Amsterdam. Katz and she (the former is a poet and playwright) have lived together for fourteen years.

Pollack's current projects includes *The Drinker of the Night*, a novel about a storyteller in a society where myth and magic have replaced materialism as the basic philosophical approach to the world. The opening chapters are set in Poughkeepsie.

*O*nce, in a kingdom near the East edge of the world, there lived a girl with skin so white, whiter and softer than a flower, that everyone called her White Rose. Now White Rose's parents had little money, so when travelers marveled at their daughter's beauty they thought, "White Rose can help us die wealthy." The mother sewed a long white dress with golden lace along the sleeves, the father sold their only cow to buy a silver comb. All day White Rose sat in the parlor by the garden, combing her long blonde hair while princes and merchants came to stare at her and court her. Nighttime, after the suitors had left, her parents told her over and over how much they loved her and how they'd all live together in a golden palace served by a thousand slaves.

White Rose only looked out the window where the flowers swayed as if they watched her. She wished the dusty pink and violet and black-speckled gold could touch her whiteness. She wished she could lie down in the green grass and feel the sun's morning blaze as it leaped off Mt. Talopel. After a time, when the princes and merchants chattered to her, White Rose just closed her eyes or shook her head, and when her parents demanded she choose someone she simply pressed shut her lips and wouldn't speak.

As the months dawdled by and the suitors drifted away, White Rose's parents shouted at her, told her how much money the gold lace and silver comb had cost, and how much money they'd spent to attract the suitors. White Rose grew more silent. She knew how hard they'd worked, how they'd spent all their money to attract the suitors, yet whenever she thought, "This time I'll say yes," the words just lodged in her throat and another rich man left the parlor angry.

Finally her parents announced that since she had cheated and robbed them they had no choice but to get their money back whatever way they could. They sold the white dress, they sold the silver comb (they'd already sold the suitors' gifts), and then they sent a message to a spice merchant who hated White Rose because she'd refused to speak to him. "We offer our daughter for whatever services a great man might require." When he read this letter the merchant slapped his chair in delight and immediately ordered the journey east.

So White Rose became a kitchen maid, the girl who scrubs the floors, who scours the pots after the merchant's family and guests and all the other servants have eaten. She wore a long grey dress with wooden sandals, ate whatever she could scrape from the dirty pots, and slept on the stone floor in a corner of the kitchen. Occasionally the merchant had her serve his guests so they could grab and scratch her; once he slapped her mouth until red blood stained her white skin. At last, however, he simply forgot her. Months and months slid past.

Then one day a carnival bounced into town, jugglers, dancers, acrobats — and one tall cold magician. His spells hurled flame-ribbons across the sky, raised snakes out of the earth. His left hand pitted a woman's face with plague, then his right hand cleared it again before she'd even screamed. His fingers shot lightning and his voice made young trees bow down like pages.

Beyond all his spells and tricks, however, the magician enchanted the crowds with another display. A dancer. His "companion" he called her, with long twisting legs and stamping feet, with fingers that coiled like snakes, and shoulders and hips that curled or snapped. Most marvelous of all was her skin, black, blacker than the dark between the stars. To watch her dance was to watch the darkness beyond the earth flicker into life. "Good people of the East," the magician smiled, "I present to you the Black Rose!"

The word darted quickly. Soon the whole town was running to the carnival. The merchant came with his family, followed by his servants and at last the cook, who jerked loose her apron with a curt "Mind the stove," to White Rose before she scurried from the house.

The moment the cook had gone White Rose turned down

the stove, washed her face, then sneaked behind buildings to the carnival. Kept in the house for months she didn't know or care what she'd see, she just thought she'd watch the show and skip back before anyone came home. Then she saw Black Rose dance.

Her head forward, her lips open, her body trembling against the coarse dress, White Rose's eyes and fingers followed every coil and spin and stamp. The world seemed a dull grey fog, with two bright lights burning towards each other — herself and Black Rose. After the dance White Rose crouched in a doorway where she watched the clowns and jugglers until the carnival day finished and the last people scattered home. Only then did she creep forward to find the magician's tent.

All night she waited between two trees, shivering, afraid to make a noise. She had almost decided to go home and face the cook when the tent flaps parted and a small darkness blotted out the starlight. The head moved side to side, curious, as if something had summoned her. "Over here," White Rose whispered. Black Rose glided towards her.

A few feet apart they stood and looked at each other. The stars shining through the trees seemed to fall back from White Rose's skin only to drop into the deep well of blackness beside her. Kneeling on the grass they touched each other's face and arms. The blackness and the whiteness twined around each other as the white and black lips pressed together. Just as the dawn touched their skin Black Rose and White Rose became lovers.

White Rose followed the carnival from town to town, always secretly, begging money on the road to live. Every night she met Black Rose outside the magician's tent, where they lay together in the grass. If the carnival camped near a woods they would wander like lost demons through the trees, wishing they could go on to the end of the world, but always coming back before the day. Once, when a soldier passed them, Black Rose leaped on White Rose's body, hiding the whiteness with her black skin. Yet, whenever White Rose asked her lover to really slip away with her, Black Rose only shook her head and wouldn't speak.

One night they found a cold stream running down a hillside. The trees along the bank bent down their delicate branches like spider webs. Their clothes tossed aside, they rolled in the water, splashing and washing each other until they fell back on the bank, locked in each other's arms, their bodies glistening in the moonlight.

Suddenly the sky darkened. White Rose looked up in surprise where a strange grey shadow, like a winged lizard, seemed to swallow the moon. About to say something she felt Black Rose stiffen, terrified as she stared over the white shoulder. White Rose spun around. The magician was there.

"So this is how you repay me," his cold voice whispered. His eyes burned, scales appeared on his neck and the backs of his hands. "I draw you from the shadows and this is how you repay me." The first and last fingers of his left hand snapped upright like knives; lightning flashed between them.

"Leave her alone!" White Rose shouted, with a dive for the magician's feet. But Black Rose grabbed her ankle and flung her across the grass.

"Black wretch," the magician cried. "Go home then. Back to the shadows." The arm came down like a sword. The fingers changed to fire sticks. For a moment sheets of blue flame covered the black twisting body, but when the flame vanished — Black Rose was gone.

Kicking and clawing, White Rose leaped on the magician. "Where have you sent her?" she shrieked. "Bring her back."

The magician, however, only slapped her away, for now he just stared at the empty spot where Black Rose had crouched. "What have I done?" he said, and shook himself like a sleepwalker waking in a strange woods. "My treasure. What have I done?"

"Bring her back," White Rose cried.

"Back?" the magician repeated, as if the wind had said the word. "No, don't you see, it can't be done. Oh my treasure."

"Then send me after her. You've got to send me after her." The magician didn't answer, only sat on the ground hugging his chest, staring at the grass. Her face soaked in tears, White Rose crawled away.

For a time she lived in the woods, kept alive by shrubs and

roots, sometimes making sounds like the foxes and owls that came to watch her white body. All day she slept in a tree, then crawled around at night, for she thought the night might show her an image of Black Rose. But the night wasn't dark enough.

Weeks drifted by. Autumn stripped the woods. One afternoon White Rose woke early to scramble down to the ground where she stood shakily and rubbed her face. With her head cocked to the side as if she might hear someone behind her, she walked away from the forest until she found a road, where she sat down in the dust.

An old woman found her. Her back bent with firewood she stopped, examined the white face beneath the dirt, then lifted the girl to her feet.

"Have you seen Black Rose?" White Rose asked. "I've lost her, you know."

"I'm sorry," said the woman, "I haven't seen your friend. If you come home with me maybe I can help you find her." With White Rose wrapped in the old lady's shawl, the two women limped home.

Through the winter White Rose lived in the woman's cottage by the river Kareena. Each day they walked to the water, the first river dredged by Ranuseeta the Prankster, who brought life into the world as a joke on Mt. Talopel. Mostly silent, they sewed long scarves for the old woman to sell once a week in the market place. At evening White Rose would draw a bucket of water and go home to cook supper for herself and her friend.

Winter passed. One evening a caravan clattered by the cottage, tall dark men on brown horses. White Rose ran out to the road and grabbed the lead horse. His purple hood thrown back, the man looked at her in wonder.

"Have you seen a woman," she pleaded, "with skin blacker than the night?"

"As black as you're white?" She nodded. "Years ago, I saw a woman like that, a dancer."

"Black Rose," the girl gasped.

"Yes, I think they called her that. But I can't say what happened to her." White Rose dropped her arm.

The caravan continued. Her eyes on the last rider, White Rose told the old woman, "I have to leave. You know that."

The woman nodded. "I hope you find your friend. But come inside now. Maybe I have something that can help you." Back in the house she reached under her cot to draw out an old mirror wrapped in red cloth. "My husband gave me this," she smiled as she polished it with the surface held towards the wall. "I liked it when I was younger."

Feeling foolishly vain White Rose peered into the mirror. Instantly she covered her eyes. The mirror had taken the room's small light and thrown it back around her like a whip. With a grunt the old woman covered it up again. "I knew your skin would do that. You take this with you. If anyone attacks you and there's even a little light just hold the mirror up behind you."

As she strapped the mirror to her back White Rose said, "I'm sorry I have to go."

Her friend hesitated. "Perhaps you will come back someday." White Rose said nothing.

Across the world she wandered, sometimes walking, sometimes on horseback, or even in a carriage. She took up begging again, quite adept at asking for money while people stared at her skin. Some asked her to pose, which she did, or to let them love her, which she did, though rarely, but if anyone said, "Dance," she walked away. If anyone tried to beat her she unwrapped the mirror and the attacker fell in the dust, holding his eyes. Everywhere she went she asked at taverns and tents and monasteries, "Have you seen Black Rose?" No one could tell her anything.

Mountains and plains, forests and ice, great cities and forgotten villages, no one had seen Black Rose. Even the terrible Walglasai Desert, the vast wasteland of sand, rock, and jungle grown from the blood of Larosha, the queen who mated with a lion, even Walglasai couldn't turn her back, though she did cross the narrowest part, Walglasai Arm. The mirror repelled the man-lions, but if Black Rose had passed there White Rose could find no sign of her.

At last she faced the West Edge of the world and stepped upon the Misty Bridge, that arches into nothingness. Wrapped in grey smoke her white body stepped out of the world until White Rose stood where no mortal had stood since the Ice

Furies — the end of the Misty Bridge overlooking the Pool of Nothingness. "Forgive me, Black Rose," she wept, "but I cannot live without you." Hugging her chest White Rose tumbled off the bridge.

Round and round her body spun, down through the cold grey mist that clung to her like a lover, on and on, while always she thought she could feel Black Rose just behind her if only she could turn around. Faster and faster fell the terrified girl until the smoke clouded her brain. White Rose closed her eyes to die.

She woke up on a cold tile floor, her legs curled into her chest, her hair shrouding her face. Very scared, she stretched her body, then stood. Before her ran a dark moat and beyond that stood a giant crystal palace, spires and spires, long halls and towers and domes with grey fog surrounding all of it. She reached around her back; good, she hadn't lost her mirror. Shakily, White Rose walked along the slender bridge that spanned the moat, while huge crystal gates swung back to welcome her.

Inside she found a great hall, big enough to hold a thousand banquetters, with all the walls and floor and ceiling formed of delicate transparent crystal. High above her the ceiling arched like a dancer's back, while all around her the walls radiated a clear soft light which made it seem —after the door had been closed — like being inside a frozen drop of water. When she looked behind her, however, she could still see the mist press the walls and door like a hungry beast.

The floor looked so delicate she was sure one step would crash the whole palace into the fog, but no, her soft feet didn't even mar the surface. Each step made a whisper of noise like a muted bell. Walking around the walls she discovered them lined with statues, hundreds of graceful creatures made from a crystal so transparent she couldn't even see them twenty feet away. Wonderful creatures, some on two legs like a woman or a swan, some on four legs or six or eight, some with coiled tentacles, some with outstretched arms, some with giant wings. But nowhere could she find a sign of anyone alive. "Hello," she called. Silence.

For hours her feet rang the musical corridors. Along the

way she stopped in empty rooms or occasionally another large hall with more statues, though nowhere any indication who had made them.

After walking miles, it seemed, she stood in a narrow high-ceilinged passage and called, for the hundredth time, "Hello. Is anyone there?" From somewhere far away, above the hum of the walls, she thought she heard a voice. She jumped; oddly embarrassed, she called again, and again came the answer, too faint for her to make out any words. She began to run, hopefully in the right direction.

She ran until she had to bend over and catch her breath, but when she called again a long silence preceded the answer. Unable to run anymore she walked on, searching the rooms — so many rooms, so many turns and circles and corridors. Several times she feared she was just passing the same place over and over, for when she called the voice seemed just as far.

All of a sudden she found herself facing a thick door made of a darker crystal, clouded and strangely ominous. A timid push swung it open to reveal a long narrow room with high walls darkly clouded. Though a window at the far end admitted the palace light the room turned it a dreary grey, and White Rose felt a terrible despair. "Hello," she called. No answer. Slowly she walked to the center of the room.

The door slammed shut behind her. White Rose spun around and there stood a monstrous brown and yellow lizard. With a wide scaly back and thick stony legs, with half-closed gashes covering its face and belly, with thin sharp fangs and a red steamy tongue that flicked back and forth across the room it slithered towards the terrified White Rose. Unable to move she watched the blood that spotted its mouth grow larger and larger.

Yet the eyes looked human. Maniacally they stared at her, while the tongue weaved towards her and the jaw dropped open, cracking in a hideous grin. The very tip of the tongue grazed White Rose's cheek.

She dove. Right at the monster's feet and through its stony legs she rolled. A horrible rattle and hiss filled the room while the long tail madly thumped the floor. The creature turned and once more slithered towards her. Desperately her fingers fumbled loose the mirror.

Like liquid fire the white radiance of her skin flung itself at the beast. Now the hiss rose to a shriek as the creature twisted its head side to side, frantic to shield its hoodless eyes. Furious, the tail thumped the floor, the tongue flicked hysterically, but White Rose stood her ground. Every time the creature turned aside White Rose scrambled after it for the fire to lash the scaly face. The scarred belly scraped and pounded the floor, sending up a furious ringing. "It's dying," White Rose thought, "I've killed it."

But then, with a sudden lurch, the creature swung sideways, and before White Rose could move, the long tail caught her chest and slapped her against the wall. Powerless without its mistress, the mirror crashed to the floor, soon smashed by the vengeful tail to a thousand chips of glass.

The rattle became a roar, almost a laugh. Now as the human eyes and the lizard tongue stalked her she could only back away until she reached the wall, where she bared her teeth in helpless fury. A glance showed her the window just too high above her head. The mouth opened, the red tongue, dripping hot oils, weaved towards the white neck.

At that very moment a bolt of black lightning shot across the room. Through the window it flashed, past the teeth, and down the monster's mouth like fire, to stick fast deep in its throat.

Gagging and choking, the lizard thrashed side to side while the human eyes screamed fury and terror. Over and over it tossed back its head in its desperation to swallow the terror lodged in its throat. Furious, the tongue lashed the face and the eyes rolled back as a red mist filled the room. White Rose whispered, "Now."

But once again the monster saved itself. With a leap backwards and a choked scream one great swallow forced the rock past the throat into the swollen belly. White Rose thought she heard a human cry of anger and despair. She too covered her face.

A noise. Strange thumps. White Rose opened her eyes to see her enemy fall on its side and kick the air. The human eyes stared at her, the lizard mouth hissed like a boiling flood. Terrible convulsions wracked the scaly body, for inside the hard belly a black fury was tearing it to pieces. Over and over it flogged the crystal floor in its agony, sounding its own crystal death bells, while hot greenish blood spouted from its mouth. The human eyes knew that nothing could help it — it had taken its enemy inside itself and this time there was no way to reach it. With one last convulsive shudder the tail and the head crashed against the floor for the last time.

A great light filled the room. Like a fog breaking up, the dreary dimness dissolved into the air. All around her White Rose heard singing, as if the walls themselves celebrated the victory, yet she herself only wept, shaking her shoulders and sobbing into her hands.

"No," she cried, and sprang to her feet. Out of the room she ran and down the corridor, deaf to the chimes her feet sounded, blind to the crystal creatures slowly coming to life. From room to room she darted until at last she found a stone table with a crystal axe. Now back again, past the lovely statues who tried to call her, back to the dead beast.

White Rose mounted the belly where she swung the axe as hard as she could, again and again, though the axe bounced off and stung her hand. A line appeared, then a crack, and she threw down the axe. Her face all twisted, she pulled and ripped until the hole opened wide enough for her to see, amid the steaming death, a huddled darkness. And so, White Rose, trembling, lifted, from the terror and the pain, Black Rose into her arms.

Though horrible sores and burns fouled the perfect blackness White Rose clasped her close as she helped her to the floor. There Black Rose lay silent and still, her eyes on her lover's face while great sobs wrenched White Rose's body.

A tear fell on the burnt cheek. White Rose bent down to kiss the sore — and where her lips touched, the skin turned clear and black again. With a cry of joy White Rose kissed her lover's body, every sore and boil and wound. Everywhere the white lips pressed grew whole again until once more the Blackness and the Whiteness held each other, their eyes bright with love. Now they saw, for the first time, the crystal creatures dance around them, heard the walls, the floor, the roof sing to them. Their arms and legs twined together, Black Rose and White Rose kissed their love.

Flowering Narcissus
Thomas N. Scortia

Thomas N. Scortia was born on August 29, 1926 in the small Mississippi River town of Alton, Illinois, twenty miles across the river from St. Louis. He graduated from Alton High School (with a brief one year vacation in a local industry) into the infantry in 1944 and managed to arrive in the Pacific as the war tailed to an end. He spent a year on occupation duty in Osaka, Japan.

From 1946 to 1949 Scortia took his undergraduate degree in chemistry and biology at Washington University in St. Louis and went on to the graduate school of biochemistry at Washington University's Barnes Hospital. It was during his undergraduate period that he first began to write fiction at the encouragement of his English professor, Lucille Codd, and her boss, Dr. George Stout.

In 1950, Scortia returned to the service during the Korean War, spending most of his time either commanding a chemical mortar company or serving in various staff functions at Fort Bragg. He was discharged in Colorado Springs, Colorado at Fort Carson and managed during that brief two weeks to meet Robert and Virginia Heinlein, a friendship that has grown with the years. On his return trip, Scortia began to write in earnest, accumulating a hundred rejection slips before selling his first story, a novelette, "The Prodigy," to *Science Fiction Adventures.* This was quickly followed by a sale to John Campbell at *Astounding* (now *Analog*). He wrote as a hobby from 1954 on, pursuing his career in the chemical and later the aerospace industry.

Scortia was chief of Advanced Propellant Research for United Technologies in 1980 when the aerospace industry collapsed. He rashly decided to pursue a career as a free-lance writer. The first year he sold a number of stories, an anthology, and a novel. Scortia developed an idea for a novel about a high rise fire and invited his friend, Frank Robinson, to join him in San Francisco as a collaborator. The book was remarkably successful as was the later movie, *The Towering Inferno.* Robinson and he subsequently collaborated on three other novels, the last being *The Gold Crew* (1981).

Scortia moved to Los Angeles in 1980 and has worked in film and television while still writing novels. Asked about his current projects, he remarks: "I have just finished a very kinky horror story, 'Green Fear,' and am now working on a very daring (for me at least) novel with the working title of *Twelfth Night.* It's a novel I've wanted to write for years but did not until the last few years have the financial security or the command of my craft to attempt. I hope it is a novel you will hear about in the future."

Honcho is dreaming. It is a simple, brutal dream. He stands spread-eagled feeling the potency in his muscles and the cold touch of leather against his bare loins. He's proud of the muscularity of his thighs and buttocks. Every time he stands in a bar (as he does now in his dream), he flexes the muscles, feeling the heavy indentation in his glutei maximi. The chicks watch him out of the corner of their eyes, their gaze telling him that they think he's a real stud. Now one gets up and comes toward him, wide hips swaying, breasts thrusting. He grabs her by the hair at the nape of the neck and pulls her head brutally. He smiles at her, exposing stained yellow teeth. Below the half-sleeves of his jacket his massive biceps bulge, the veins writhing like ropes. He is going to push her to the floor and use his boot on those inflated boobs, but. . . .

It all dissolves.

He is lying with his eyes closed. He feels the pressure of sheets against the hair on his torso. He tries to open his eyes, but they seem glued together. He is cold, colder than he has ever been in his life in spite of the warmth the sheets are exuding. He doesn't remember being this cold, certainly not in California, certainly not in the dead of summer with the heat devils dancing over the blacktop of the freeways and his wheels kicking up a cloud of dust and grit behind him.

Then he remembers. The kooky egghead in Berkeley. He needed the bread and the ad in the *Barb* sounded nutty enough so that he thought he could con the gink out of a few bills. Only the little guy had been legit; he even taught at UC and he wanted Honcho to go through with it. It was perfectly safe, he said. Three bills for just going to sleep for a week. Well, Honcho decided, trying to unglue his eyes, the week was over and he'd have enough money for a couple of lids and a brace of poppers for the club run the end of the month.

"Damn it," he yells when he tries to move and finds his arms strapped to his sides. "What kind of trip is this?"

From some distance he hears the sound of feet scraping against the floor, then the squeak of a door. Now somebody is in the room and he senses a presence crossing, bending over him. Something moist swabs at his eyes. They burn like fire but suddenly the lids are no longer glued and he can part them.

Honcho opens his eyes slowly, painfully because the light hurts. It feels as though he has been holding his lids tightly compressed for hours. The air fills with spots of light and crawling shadows. Beyond these he makes out a shape. Human? He can't tell, but he knows it is probably the face of the little egghead who has put him in this trip. He waits for the image to clear and, sure enough, he begins to make out the shape. It's a man's head, he sees. Bald, not a trace of hair. Beyond this he cannot yet make out facial details.

He closes his eyes and tries to rub them. His hands are still bound. The man above him makes a movement and his hands are free. He scrubs vigorously at his eyes, ignoring the copious flow of tears. Then he opens his eyes. He can see again. Purple and black spots still float before his eyes, but he can see. The face above him floats into focus. It is not the face he expects.

"Who the hell are you?" he demands.

"Take it easy," the man says. "You'll be all right."

Honcho realizes that he has assumed it is a man, but the voice is high and gentle-sounding, not at all masculine. The head is bald, shaved maybe, and the build is slight. He (she) is not over five three and slim to the point of emaciation. The body is covered by a single loose-fitting tunic. There are no signs of sex in the clothing cut, no indication of breasts. Honcho decides that it must be a man, even though he can see no trace of beard.

Honcho sits up and flexes his biceps. He laughs, feeling the sudden animal pleasure of being alive. The bald gink looks at him with wide eyes. Man, he thinks, ain't you ever seen a guy with a man's build. Then he digs. The gink is looking at him with admiration and Honcho says to himself, That kind of scene? Ugh. Eat your heart out, baby. And he feels damned good.

"Where's the professor?" Honcho demands.

"Professor?" the little man says. "Oh, you mean Dr. Liebowicz?"

"That's right. The little ginch with the four eyes."

"He's dead," the man says. "He's been dead a long time."

"Hey, baby, don't give me that shit," Honcho says, springing from the bed and grabbing the little guy by the loose cloth of his tunic. "Nobody cons me, sweetie."

The little man pushes Honcho's hand away, not so much with strength as with the sudden solemn authority of his large eyes. "It's true," he says. "Liebowicz is dead. He died in prison over a century ago."

"Oh, God," Honcho says and sinks down to the bed. A century ago. "Somebody's going to pay for this," he yells. "Somebody's going to fork over lots of bread. It was only supposed to be a week."

"One hundred fifteen years and... ah... four months," the little guy says.

"Who the hell are you?"

"CTX-25, series ten," the little guy says.

"What kind of a name is that for a human?" Honcho demands.

"I am not human," the little guy says.

"You sure ain't no Martian."

"No," CTX-25 says. "I was built."

"Huh, call that a build," Honcho says.

"By humans," the little guy says, dropping his eyes and making a funny motion of respect with his right hand, two fingers extended. "Before the plague," he says.

"Hey," Honcho says. "You're coming on too fast. What plague?"

"Why, the plague that destroyed the human race," CTX-25 says and before Honcho can answer he leaves the way he came.

Honcho feels weak and he falls back onto the bed. He is suddenly scared. He doesn't like it one bit. Somebody is having a great day with him, he decides. He yawns and says, "What a hell of a note; sleepy after sleeping a century." But he falls back, his head touches a pillow, and he is sound asleep, filling the air with rasping snores. He does not dream now.

When he wakes up, he yells out, "Damn it, what do you have to do to get some chow around here?"

The door magically opens and another little guy wheels in a cart with a steaming steak, a big baked potato awash with sour cream, peas and a frothy mug of beer. "You read my mind," Honcho says to the little guy who is not CTX-25.

"That's right," the little guy says. Then, "I brought you a viewer." He points to a thing that looks like a portable TV on the cart and then, without saying another word, leaves. Honcho dives in. He is not one for niceties. He rapes the steak, mauls the potato, gulps the beer, and smears the grease away from his lips with the hairy back of his hand. Then he starts to fiddle with the viewer.

There are two knobs. One turns on the gadget; the other presses inward to flip view after view on the screen. There are old newspaper clippings about Liebowicz, who is accused of illegal experimentation on humans. He is tried and convicted while a bunch of deadhead students demonstrate outside the courtroom. The court psychiatrist decides he is spaced out and they send him to Vacaville, where eventually he is killed when one of the other inmates doesn't like the way he parts his skin. There's some crap about building a place to keep the sleeping Honcho. They even have Honcho's biography and a picture of him mounted on his competition Dunstall-Norton 750, leering at the camera. (What a pile that machine cost him, a beautiful hog and probably all rust now.) He can't believe the biography. He wonders who fed the newspapers all that Sunday-school crap. Boy-wonder mechanic, cyclist, man among men. (Well, sure, but not that goody-good.) He flips the knob in disgust.

There's some stuff about new developments in biochemistry. Some doubledome named Whitfield creates artificial tissue in the lab, and later a guy called Nobel Laureate Valdez builds something called an android. There are pictures, and Honcho recognizes something that looks like CTX-25. (The article says they're sexless, which to Honcho makes no sense, and his original suspicions about CTX-25 return. Imagine a world peopled by artificial faggots. He laughs out loud at that thought.)

After that he reads about the war between the Chinks and the Russkies and how one side or the other starts to use virus warfare. Only it gets out of hand and sweeps the world. There's one final item. By now apparently the androids are publishing the newspapers, because the final item says, "Last human being dies." After that there is nothing. The dateline is seventy-five years after Honcho began his big sleep.

When CTX-25 comes in later, Honcho is in a brown mood. "That's a lot of crap," he says, pointing at the viewer. "Ain't it?" he asks hopefully.

"No, it is history," CTX-25 says.

"You mean I'm the only human alive in the world," he demands.

CTX-25 asks, "Are you feeling better? Is the food all right?"

"Damn it, I asked you a question," Honcho roars.

"We'll answer your questions later," CTX-25 says with a pale smile. "We have to make sure you're in good health."

"I can chew up a pansy like you and spit out the pieces," Honcho says.

CTX-25 hands him some clothes. Honcho is delighted. Jackboots with a chain across the insteps, just like he used to have. Black leather chaps and Levi's, a shirt and black leather vest topped off by a leather cap filled with badges. The slogans on the badges don't make much sense, but the image is good. The Levi's are neat and clean and pressed. While CTX-25 watches, Honcho rumples them and drags them across the floor. He thinks maybe he should christen them like they do for the new guys in the Satan's Wheels but it takes too damned long for them to dry. So he puts them on that way. A few days and they'll feel decent, he decides.

CTX-25 takes him down to a gym where a couple other sexless ginches are waiting. They put him through all sorts of tests on what they call a dynamometer. They make him run on a treadmill, listen to his heart, wire him up to a fancy gadget that flashes out patterns on an oscilloscope. While they watch and chatter among themselves, he grabs an overhead bar and chins himself thirty-five times. Not as good as usual, but the little guys are impressed.

"Look," he says, "I played your game, but you guys owe me something. From what you tell me, you were built to serve humans."

"That's right," CTX-25 says.

"That still operates, don't it?"

"That's right," the android says.

"Okay," Honcho says. "Then I ain't happy the way things are going. You guys gotta get me what I want."

"Food?" one of them asks.

"Hell, no," Honcho says. "I want a pad. I'll tell you what I want. Then I want a hog."

"Hog," CTX-25 says. "An animal?"

"A bike, damn it," Honcho says, "and make sure there's someplace to ride it. You got roads, ain't you?"

"There will be roads," they promise him.

"And a babe," Honcho says. "A twist, a snatch."

"A woman," CTX-25 says with a vague smile. "We are working on that."

"See that you get it right." Honcho pauses. "And none of your androids. I don't go for that."

"There is another in sleep," CTX-25 says. "We are reviving her. I think you'll like her."

"Huh," Honcho says. "I damn well better."

The next day CTX-25 takes him down an elevator and out in front of the building. There, leaning on its kickstand, is a bike. "You read my mind," he yells excitedly, running over to the machine.

"Precisely," CTX-25 says, but Honcho ignores him. It's the very same, the Dunstall-Norton 750, just the way he remembers it. His hand caresses the reshaped exhaust ports with their gleaming metal. He can see where the combustion chambers have been resphered when he looks into the engine. He knows that they're five millimeters greater in diameter and he knows all the other things that have been done to the standard Norton: the steeper inlet valve angles, the larger inlet valves and ports, the greater compression ratio. Then he sees the nick on the throttle handle and the pit on the accelerator dial and he knows this isn't just another machine.

"How the hell?" he yells. "It's my own baby."

"We tried to duplicate it completely," CTX-25 says proudly. "We're very good at that."

Honcho mounts the cracked leather seat, opens the petcock, and throws his weight on the starter. The engine turns over with a roar and he grips the throttle with his left hand and starts to feed it gas. The smell fills his nose like whiskey and he feels his heart race with the excitement. Ignoring CTX-25, he kicks up the stand, engages the clutch, and he's off, roaring down the concrete incline and out onto a broad concrete road that circles away from the low building and into the trees.

The wind is whipping past his head and biting into his eyes. He wishes he had goggles, but he feeds the hog gas and watches the needle climb. The hydraulic front shocks are singing and the whole beast feels like something alive between his legs. It feels like an extension of his meat, and he hugs the frame with his knees, remembering the excitement the last time the Wheels went to Monterey on a run and they strung the gremmy up by his thumbs to one of the trees and worked him over while Seven-times Cindy came over and emptied her beer all over his bare butt. Far out.

Only the road doesn't go anywhere. He circles, and suddenly there is the sprawling white building and there's CTX-25 waiting for him, a cold smile on his face. "You can take the back road next time," he says. "That goes into the city." Honcho sees that a ribbon of concrete runs to the rear and arrows out toward a distant hill. There's no sign of a city and he assumes that it is over the hill.

"I'll just do that now," he says.

"No," CTX-25 says. "I have another surprise for you."

Honcho reluctantly dismounts and kicks down the stand on the bike. The machine smells excitingly of hot metal and gasoline. He follows CTX-25 up the steps into the building. They walk down the long corridor and downstairs into another level. CTX-25 gestures at a door and Honcho pushes through into a room very much like the one he awoke in. There's a bed, and several pieces of cryptic apparatus stand in the corner. In the bed is a form.

She's still unconscious, her huge breasts rising and falling under the sheet. The nipples make sharp indentations in the fabric. She's big, Honcho sees, maybe as tall as he is with wide amazon hips and a big face with sensuous lips and long black hair. She looks like quite a piece and he turns to CTX-25.

"Is this another of your kind?" he demands.

"No, she's not android," CTX-25 says. "She will awaken soon and then she's yours."

Honcho licks his lips and feels his groin tense. Suddenly he's horny as hell and he can't wait. She looks like every doll he's ever had. He knows every contour of her body and the way she'll kiss and ball and he can't wait.

CTX-25 prods him out of the room and conducts him back to his quarters. They're new quarters now with deep leather chairs and bike pictures on the wall and a refrigerator with beer and Dago red. There's a chest with smokes and poppers and a lid of grass. Somebody has scrawled "Acapulco Gold" across the label and he opens it and sniffs it. The real stuff, he decides, and not cut with a lot of syrup.

"When's that piece going to wake up?" he demands.

"Soon," CTX-25 assures him and leaves him to himself.

There's a hi-fi at one end of the room and he finds a Led Butterfly album he likes. (Where did they get the thing? he wonders.) With the music blasting around him, he pours himself a glass of Dago red. Everybody tells him the stuff should be drunk hot but he likes it cold and bitter. He kicks off his boots, wiggles his toes in their sweat-stained socks to the music, and starts to get high. After a while he rolls himself a joint and alternates between puffs and a gulp of wine. In no time he is floating, not tripping out exactly. . . but floating.

He thinks about the snatch below who must now be awake and wonders how the hell she got in the middle of the next century. He feels a kind of gratitude to CTX-25 and he smiles to himself contemptuously. Poor bastard, never humping it. What a way to live, but he apparently understands what Honcho needs. He begins to feel the secondary effects of the pot and a kind of suspicion begins to grow.

Just what's in it for the creep? he wonders. He's given Honcho everything he wants and now he's found Honcho a woman. Of course, his kind was built to serve humans. Only there ain't any more humans, none except Honcho and the piece below. Which brings him around to the question again. Why?

And suddenly Honcho knows. He spits wine halfway across the room and yells. "That bastard." Of course he'll get Honcho a broad. Why? Because there are no humans to serve and he and his kind are built to serve humans. They need it like a head needs his fix. So, where does that leave Honcho? Honcho and the broad? Of course! The bastard expects Honcho to father a whole horde of sniveling snotnose kids just so CTX-25 and his crowd will have somebody to serve.

"Not damn likely," Honcho announces to the walls, drowning out even Led Butterfly. "That ain't my scene, baby," he tells nobody in particular. He's mad now and if CTX-25 were in the room he would deck the ball-less wonder. He throws the half-filled glass at one of the hi-fi speakers and starts to pull on his boots.

He stands up and finds he's weaving on his feet. No matter. He knows what to do. He'll cut the ground right from under them and wind it all up with an orgy of laying that'll leave them panting. He puts on his cap and stumbles out into the hall. There's no one around, which is just fine. He walks the length of the hall, finds the steps, and goes down and down to the level where the broad is. He finds the room and pushes open the door.

She's asleep, her heavy breasts rising and falling regularly. Part of the sheet has twisted around her, outlining her full figure, and Honcho licks his lips at what he sees. One heavy thigh protrudes from the cover and he marvels at the heavy musculature. He can imagine those heavy thighs tightening around his waist as he drives in and possesses her violently.

She opens her eyes and says, "Hey, man, what makes?"

"You know what those bastards are up to?" he says dreamily.

"You're high," she accuses.

"So what?" Honcho says. "That doesn't keep me from knowing they want us to start breeding a lot of brats so they can have a human race to worship and serve."

"Baby, you can get yourself another girl," she says. "I'm not about to be anybody's bitch."

"I got other plans for you," Honcho says. "We gotta get out of here."

"I'm for that," she says.

"What's your name?" he says.

"Mary," she says. "Ain't that a laugh?"

"Get your clothes on," he says. "I got a beast outside and we'll split before they know we're gone."

"Ain't got no clothes," she says. "What the hell, who needs clothes?" She gets to her feet and wraps the sheet around her.

They make it out the door and down the corridor, up one flight of stairs, and out into the cold night where the hog waits patiently, leaning against its stand.

"Man," she says, "that's a beast. What'd it set you back?"

"Originally?" he says. "Hell, I saved for three years. You don't get that kind of bike cheap."

He mounts the seat and she wriggles on behind him. The sheet is wrapped tightly around her lush figure but he can feel the heat against his body, even through the leather vest. She has a kind of raunchy female smell about her that excites him. He reaches around and gropes in a strategic spot. She moans as his hand closes brutally on her. She's all woman, Honcho assures himself, and she's just what he needs to take the edge off his appetite.

He throws his weight on the starter and the Norton comes alive. She grabs onto him as he throws in the clutch and they speed down the concrete ramp and take the road that circles around the building. As they leave the area, they arrow through a grove of trees and the road stretches like a ribbon before them, the moonlight painting it a scabrous yellow.

He guns the machine and watches the speedometer creep upward: sixty, seventy, eighty. There is no sign of pursuit, and he roars his defiance into the wind that is biting his face. Behind him she clutches his chest and shivers. She starts to insinuate her fingers past the vest and into his shirt, rubbing the hair on his chest until he is roaring no longer with defiance but with sheer lust.

Damn, he feels like Gene Romero tooling the Sacramento track. All balls and a mile wide. They're halfway to the rise now. On the other side, if he can believe the little creep

CTX-25, is the city and he wonders what he will do there. Her hands are all over him now. She's excited and the excitement is spreading to him. He sees a grove of trees ahead and he says, What the hell, to himself. He slows, kicks at the ground with his left foot, which is partly protected by a metal mask over the boot, and tears into the grove. His hand bears down on the brake, and they almost fly over the bars as he stops, dismounts, kills the engine, and kicks the stand.

"What's up, stud?" she challenges. Her grin tells him she knows what is up.

He grabs her, yanks her from the seat, and *pulls* her to the ground. The sheet falls half away and his hands are brutally over her. He seizes her head, forcing it down while he jerks at the lacing on his chaps. Man, he thinks, this is what I've been waiting for.

Only there's a beam of light plunging out of the sky and outlining them. It's some kind of whirlybird, he thinks, and they're after them. "Honcho," a voice says from on high. "Come back. You don't have to do this."

He bundles her back in the sheet, ignores the loose lacing on his leather chaps, and they're back on the machine. The thing roars and they're on the road while the machine overhead flops clumsily, following them while the light shoots down and the voice pleads with them to return.

They're approaching the crest of the hill and he knows that if he can get over it they can dodge the flopter and hide. At the crest of the hill he sees that they won't make it. It's all a camouflage, a fake. There's nothing beyond the hill, no road, no city, no nothing.

The bike leaps out into space. He can see a place to bring it down, if he's lucky, a flat spot, graveled and level. Like ole Knievel, he thinks. Hell, jump twenty automobiles. This takes guts.

Then they hit and the tires spit gravel. The machine flips into the air and he is turning slowly, agonizingly. He hits and all is pain and darkness.

Honcho is dreaming. It is the same dream, a brutal dream of gross masculine sexuality. His eyes are gummed together but shortly someone swabs them and he opens his eyes to the same room. CTX-25 is waiting for him.

"You bastard," he says. "You caught us. If you think I'm going to be a breeding stud for you—"

"No, we didn't catch you," CTX-25 says.

"What the hell," Honcho says, ignoring him. "Am I hurt?"

"No, the body is perfectly sound. That body at least."

"What's that gibberish supposed to mean?"

"You were killed," CTX-25 says sadly.

"Bullshit," Honcho says. "I'm more alive than you are."

"This Honcho is," CTX-25 says.

"You're out of your mind," Honcho says.

"No," CTX-25 says. "We were forced to clone you again."

"Clone? What does clone mean?"

CTX-25 tells him. The Honcho that Liebowicz threw into suspended animation did not live. That is, he could not revive. There were not other humans available to them. There was only one solution. Take a single cell, this time from the esophagus. It contains all of the chromosomes necessary to produce the complete individual. They grew a new Honcho. But wanting him to be completely human, they scanned the sleeping mind, impressed the new brain by their techniques with the old personality. For practical purposes, the new Honcho was a continuation of the old — all the good, all the bad.

"When Honcho died in the cycle crash, we had to do it all over again."

"What about the babe?" he demands. She survived, he is told. Is she deformed, crippled? he wants to know. No, their science is equal to such injuries.

"Damn it, I want her," he says.

"Don't you understand who she is?" CTX-25 wants to know.

"She's another one who survived or maybe you recreated her. Never mind, she's all broad."

"Only one living creature survived," CTX-25 insists.

"I survived," Honcho roars, "and so did she."

"No," CTX says slowly, watching his face. "She came from the same process you did."

·146·

Honcho stares at him. A sickness arises in him. He cannot accept what the android is telling him.

"It's easy," CTX-25 is saying. "At one stage in the development, the fetus has the potentiality of either sex."

"That's queer!"

"Do you want to be alone?" CTX-25 says, and he leaves Honcho to contemplate the problems of this, his third life. He thinks for a long while, and while he thinks he remembers the full exciting body. Fake or not, it was a damned good one. His hand massages himself and he thinks, Well, what the hell, better than mother thumb and her four daughters.

He is quite prepared when the door opens and she enters the room. He had thought she looked familiar and now he knows. Hell, how can he be disgusted with himself? The idea sort of appeals in a way. He always had a good opinion of himself.

"You all right?" she asks.

"Come here," he says.

She walks over to the bed and sits down, looking at him with eyes that say animal things. He rises until he is sitting upright and grabs at her.

"I thought you'd never do that," she says.

He kisses her, bruising her lips with intensity while his hand slides down and finds the secret place he knows. She is all woman, that's for sure.

"Man," he says fiercely. Then he corrects himself and says, "Babe, we're really going to make it with each other."

"We sure as hell are," she says, returning the fierce urgency of his kiss.

"We are really gonna make it, you and me," he says again. "Baby, we were made for each other."

"You can say that again," she says, pulling away from his lips and lowering her head to bite painfully at his distended nipples.

Nuclear Fission
Paul Novitski

In 1975, when Vonda McIntyre and Susan Anderson were assembling their anthology *Aurora: Beyond Equality*, Paul Novitski wrote a story called "Occupational Hazard," portraying some of the problems he thought people might still face once gender equality had been achieved. The manuscript was rejected, which is just as well: gender equality, in the sense he had originally meant it, can never be realized. Human differences, by the definition of "human" he used then and now, must exist. "What human beings *can* do," argues Novitski, "is to deal with those differences responsibly. What we *will* do is deal with them." Therein lies the story.

A year later Novitski had reworked that manuscript into "Nuclear Fission." At the Milford and Clarion science fiction workshops it was both loved and loathed but rarely elicited an ambiguous reaction — a mark of efficacy if not necessarily merit. The next year Terry Carr bought in for *Universe 9*.

The first story Novitski sold was to *Amazing* in 1972, when he was twenty-two. Since then he has written, and sold, an average of one short story every two years. "Exhausted from this furious pace," he notes, he paused in 1979 to become a "workaholic." He is currently self-employed as a free-lance computer programmer in Seattle.

"Until three years ago," observes Novitski, "I thought computer programming was a vice and probably dangerous to one's health; now I *know* it is. I find it very much like writing fiction and nearly as pleasurable. The major differences are of result, not act, and even then there are strong structural similarities. Although the readers of programs are, for the most part, machines, their users are people, and the human element is not altogether lacking. There is, however, a paucity of emotional content to most programs, so I am turning my attention back to busting some more characters loose from the hoosegow of my mind."

As dark hills rolled beneath the zeppelin, the sun rose behind it to cast pale, gold tendrils up the ridges of the coast range ahead. Spider lay curled in a hammock in the port cabin, watching through the wide window as the Willamette landscape began to appear beneath the fading stars. Somewhere in the folds of the foothills ahead lay the cluster of domes that was her home, nestled in fir and rhododendron. She stretched out in the sling and yawned. Her brother Fuchsia would probably be the only one up this early — he always got up before dawn, trudged up the hill to the pottery to throw a few before breakfast. But the others would still be asleep.

Spider yawned again. For her it was too late at night — or too early in the morning — to be fully awake or asleep. These annual transcontinental flights always threw off her circadian rhythms. When she had boarded the zeppelin in Pennsylvania it had been nine at night; during the flight the sun had risen behind them, arced overhead, and set in their eyes. Now it was rising again, and although she had caught one full night's sleep during the thirty-hour trip, she felt exhausted.

She turned and slipped quietly out of the hammock, flexing her shoulders in the cool, dark air. Several other hammocks in the long cabin bulged with softly snoring shapes. Spider moved along the sleepers to the hatch.

She stopped in the head, to squat, for a minute, over the toilet set into the floor. Stood, threw cold water from the tap onto her face. With long fingers she brushed back her shaggy white Afro and contemplated her flat, thick features in the mirror. In the pale light from the bathroom's tiny window she seemed to float in the mirror like a ghost, like the afterimage of someone who has suddenly disappeared. She shivered, dried herself quickly with the rough towel, and stepped back into the corridor.

The first hatch on the left opened to her push to reveal the pilot and console silhouetted against the dawn-lit mountains. She could hear the burr of the engines more clearly here. She slid into the empty co-pilot's couch and sighed.

The pilot glanced over. "Howdy. Up already?"

"Still, you mean. Never really got to sleep. I'm your passenger for Noti."

"Oh, right." The pilot's face was serene in the dilute glow of dawn. "Well, you haven't got long to wait. We're due to touch down in about forty minutes."

"Eugene?"

The pilot shook her head. Her hair was so short it looked like fur. "No, yours is the only stop until we turn up the coast. I've got time to take you right to your door."

"Great! I wasn't looking forward to that three-hour bike ride."

The pilot snapped her finger against the radio mike. "Yep, it's been a real quiet night. No one to pick up till we get to Astoria. Folks don't travel much this time of the year. They're all at home, putting in gardens, pruning trees—"

Spider groaned. "Don't remind me! I've been gone three weeks to that G.R.C. conference in the East, and I just know that no one in my household will have gotten round to pruning my dwarf apples."

The pilot laughed. "Yeah, I know what you mean. After I'm done with this circuit I'm going to stay home for the summer. I miss my folks."

Spider put one foot up on the edge of the console, crossed it with the other. "Where's that?"

"Place in the Cumberlands. We've got a big old farm out there, sheep, chickens, soy, hemp. About twenty of us live there full time, sixteen wives and four daughters."

Spider looked over at the pilot with surprise. "You're married?"

"You bet. I like that commitment. We've got the best ten-year contract this side of the ocean." She threw a row of switches with her toes. "And yourself?"

Spider waved vaguely. "Oh, just a small extended family. My son, his father, *his* mother, me, my brother, his lover, *his* daughter. We've never wanted to get married. A few years ago we all changed names together, but we haven't wanted anything more formal than that."

The pilot sniffed. "Sounds like a pretty tight little clan."

Spider frowned, picked at a button on her shirt. "I guess."

"You don't sound so sure."

Spider shrugged. "People change. Right now I'm closer to someone in another household." She was silent for a while. The world outside was getting lighter, the hills steeper and greener. The white peaks of the coast range were visible in the distance, where they melded with the clouds. She glanced over at the pilot. "You have any kids?"

"Hm? Yeah, like I said, we've got four on the farm—"

"No, I mean—"

"*Oh.*" The pilot frowned, adjusted a lever and snapped a switch. "Since you ask, yes, I do. Had a couple of them years ago." She glanced up. "Boys."

"Where are they now?"

"Who knows? Wherever their father is, most likely."

Spider ran her hand across the flat of her stomach. "I got tied after Sparrow was born."

"Really?" The pilot shook her head. "Not me, sister; I don't want *no*body poking around my insides."

Spider gasped. "You mean you've had two kids and you're not tied? Gods! If you could only see the global starvation figures I have to work with every day!"

The pilot turned in her couch and cupped Spider's cheek with her hand. "Lady," she smiled wryly, "there's no *way* I'm going to get pregnant where I am now."

"Oh." Spider felt her face get hot, swallowed hard. "Sorry, that was stupid of—"

"Forget it." The pilot turned back to her board.

Spider searched for a way to reconnect. "My lover is pregnant," she said at last.

"You don't say."

"That's why I'm coming back early from the conference. She wanted me to be there."

The pilot shrugged. "Why didn't she just postpone it?"

"No, she decided on the date more than a year ago. Today's the cusp."

The pilot snorted. "I never paid much attention to that

astro stuff in school. When I had my two boys, I just went about my business and let my body handle the whole thing." She shifted several toggles on the board and Spider felt a slight descent. The hum of the distant engines rose in pitch.

"Actually I feel the same way. I had my boy naturally. Walker still hasn't convinced me that controlling the gestation period doesn't harm the fetus." The pilot did not reply, and Spider sat back to watch the details appear in the landscape as they descended.

"Tell me where you live exactly," said the pilot, "so I can put this thing down."

Spider blinked, then rummaged in her shirt pocket for a pen and a scrap of paper. "Come to think of it," she said, "I'd like to ask you the same thing."

Sunlight spilled like warm syrup over Sparrow's face, blood-red through his eyelids as he squirmed on the mat. Reluctant to waken, he grasped at the melting splinters of recent dreams, but those visions, touches, and smells trickled only more swiftly between his mental fingers, leaving him beached, finally, on the broad round morning.

He blinked and rubbed his face, shifted across the mat so that the sun, shining through the eastern window, was out of his eyes. A cool morning breeze swept smells of tree blossoms gently through the room. With dawn, the top of the little dome had opened like a flower, spreading back petals from the sun's warmth. That old familiar branch snaked across his circle of sky, shaking clusters of pinky-white blossoms in the morning breeze.

Sparrow took a deep breath of the cool mixture of smells and let it slowly sigh away. Way up in the sky, a solitary black speck drifted amid the blue. He squinted one eye. What was that bird seeing way up there? A shaggy beard of woods, most likely, spread across the mountains' face, creased by veins of streams and road. And here, in a patch of morning sun, a handful of domes like warts.

Sparrow giggled to think he was living in a wart. Was the world really like a face, like the face of the moon? When Spider used to let him sit in her lap, he liked to run his fingertip across that bump below her left ear that sprouted three thick, white hairs like cats' whiskers. He shook his head to clear away the memory. Thinking about Spider made him feel too lonely. The world was like Coyote's face, but with a green beard, not red.

He sat up, shivering as the sheet fell from his brown chest, round belly. He brushed the long squiggles of hair from his face, let his head fall back, and froze in mid-yawn. That wasn't a bird up there! The speck had grown to a blob, and now he could make out its shape, long and rounded.

Spider was home!

He jumped up from the mat and padded down the short tunnel that connected his room with the main one of the house. He flung aside his flannel door and stepped into the wide, cool room. The cozy smell of carob permeated the air. Prints and paintings, familiar pillows, and shelves stuffed with ragged books lined the main dome's wall. The thick round rug that hugged the floor was shaggy with forest colors. All the doorways that led to the other domelets wore different cloth doors, emblems of their occupants. Only three were tied back with thongs — Coyote's spare landscape in black brush, Swann's ancient psychedelic print, and Fuchsia's brown fuzzy rug. The others must still be asleep. Fuchsia always got up first — he'd be up in the pottery — but Coyote and Swann....

Sparrow circled the room toward the kitchen alcove, taking the longer way around to stop in the toilet to pee. His narrow yellow stream fell away into the darkness of the composter. He remembered to close the lid after himself, rinsed his hands briefly under the tap, and shook them dry on his way to the kitchen.

He crept the last few steps and peeked around the fireplace. Swann lounged at the kitchen table sipping carob, engrossed in a book, while Coyote knelt at the garden bin peeling breakfast. He glanced up, saw Sparrow, and waved.

Sparrow walked over and plopped down on a pillow at the low table. Swann, wrapped in a thin green robe, looked up from her book and murmured something, the branching lines of her face congealing in a smile. Sparrow grinned back, savoring his secret, and poured a mug of orange juice without spilling much. The cool, thick lip of the mug met his mouth. Sweet juice.

Coyote put a bowl of sectioned fruit on the table and sat across from Sparrow. His lips moved behind his bushy red mustache: "What's new?"

Sparrow signed with his hands: *I know a secret!*

Coyote gaped in mock astonishment. "Well, don't keep us in suspense!"

Swann put her book down. "What is it?"

Sparrow jumped up from the table and ran a circle around the room, head down, cheeks puffed, arms straight at his sides. One quick circuit of the kitchen and he sat down again, grabbed a handful of fruit, and looked slyly at Coyote and Swann as he sucked on a piece.

Swann and Coyote looked at each other in bewilderment.

"Let's see," said Coyote thoughtfully. "You saw a bee!"

Sparrow shook his head.

"The bull in the meadow," said Swann.

Wrong again, he sighed.

Then Swann leaned over and laid her hand on Coyote's shoulder. He cocked his head, frowned, then broke into a grin. "That must be the ship!" He got to his feet and went to the window, the sun electrifying his bush of red hair. Swann joined him, and a sudden shadow fell across the room, turning off Coyote's hair. A low fluttery feeling was happening in Sparrow's stomach. Coyote turned around and abruptly stopped grinning.

You cheated! Sparrow's hands jerked in the air. *You didn't guess, you cheated!*

"Oh, come on," said Coyote, kneeling in front of him. "Don't be like that. I can't help it if I can —" He blinked, tried to grin again. "Hey, Sparrow," he said, "let's go outside and see it land!"

Sparrow set his jaw and turned away. His secret excitement had drained away, leaving him sad and tired. He wanted to see Spider land, but not with dumb old Coyote and Swann and Rabbit and the others all crowding around. His eyes started to hurt and he brushed away the wetness. He tore a ragged piece of fruitflesh with his teeth and chewed it hard. When he finally looked around, both Swann and Coyote were gone.

He jumped up and ran from the kitchen, then froze for one

agonizing minute in the main dome. The tremor in his stomach was stronger now, a low, pulsing vibration. He ran, then, not outside, but back through his own flannel door, down the short tunnel to his room.

His mouth fell open, slowly closed. Filling nearly half the sky was the gigantic bulge of the zeppelin, dark red in the morning light. He climbed onto his clothes trunk and stood on tiptoe, peered over the edge of the open dome. The zeppelin hovered above the meadow next to the house, two tiny figures standing underneath — that was Coyote's rusty bush of hair, Swann's gray shag — as a bubble descended on a long cable from the shadow of the ship's belly. Sparrow caught sight of Fuchsia's dark body moving down the hill from the pottery, and Rose appeared beyond the curve of the main dome with Rabbit in his arms, strolling out to join the others.

The bubble, which had been tiny beneath the bulk of the airship, turned out to be much larger than the people standing below. It swung gently on its cable and touched down on the grass. A doorway appeared and Spider's familiar white cloud of hair popped out. She swung onto the lawn and reached back in for her bags. The bubble rose quickly into the air as everyone crowded around Spider. Sparrow chewed his lip, flexed his cramping feet. Everybody was hugging everybody else, then they turned and started back toward the house.

The zeppelin was already rising, moving away. The rumbling in Sparrow's gut began to lessen. He stepped down from the trunk and stood wavering in the middle of his room, then lunged for the window, jerked it open, and scrambled outside.

Coyote paced across the main dome rug, rubbed his palms together, and paced back again. Where had Sparrow run off to now?

"Hey," said Spider from across the room. "Will you sit down and stop worrying? He'll be okay." She sat against the wall beneath the blue Picasso print, Swann beside her and Rabbit on her lap. Rose and Fuchsia had long since gone, Rose to work in the village garden and Fuchsia back up the hill to work on his pots.

Coyote turned and recrossed the room. "It's really my

fault," he said. "If I hadn't come out with that stupid remark about being able to hear, he would have gone out with us to meet you and this whole dismal business—"

"Coyote!"

He stopped.

Spider looked weary. "Come on, would you please just sit down and be quiet for a while? You're making me nervous, and I've only been home an hour. Sparrow has to work out his own problems, that's why he's not here. He's got to learn sometime that people who can hear have certain advantages over him, and he'll be lucky if the lessons are only as harsh as losing guessing games. Don't be overprotective."

Coyote folded his arms and pursed his lips. "You would call it overprotectiveness, wouldn't you? Sometimes I think you don't care about Sparrow one way or the other."

Spider looked away with a tight jaw.

"Now, Coyote," said Swann quietly, "keep in mind what the doctors said about—"

"The doctors can go rape themselves!" he yelled.

Rabbit screwed up her face and began to wail. Spider hugged her saying, "There, Rabbit, it's okay," and giving Coyote an angry look over the little girl's shoulder. Swann, startled, said nothing.

Coyote took a deep breath and tried to speak more calmly. "I'm sorry I shouted, I'm just worried about Sparrow. Swann, those doctors didn't know the boy. They were just bumbling behaviorists, trying to juggle their statistics to come up with something meaningful. Professionals are all alike."

Spider made a choking noise, looked incredulous.

"The doctors did say," said Swann, "to go easy, not to push."

"Push!" Coyote shook his head. "You think I'm pushing? I'm just trying to help my child grow up emotionally balanced."

"Then you're trying too hard," said Spider.

"Don't you think I love that boy?"

"Shh!"

"You—" He turned away, turned back. "You make it seem like I'm on some kind of ego trip."

Spider looked startled, and laughed.

He walked to the door.

"It's hard," came Swann's low voice behind him. He gripped the molding around the doorway, slowly inhaled.

"What?" he said.

"Love," said his mother. "It's hard to share."

Coyote grunted and pushed himself outside. The sun was already halfway up the sky, scattering small clouds before its brilliance. It was going to be a warm day. Hands thrust deep in the pockets of his skirt, he shuffled around the curve of the dome. Why did he have so much trouble talking to Spider? It had been like this for months. She was distant, critical, and argumentative. She ignored him; worst of all she ignored her own *son*.

It wasn't, he decided, that he minded taking most of the responsibility for Sparrow. After all, the boy was his son, too. And he admitted that Spider's work was demanding and liable to make her touchy, preoccupied. But. . . well, hell, just look at her now. She found lots of time to snuggle with Swann for long, intimate conversations, and she spent *hours* with Rabbit every week that she could have been spending with Sparrow. Coyote was sure he had caught jealous looks in Sparrow's eyes when he saw his mother and Rabbit together. And wasn't that just what an extended family was supposed to prevent — jealousy? If the cultural revolution had one major flaw, he thought, it was that it had to use the people of yesterday's world. Coyote kicked at a dirt clod and shook his head.

And then there was Walker. Wasn't there something a little perverse about Spider's relationship with her? No, not the sex — Coyote was an adult, he'd had his quota of homosexual flings in the past, there was nothing wrong with that. No, it had to do with the emotional intensity of Spider and Walker's affair. There was something unhealthy, he felt, something *adolescent* about their lovey-dovey manner. Their relationship was too exclusive. He felt completely and utterly left out of their lives, and was sure the others felt that way, too. It wasn't that he was *jealous* — Gods, it had been months since he and Spider had coupled, longer than that since they had really been friends. It wasn't his problem, it was theirs—

He rounded the side of the main dome and headed toward

the garden. It was good to see it sprouting so soon. He had designed and built the garden that very first autumn after he and Spider had moved here, replacing the traditional flat garden plot that Swann had used for years. Coyote's garden rose in a slow shape of earth from the surrounding lawn, the shape, as it happened, of Spider's left breast when she slept, though he never told her that. She would criticize him for perpetuating some fertility goddess myth or other. Whatever the image, it was a good, functional design. Where the nipple would be, a pool of water slowly crested, fed from the household well by a windmill not far away. The water trickled through a network of stoneware pipes that fed the plants. The planting rows spiraled down from the pool, cut by several radial paths that ran straight down from the peak. Coyote mounted the shallow slope, choosing the longer, spiral route to the top. As he rounded the curve of the garden he saw Sparrow, crouched low, playing in the dirt on the other side. He paused to take three deep breaths before approaching.

Was that a weed? Sparrow leaned over the mound of dirt to study the tiny sprout. Its leaves were sharper and more jagged than the tomato leaves popping up along the row. His fingers reached out to pluck it, then paused, stroked the little plant instead. Even dandelions were good in salads, and good for making wishes later in the year. Why was a particular plant good in some places and bad in others? Why did they call them *weeds?* Poor little dandelion, thought Sparrow, you're not really bad, you're just growing in the wrong place, is all. And that's not your fault. Weeds don't decide to be weeds!

A sudden shadow fell across the dirt and Sparrow jerked away. Coyote loomed over him, smiling, leaning down. Sparrow caught his breath, then glanced down again and saw that he had accidentally gouged the little weed out of the dirt with his fingers. He began to cry, and Coyote's arms came around his shoulders, but he moved out of reach and picked up the dandelion sprout carefully. Its hairlike roots held a few crumbs of dirt; already it looked like it was wilting.

He glanced reproachfully at Coyote, who looked concerned and said, "It's okay, we can plant it back again."

Sparrow shook his head and held the plant up for Coyote to see.

"Ah," said Coyote. He looked around, then pointed toward the meadow. "Let's transplant it over there."

Together they walked down the garden slope and across the bright green clover and grass. Coyote knelt and dug into the soft earth with his thick, stubby fingers. Carefully they filled crumbs of dirt in around the fragile roots until the sprout looked just as safe and sound as it had in the garden.

Sparrow nudged Coyote's shoulder and made signs with his hands. *Will it be okay now?*

Coyote smiled. "I think so. Weeds are pretty tough critters."

Sparrow sighed and sat back on his heels. This little patch of dirt, not much wider than his hand, with its single sprout, was his very own garden. He decided he preferred it to the big family plot. He would come out and water it every day, make sure his dandelion grew big leaves and a bright yellow flower. And then in the fall—

Coyote took his hand. "Come on," he said, "it's time to get cleaned up."

Sparrow frowned, signed with his free hand: *What for?*

Coyote pretended to swoon with amazement, making Sparrow laugh. "Have you forgotten already? This is the day of Walker's big surprise!"

Spider pulled a bicycle off the rack and wheeled it out of the shed into bright sunshine, where Fuchsia stood holding Rabbit in his arms. Spatters of slip had dried white against the rich brown flesh of his face, clung in tiny hard droplets in the hair of his chest and arms.

"Hey," he said to her, "thanks again. Rose said he wouldn't mind taking her if you changed your mind."

Spider shook her head and smiled. "No, really, I'd like to. It'll be fun." She laughed, adjusted her sunglasses. "Rabbit's too young to give me any flak. Aren'tcha, girl?" She lifted Rabbit from her brother's arms, the white of her hands stark against even Rabbit's pink skin, and sat her in the babybasket between the handlebars. "Okeedoke?"

Rabbit gurgled. Fuchsia waved and started back toward the house.

"Hey!" she called. He turned his head. "You," she said, grinning, "are the only man in the world I can really get along with." Fuchsia laughed, then faltered, his dark eyes caught on something behind her. She turned and found Sparrow and Coyote walking up, hand in hand. Coyote's cheeks were sucked in, but he was smiling — she glanced back at Fuchsia, but he was gone around the curve of the dome. She blew a long breath between her teeth, attempted a smile and turned back.

"Well, hi there, Sparrow, how's my man?"

Sparrow smiled back, glanced once at Coyote, and ran the last few steps. Spider leaned down to hug him, but the top-heavy bike began to tip and she had to stagger on one foot to keep from falling. With the jolt her sunglasses fell off — she swore and clenched her eyes against the glare — and Rabbit started to cry. "Hey, Rabbit, hey," she said, "Sparrow, could you hand me those — oh, thanks." She took the glassses that were slipped into her hand and put them on, blinked. Coyote stood beside her, biting his lip.

"Oh, thanks," she said again. "Where's Sparrow?"

"Ran off. What do you expect? Want me to—?"

"No, no, that's okay, I'll talk to him later." Gods, she thought, I'd rather he screamed at me than looked like that. She tried to smile, and immediately wished she hadn't. "Hey, look," she said. "I'm going on ahead to spend some time with Walker. The rest of you catch up later, okay?" She pushed off quickly, wasn't sure if she heard a reply, pedaled past the domes and across the meadow into the woods. As soon as she felt securely out of sight she sat back on the bike seat and coasted, trying to take deep, slow breaths. She could feel her shoulders trembling. Gods above, why did Coyote affect her like that? Rape that man anyway! she snarled to herself, and waited for the instant remorse. Nothing came. She just felt tired and relieved to be alone. At least little Rabbit wouldn't yank her into some ugly scene.

She began to pump again along the narrow paved path, sailing quietly through the soft, scattered light and sounds of the forest. Beneath the trees, the sunshine wasn't nearly so painful.

The thick pine-needle bed of the woods absorbed almost all sound, exuding in return a rich, exhilarating smell, a sexual smell, a smell of lazy combustion as the acidic needles turned into warm earth. She could make out four species of bird by their calls. As she picked up speed, the breeze washed across her face and through her cloud of hair, and tired though she was she laughed and put some muscle into the bike.

Rabbit was happy in her basket, swinging her legs, waving her arms in some private dance, singing to herself in minor keys. Spider topped a short rise and coasted down the other side, letting go the handle bars and spreading her arms like wings. She sang some lines from an old, sad song that Swann liked to play on her guitar. *I wish I had a river soooo long, I would spread my wings and fly-yyyy....*

At the bottom of the hill, the pavement forked at a thick, craggy-barked old fir that everyone called Douglas, the oldest in the forest. One way led to the community center where Swann and Coyote and Rose worked part time to fulfill their household's community quota. Spider took the other path, that circuitous route that passed by every other homestead on this side of the valley. From here it would be a good fifteen-minute ride to Walker's farm.

All told, there were forty-seven households in the village of Noti, some as large as twenty or thirty people, a few triples, couples, and solitaires. Their homesteads were sprinkled over six square kilos of the valley, separated by woods and fields, joined by the bike paths and the loose, co-operative anarchy with which they conducted community affairs. Noti had been one of the first rural ghost towns repopulated with the dissolution of the cities in the techno-cultural revolution, and though from time to time some of the inhabitants had fallen short of manifesting the revolution in their own lives, the community as a whole had been functioning successfully for nearly a decade.

Each of the households was self-sufficient in survival needs — food, clothing, shelter, and affection — but large groups of people can accomplish things that handfuls cannot. Not, at least, so enjoyably. The Noti neighbors came together for dome-raising, harvesting, path-paving, and well-digging, for the collective purchase of raw goods, for dances and for theater. While the majority made their living by household craft and labor, trading their surpluses within the village population, a few such as Spider worked at outside jobs.

Spider was a programmer for Global Relief, an international government corporation that designed food distribution systems and agricultural prescriptions for places hard hit by the turn-of-the-century droughts. Spider's current project was the Midwest American Desert Reclamation Project. She had a remote console at home, through which she did most of her work. The only physical manifestation of the corporation was its annual conference.

As she rode the bicycle farther down the valley, Spider left the forest and glided through the rye fields that surrounded Walker's home. She passed one or two old frame houses, relics of the early nineteen hundreds, now unusably rotten and left to compost at their own easy pace. She swerved to avoid a couple of pedestrians, waved back to them, and shortly pulled up in front of the main house of the farm, a tall tetrahedral barn of rough cedar shakes. She parked the bike with the jungle of others and carried Rabbit through the cool, refreshing light of the grape arbor and into the kitchen. Several folks lounged around a table in conversation. Some looked up, waved.

"Howdy," said Spider, setting down Rabbit, who crawled away toward other children. "Hi, Walker." She bent to hug her friend. Walker's belly was huge and warm between them.

"Hey, lover, I'm glad you made it back." Walker ran her fingers over Spider's eyes, her cheeks, across the broad flat nostrils of her nose to her mouth. They kissed, tongue caressing tongue, and parted. "Until I heard the ship this morning," murmured Walker, "I'd nearly decided to wait another day."

Spider laughed. "Silly, I told you I'd be back in time. You've had your heart set on the cusp for months now." Spider stood. "Hey, I want you for myself for a while."

Walker grinned. "Twist my arm, will you!" She eased herself to her feet, brushed back her short hair, and found Spider's hand. "Be back in a while!" she called back as they walked out the door.

They crossed the stubbly lawn and stretched out beneath a cherry tree's shimmering white masses. Spider plucked a thick blade of grass and nibbled its tip, watching the subtle changes of color in Walker's eyes, cloudy as agate.

"So when's the big event?"

"I finally decided on three forty-two," said Walker. "I started the contractions this morning. I had been planning for seven this evening but I changed my mind. This way I'll lose that conjunction of Venus and Mars, but I'll get a beautiful trine, and it puts the moon in Cancer, which is all right with me."

Spider had to laugh. "You know, I haven't the foggiest idea what you're talking about."

Walker's bushy eyebrows rose. "You should at least be aware that your Moon's in Cancer, too!"

"Great," said Spider. "We'll start a club." She leaned over to kiss Walker's cheek. "But don't you think you ought to have consulted you-know-who about the time?"

Walker frowned — "Who? Oh!" — and laughed, saying "Silly, that's the whole point; I decided what would be the right time by tuning in on what's happening inside. I wouldn't try to force anything! This will be the most important day in this new life." She ran her hand across the fabric on her belly.

Spider bit a lip. "Hey, Walker?"

"Hmm?" Walker turned her head toward her, though her eyes seemed to look somewhere over Spider's left shoulder (Spider fought the urge to glance back). "What is it?"

"I wanted to say... to ask... well...."

Walker's fingertips found Spider's lips and pressed against them gently. "Yes," she said softly, "I've already started asking the others. I think it will be fine."

Spider kissed her palm. "You haven't read my thoughts completely."

Walker's eyebrows came together into one long, thick hedge. "I thought — I mean — don't you want to move here?"

Spider took a deep breath and let it sigh away.

"Oh," said Walker finally. "Oh. Of course." She lifted her hand off the grass. "Do they bother you so much?"

"Yes," said Spider at length.

"Oh, I love you dearly, but you have to understand that I

can't leave my family now."

"Your family per se doesn't bother me," said Spider. "It's just the men."

"I know that's what you mean. But why?"

Spider blew out a breath, sat up, pulling at her hair and rubbing her forehead. "I don't know. I mean I do, I know the feeling inside and out; it's been getting stronger and stronger for the past year or two. Why it's come to me, that I can't say, unless it's the particular men I've been around. They just don't. . . connect, you know? With anything that's me. Call it a lack of common experience. All I know is that I don't want to live with them any more." She glanced down at Walker and shifted slightly to intersect with Walker's gaze.

"But Spider, you have to understand, here I feel like I can finally relax. I have a home for the first time in years. I would love for you to join us, I know you're not happy with Coyote and the rest, but please don't ask me to trade my family for you. Because I would have to say no." Her fingertips moved up Spider's face, the lines of her mouth, her eyes, the ridges of her brows. "Don't be sad," said Walker. "Lover, people are never happy as commodities."

Spider ripped a tuft of grass, threw it on the breeze. She felt that terrible weariness wash over her again. "But it's not as if I wanted you all for myself," she said, hearing her voice quaver. "I want a big household, I do. I'd just like it to be all women. . . ."

Walker's finger tip on her cheek abruptly left a wet track. "Oh Spider, Spider. . . Look, what if my baby is a boy? Would you refuse to live with him? Spider — lover — my commitment is stronger than that. I'm settled here. That's why I decided to have this child. I have a home. I need that."

Spider moved away slightly. "So it's settled."

"Settled! Spider, I'm settled."

She felt the muscles of her chin tug down, those above her eyes pull back. She wiped one cheek with the back of her hand, swallowed. "God damn it." Her fingers clutched cool grass. "If only I'd found you a couple years ago. If only you weren't into this pregnancy mode. . . ."

Walker's eyebrows arched. She shook her head slowly.

"Spider, just listen to yourself! Do you realize how you'd react if any man made a crack like that? Now, come on. Be my sister today. I want you to *be* with me."

Spider sobbed so hard it hurt her throat, pulled Walker to her chest and held her tight.

"Hey!" cried Coyote. "I'm for a shower! Who's with?"

"Me," said Fuchsia, flecked with clay.

"Sure," said Swann, coming in dusty.

Sparrow grabbed Coyote's hand and led the way.

Water fell, like heavy light, in cold, thick blue drops. Coyote and Sparrow and Fuchsia and Swann jumped and danced in the indoor rain, rubbing each other with sponges and flinging wet hair.

"Who will scrub my back?" asked Fuchsia.

"I will," said Swann and Coyote at the same time. They laughed and set to work on either side.

"Ahhh," said Fuchsia, "you two do a heavy job."

Sparrow caught their attention with a flutter of hands. *Fuchsia's peeing in the shower!*

"Huh?" said Fuchsia. He blinked and looked down.

Coyote laughed and tapped Sparrow's shoulder. "Look again," he said. "That's just water running down."

Sparrow looked confused.

"Just look at me! Just look at yourself!"

Sparrow peered down across his rounded belly, then giggled delightedly. The water ran down his sleek brown skin, coursed around his navel, and dribbled off his penis, arcing through the air to the slatted floor.

Swann bent down to rub shampoo into Sparrow's frizzy hair. "Occupational hazard," she said. Like her face, her body ran with wrinkles. Her breasts hung low and bobbled in the wet light.

I didn't see that word, signed Sparrow.

"Occupational hazard," enunciated Swann. "It's an old expression that means, well, that there are certain things that happen to you as a result of what you do for a living."

What kinds of things?

Swann cleared her throat and frowned. Fuchsia knelt

beside her and poked Sparrow in the belly, eliciting a giggle. "For example," he said, "you were born with knees, so whenever you fall down on something rough and hard, you skin them. That's the occupational hazard of having knees."

Swann was shaking her head. "That's the occupational hazard of running around!"

Coyote squatted, too. "And we," he said, "have penises because we were born male, so it looks like we're peeing in the shower. Even when we're not!"

Sparrow laughed, then looked at Coyote's groin, at Fuchsia's, at Swann's, then at his own small stub.

"All done?" said Swann, rinsing under the shower.

Fuchsia stepped to the wall and turned off the water with a wisk.

"I'll get the towels," said Coyote, but Swann caught his arm.

"Not for me," she said. "It's quite warm enough outside for me to dry off."

"Same here," said Fuchsia.

Me, too, signed Sparrow.

Coyote shrugged. "Me, too." As a group they strolled outside, picked clothes off the line, at length chose bicycles from the rack in the shed, and pushed off down the trail.

Sparrow parked his bike with the others and wandered off alone to explore the farm. He had been here only once or twice before, never with so many people around. The largest building of the homestead was a huge pyramid made of wood. Its windows, and sections of its walls, were thrown open like so may tongues to lap up the day. Sparrow avoided the crowd of kids on the lawn and circled the house, peering into open rooms. In one, about ten people sat in a circle holding hands. They all had their eyes closed, and he guessed they must have been omming. Fuchsia had taught him to do that last fall. It made him feel good, especially when he felt it through his hands from the people next to him.

He slipped through a low arch in the hedge and came out in the garden. Flowers of all colors spread beneath the bright sun. Beyond some bushes, a thick cherry tree gnarled its way into the sky where it burst with a cloud of white blossoms. Several pairs of legs dangled down, and higher up a section shook, releasing a minor snowstorm to the breeze. Sparrow padded carefully through the bushes past the tree, grinning gleefully at the thrill of secrecy that shivered up his spine.

He ran around a corner of a hedge and found himself abruptly in the middle of a group of people lounging on the grass. Several looked up at him. He couldn't move. One woman flailed at a guitar and everyone swayed openmouthed. He couldn't make out the words: their lips didn't move enough. With an effort he jerked away and ran in another direction.

Some secrecy! He found a large bush and crawled inside, crouched in the flat, dry space surrounded by leaves. This was more like it.

He really wondered, sometimes, what it must be like to know about things you couldn't see. He could feel some things, like drums, and omming, and the zeppelin that morning. He felt those things in his stomach and with his fingertips, and when he laid his hand across the throat of someone who talked or sang. But what was it like to feel someone whose back was turned talking across the room? What was it like to feel a bird's throat ripple in the trees? To feel the wind shiver through the branches of a tree? Could other people really feel those things from far away?

His attention was caught by movement through the leaves. He leaned forward and peered out. Everyone was walking in one direction — towards the house. It must be time! But how did they know?

The kitchen was crowded and noisy when the bell began to ring, high in the apex of the house. For the space of one breath, everyone around Coyote fell silent, then began to talk again, but softly now, with a different tone. They started to move toward the door that led to the commons. Coyote set his cup of tea on the table and followed, feeling socially detached and at the same time somehow clear, inside, riveted to the moment. He smiled and nodded when his eyes met those of friends, but he didn't feel like talking to anybody, and no one tried to talk to him. The grandfather clock in the hall read three-fifteen, its long pendulum tocking slowly back and forth behind the window in its case.

The commons was a two-story-high pointed space. Walker sat in lotus in the middle of the floor as her friends filled up the room around her, children toward the center and the tallest adults lining the three walls. Coyote sat near the middle with people his height. It looked to him like nearly a hundred people. Some of them he recognized as members of this household. He caught sight of Swann and Fuchsia sitting together over to his right, their backs against the wall, but neither of them glanced his way. In fact, nearly everyone was facing Walker now. Coyote turned back, shifted his legs into a comfortable half-lotus, and noticed Sparrow's skinny silhouette in a doorway across the room. He wished the boy would look his way. . . .

The group began to breathe with Walker. Her diaphragm pulled in, relaxed, her nostrils flared visibly with each inhale. The only sounds were the unison breathing and a handful of children and dogs yelping outside. Walker's vast belly shuddered. A low, whispered chant began to grow among the members of the gathering, in time with her breathing, in time with the contractions of her uterus. Coyote cleared his throat and added his own murmur to the group. They were like an ocean to Walker's moon, he thought, and tucked the conceit away in a safe place where he might find it the next time he worked on his poetry.

Like an incoming tide, the chanting rose and fell in successively stronger waves. One of the three midwives held a wristwatch in his hand and murmured occasional cues to Walker, though all of her attention seemed to be focused inward. Her eyelids were closed, her mouth half open. Several times she changed position, working into progressively higher stances till she squatted, her buttocks clear of the floor. The hands of another midwife (Coyote recognized her from the community garden — her name was Gael) rested on Walker's shoulders for balance, while a third lay on the sheet to massage Walker's belly, her groin, her enlarging vagina. The chanting reached its final peak as Walker make the sharp, high noises of ecstacy and pain, and with surprising suddenness the red, wet bulge of the baby's head appeared between Walker's thighs. Walker leaned back into Gael's arms, while the third midwife cradled the emerging baby in her hands. The hips, the knees, the tiny feet came out, and the woman brought the infant up and laid it on Walker's stomach. Walker's hands groped and found the little hands and head and briefly she smiled. Coyote thought she looked exhausted. Gael had slipped a pillow under her head. The room was very quiet, remained so until after some minutes the baby began to use its lungs — a small cry escaped to mark that moment — and people began to murmur, began to talk, began to cry and laugh.

Coyote didn't stay to see the cutting of the cord or the after-birth rite. He rose stiffly to his feet and joined several others outside. No one said very much, just smiled or looked serene. Someone over by the garden was getting sick, helped by friends. One man Coyote didn't know laughed out loud with wet cheeks and spread his arms to the sun.

Coyote began to look around for Sparrow.

"But just look at the eyes! Hey, there, little one!" Spider stroked one tiny palm with her fingertip, and the hand closed around her knuckle, the little eyes tracked, and tracked again. Spider grinned down at Walker. "See that?" She took Walker's right hand and folded it gently around the baby's hand holding her finger. "See? I mean, feel? That's an instinctive mechanism left over from when we all had hair on our bellies and backs that babies clung to."

Walker's marbled eyes were wet, seemed to look somewhere near the ceiling. "I do see," she said.

Spider grinned and kissed the woman's fingers. "You did all right for yourself, lady, you did okay! She's even a she."

Walker smiled wearily and shook her head. "You know, my love, I have long maintained that birthing is not so much a woman thing to do as a human thing. It's only to be regretted that nearly half our population are incapable of experiencing this god-awful exhaustion."

Spider laughed. "Hush, we'll talk politics later." And sud-denly she felt sad. The commons was nearly empty now, the sun was falling in the sky. Or rather, Spider thought, the earth is rolling up. And felt a trickle course down her cheek. "Walker?" She fumbled in her pocket and found the scrap of paper.

"Mmm?" Walker looked almost asleep.

"I'll see you later, huh?"

She nodded dreamily.

"Say. . . in about a year?"

Walker opened her sightless eyes.

"I'm going," Spider said with an effort. "I don't know, East, I think. I want to see Virginia. I want to get some dust between my toes, try some other styles." She waited for Walker to say something, but no reply came. "I'll come back next spring, I promise. Just think! This little lady will be running the place by then."

Walker laughed then, with tears. "I really doubt that!"

"I love you," said Spider.

"I love you, too."

Spider bent down to kiss her cheek, her lips. She nuzzled the infant, rose, and quickly walked away.

Bike? No, walk. Leave the asphalt path and take the deer trail through the woods. Fir tree, bushes, brambles, and that thick, sweet smell of afternoon. Sparrow ran along the path until his breath got hard. He rested, pulled down his pants and stooped, watched a pale green frond that was just beginning to lift from the crumbs of earth at the base of a tall, thick tree. Baby plant, baby girl. Dying, being old. Being himself. Was Swann ever a baby? Sparrow shook his head in slow thought.

He wondered if everyone looked like that at birth. So quiet, so messy, glistening, dripping, caked with cheesy stuff, so red and blue and small! Sparrow was nearly six, a lot older than Walker's baby, but he was still a baby compared to Swann. And Swann was a baby compared to. . . well, to Douglas. Just where did that end?

He shivered and found himself in shadow. He got to his feet jerkily, tugged up his pants, and trudged on down the path. The low red sun flickered among the tree trunks as he passed along. The trail meandered around and down and then rose steeply, rounded a ridge, and deposited him on the edge of the woods, just meters from the main dome door.

The screen door slammed against the late afternoon, and footsteps pattered down the ramp. Coyote glanced up from his sewing. "Hey—" His gray eyes tracked across the room, followed Sparrow's flight through the blue flannel door. "Huh," he said, "I wonder what his hurry was."

Swann, beside him, ejected a wooden egg from a sock and cast her eyebrows toward her son. "Didn't you see the tears?"

"What?" Coyote lifted his thin shoulders against his cloud of rusty hair. "But—"

"I was watching Sparrow through the whole thing," came Fuchsia's voice from behind a pair of trousers. Flip, flop, folded, they landed with a whump on the pile of clothes. "I think Sparrow took it... specially..." he said. "I think that in some special, five-year-old way, he really understood."

For a minute the room was silent, but for the sounds of cloth against cloth. Then Coyote said, "Oh, God...."

"I think Sparrow was touched," said Swann, "in a religious sense."

Coyote regarded her silently for a moment, then speared the patch he was sewing with his needle and stood up from the rug.

"Now, Coyote—" Swann began, but he was gone. She settled back, shaking her head and thrusting out her lower lip. "My lord, when will that man learn to leave well enough alone."

Spider pushed aside her door (a snapshot of a spiral molecule, silk-screened on burlap) and walked into the room. "Swann," she said, "I've got something to—"

"He just doesn't listen," said Swann. "And Sparrow *can't.*"

"Swann—"

"Oh well, I suppose we'll have to leave them to find their own answers together." She shook her head again.

Spider sighed. "I guess you're right."

Fuchsia nudged Swann, cleared his throat. "Spider?" he said. "Were you about to—"

Spider smiled wanly at her brother and shook her head. She turned her head and went back into her room to finish packing.

Coyote found Sparrow huddled inside a tangle of blanket

against the domelet wall. "Hey," he said, gently shaking Sparrow's shoulder. "It's me." He eased the boy over onto his back and regarded the red, wet eyes. "Hey, what did you think of the birth today? I thought it was beautiful, didn't you?"

Sparrow nodded, shaking brown frizz.

"Well, what did you think? What did you feel? I really want to know."

Sparrow frowned, nearly smiled. Then started to sob. Coyote found a hand and squeezed.

"Wasn't she pretty?" he said. "I've seen three births in my life — one of them was *you* — and each time it was just too good to believe, just too beautiful to compare."

His son turned away, crying freely into the blanket.

"Hey," said Coyote, "hey," and ran his hand along the small, skinny arm that showed. Sparrow released a long, low wail that made Coyote shiver. With care he turned the boy over again. Sparrow looked at him with bright, wet eyes, and worked his other hand free from the blanket. His fingers shook, but Coyote could still read what they said.

"Why, sure," he replied, smiling with effort. "I don't see why not. A lot of people have babies when they get old enough."

"Ah-ahhh," cried Sparrow, shaking his head, butting his head against Coyote's, skull meeting skull through scalps and soft hair. The boy made another sign, the one that stood for *impossibility*.

"Oh," said Coyote, "now where did you get that idea? Anyone can have a ba—" His jaw went slack. "Oh, God," he said, and hugged the boy to him. "Oh, Sparrow, I'm sorry, I didn't understand." He kissed his head, his face, his hands. "I'm sorry," he murmured. "I wish I could change you, if that's what you want, but I can't. We all have to live with the way we were born."

He pulled away, moved Sparrow's face so the boy could see his lips. "I love you," he said, "just the way you are." And for a while, then, both of them cried.

When Spider slipped in to say good-by, she didn't wake either of them.

Passengers
Robert Silverberg

Robert Silverberg was born in New York City but has lived for many years in the San Francisco Bay area. He studied comparative literature and philosophy at Columbia University and began his writing career while still an undergraduate: his first short stories appeared in 1954 and a novel, *Revolt on Alpha C,* in 1955. Since then he has written hundreds of short stories, more books than he has troubled to count, and a great many magazine articles. His work has been featured in *Omni, Playboy, American Heritage, Horizon, Harper's,* and other such periodicals.

Among Silverberg's best-known novels are *Tower of Glass, Downward to the Earth, Son of Man, Dying Inside, The Book of Skulls, To Live Again, Hawksbill Station, Nightwings, A Time of Changes,* and *Lord Valentine's Castle.* His literary triumphs have won him numerous Hugo and Nebula awards — the most coveted awards in the field. In 1967-68, he was president of the Science Fiction Writers of America, and in 1970 he was guest of honor at the World Science Fiction Convention in Heidelberg, Germany.

Silverberg's reputation in the science fiction field derives, in large part, from the work that he produced in the middle 1960s. He proceeded, then, to become far more elitist, more and more literary, to the point of no return, to the absolute vanishing point of his career. In 1974, Silverberg did the unthinkable. After a successful twenty-year career in science fiction, he quit.

Today, Silverberg is writing again. After a five-year hiatus he returned to the field to write the epic adventure, *Lord Valentine's Castle*, which captured the plaudits of critics and readers alike. The publication of this book marked a turning point in Silverberg's career. This work, like the others which have followed, is far more accessible, far more human, far more concerned with matters of narrative rather than style.

When not at his typewriter (word processor, actually), Silverberg keeps busy in his garden of exotic sub-tropical plants, travels widely, and diverts himself at restaurants specializing in alien cuisines.

There are only fragments of me left now. Chunks of memory have broken free and drifted away like calved glaciers. It is always like that when a Passenger leaves us. We can never be sure of all the things our borrowed bodies did. We have only the lingering traces, the imprints.

Like sand clinging to an ocean-tossed bottle. Like the throbbings of amputated legs.

I rise. I collect myself. My hair is rumpled; I comb it. My face is creased from too little sleep. There is sourness in my mouth. Has my Passenger been eating dung with my mouth? They do that. They do anything.

It is morning.

A gray, uncertain morning. I stare at it awhile, and then, shuddering, I opaque the window and confront instead the gray, uncertain surface of the inner panel. My room looks untidy. Did I have a woman here? There are ashes in the trays. Searching for butts, I find several with lipstick stains. Yes, a woman was here.

I touch the bedsheets. Still warm with shared warmth. Both pillows tousled. She has gone, though, and the Passenger is gone, and I am alone.

How long did it last, this time?

I pick up the phone and ring Central. "What is the date?"

The computer's bland feminine voice replies, "Friday, December fourth, nineteen eighty-seven."

"The time?"

"Nine fifty-one, Eastern Standard Time."

"The weather forecast?"

"Predicted temperature range for today thirty to thirty-eight. Current temperature, thirty-one. Wind from the north, sixteen miles an hour. Chances of precipitation slight."

"What do you recommend for a hangover?"

"Food or medication?"

"Anything you like," I say.

The computer mulls that one over for a while. Then it decides on both, and activates my kitchen. The spigot yields cold tomato juice. Eggs begin to fry. From the medicine slot comes a purplish liquid. The Central Computer is ever so thoughtful. Do the Passengers ever ride it, I wonder? What thrills could that hold for them? Surely it must be more exciting to borrow the million minds of Central than to live awhile in the faulty, short-circuited soul of a corroding human being!

December fourth, Central said. Friday. So the Passenger had me for three nights.

I drink the purplish stuff and probe my memories in a gingerly way, as one might probe a festering sore.

I remember Tuesday morning. A bad time at work. None of the charts will come out right. The section manager irritable; he has been taken by Passengers three times in five weeks, and his section is in disarray as a result, and his Christmas bonus is jeopardized. Even though it is customary not to penalize a person for lapses due to Passengers, according to the system, the section manager seems to feel he will be treated unfairly. We have a hard time. Revise the charts, fiddle with the program, check the fundamentals ten times over. Out they come: the detailed forecasts for price variations of public utility securities, February — April 1988. That afternoon we are to meet and discuss the charts and what they tell us.

I do not remember Tuesday afternoon.

That must have been when the Passenger took me. Perhaps at work; perhaps in the mahogany-paneled boardroom itself, during the conference. Pink concerned faces all about me; I cough, I lurch, I stumble from my seat. They shake their heads sadly. No one reaches for me. No one stops me. It is too dangerous to interfere with one who has a Passenger. The chances are great that a second Passenger lurks nearby in the discorporate state looking for a mount. So I am avoided. I leave the building.

After that, what?

Sitting in my room on bleak Friday morning, I eat my scrambled eggs and try to reconstruct the three lost nights.

Of course it is impossible. The conscious mind functions during the period of captivity, but upon withdrawal of the Passenger nearly every recollection goes too. There is only slight residue, a gritty film of faint and ghostly memories. The mount is never precisely the same person afterwards; though he cannot recall the details of his experience, he is subtly changed by it.

I try to recall.

A girl? Yes: lipstick on the butts. Sex, then, here in my room. Young? Old? Blonde? Dark? Everthing is hazy. How did my borrowed body behave? Was I a good lover? I try to be, when I am myself. I keep in shape. At thirty-eight, I can handle three sets of tennis on a summer afternoon without collapsing. I can make a woman glow as a woman is meant to glow. Not boasting; just categorizing. We have our skills. These are mine.

But Passengers, I am told, take wry amusement in controverting our skills. So would it have given my rider a kind of delight to find me a woman and force me to fail repeatedly with her?

I dislike the thought.

The fog is going from my mind now. The medicine prescribed by Central works rapidly. I eat, I shave, I stand under the vibrator until my skin is clean. I do my exercises. Did the Passenger exercise my body Wednesday and Thursday mornings? Probably not. I must make up for that. I am close to middle age, now; tonus lost is not easily regained.

I touch my toes twenty times, knees stiff.

I kick my legs in the air.

I lie flat and lift myself on pumping elbows.

The body responds, maltreated though it has been. It is the first bright moment of my awakening: to feel the inner tingling, to know that I still have vigor.

Fresh air is what I want next. Quickly I slip into my clothes and leave. There is no need for me to report to work today. They are aware that since Tuesday afternoon I have had a Passenger; they need not be aware that before dawn on Friday the Passenger departed. I will have a free day. I will walk the city's streets, stretching my limbs, repaying my body for the abuse it has suffered.

I enter the elevator. I drop fifty stories to the ground. I step out into December dreariness.

The towers of New York rise about me.

In the street the cars stream forward. Drivers sit edgily at their wheels. One never knows when the driver of a nearby car will be borrowed, and there is always a moment of lapsed coordination as the Passenger takes over. Many lives are lost that way on our streets and highways, but never the life of a Passenger.

I began to walk without purpose. I cross Fourteenth Street, heading north, listening to the soft violent purr of the electric engines. I see a boy jigging in the street and I know he is being ridden. At Fifth and Twenty-second a prosperous-looking paunchy man approaches, his necktie askew, this morning's *Wall Street Journal* jutting from an overcoat pocket. He giggles. He thrusts out his tongue. Ridden. Ridden. I avoid him. Moving briskly, I come to the underpass that carries traffic below Thirty-fourth Street toward Queens, and pause for a moment to watch two adolescent girls quarreling at the rim of the pedestrian walk. One is a Negro. Her eyes are rolling in terror. The other pushes her closer to the railing. Ridden. But the Passenger does not have murder on its mind, merely pleasure. The Negro girl is released and falls in a huddled heap, trembling. Then she rises and runs. The other girl draws a long strand of gleaming hair into her mouth, chews on it, seems to waken. She looks dazed.

I avert my eyes. One does not watch while a fellow sufferer is awakening. There is a morality of the ridden; we have so many new tribal mores in these dark days.

I hurry on.

Where am I going so hurriedly? Already I have walked more than a mile. I seem to be moving toward some goal, as though my Passenger still hunches in my skull, urging me about. But I know that is not so. For the moment, at least, I am free.

Can I be sure of that?

Cogito ergo sum no longer applies. We go on thinking even

while we are ridden, and we live in quiet desperation, unable to halt our courses no matter how ghastly, no matter how self-destructive. I am certain that I can distinguish between the condition of bearing a Passenger and the condition of being free. But perhaps not. Perhaps I bear a particularly devilish Passenger which has not quitted me at all, but which merely has receded to the cerebellum, leaving me with the illusion of freedom while all the time surreptitiously driving me onward to some purpose of its own.

Did we ever have more that that: the illusion of freedom?

But this is disturbing, the thought that I may be ridden without realizing it. I burst out in heavy perspiration, not merely from the exertion of walking. Stop. Stop here. Why must you walk? You are at Forty-second Street. There is the library. Nothing forces you onward. Stop a while, I tell myself. Rest on the library steps.

I sit on the cold stone and tell myself that I have made this decision for myself.

Have I? It is the old problem, free will versus determinism, translated into the foulest of forms. Determinism is no longer a philosopher's abstraction; it is cold alien tendrils sliding between cranial sutures. The Passengers arrived three years ago. I have been ridden five times since then. Our world is quite different now. But we have adjusted even to this. We have adjusted. We have our mores. Life goes on. Our governments rule, our legislatures meet, our stock exchanges transact business as usual, and we have methods for compensating for the random havoc. It is the only way. What else can we do? Shrivel in defeat? We have an enemy we cannot fight; at best we can resist through endurance. So we endure.

The stone steps are cold against my body. In December few people sit here.

I tell myself that I made this long walk of my own free will, that I halted of my own free will, that no Passenger rides my brain now. Perhaps. Perhaps. I cannot let myself believe that I am not free. Can it be, I wonder, that the Passenger left some lingering command in me? Walk to this place, halt at this place? That is possible too.

I look about me at the others on the library steps.

An old man, eyes vacant, sitting on newspaper. A boy of thirteen or so with flaring nostrils. A plump woman. Are all of them ridden? Passengers seem to cluster about me today. The more I study the ridden ones, the more convinced I become that I am, for the moment, free. The last time, I had three months of freedom between rides. Some people, they say, are scarcely ever free. Their bodies are in great demand, and they know only scattered bursts of freedom, a day here, a week there, an hour. We have never been able to determine how many Passengers infest our world. Millions, maybe. Or maybe five. Who can tell?

A wisp of snow curls down out of the gray sky. Central had said the chance of precipitation was slight. Are they riding Central this morning too?

I see the girl.

She sits diagonally across from me, five steps up and a hundred feet away, her black skirt pulled up on her knees to reveal handsome legs. She is young. Her hair is deep, rich auburn. Her eyes are pale; at this distance, I cannot make out the precise color. She is dressed simply. She is younger than thirty. She wears a dark green coat and her lipstick has a purplish tinge. Her lips are full, her nose slender, high-bridged, her eyebrows carefully plucked.

I know her.

I have spent the past three nights with her in my room. She is the one. Ridden, she came to me, and ridden, I slept with her. I am certain of this. The veil of memory opens; I see her slim body naked on my bed.

How can it be that I remember this?

It is too strong to be an illusion. Clearly this is something that I have been *permitted* to remember for reasons I cannot comprehend. And I remember more. I remember her soft gasping sounds of pleasure. I know that my body did not betray me those three nights, nor did I fail her need.

And there is more. A memory of sinuous music; a scent of youth in her hair; the rustle of winter trees. Somehow she brings back to me a time of innocence, a time when I am young and girls are mysterious, a time of parties and dances and warmth and secrets.

I am drawn to her now.

There is an etiquette about such things, too. It is in poor taste to approach someone you have met while being ridden. Such an encounter gives you no privilege; a stranger remains a stranger, no matter what you and she may have done and said during your involuntary time together.

Yet, I am drawn to her.

Why this violation of taboo? Why this raw breach of etiquette? I have never done this before. I have been scrupulous.

But I get to my feet and walk along the step on which I have been sitting until I am below her, and I look up, and automatically she folds her ankles together and angles her knees as if in awareness that her position is not a modest one. My eyes meet hers. Her eyes are hazy green. She is beautiful, and I rack my memory for more details of our passion.

I climb step by step until I stand before her.

"Hello," I say.

She gives me a neutral look. She does not seem to recognize me. Her eyes are veiled, as one's eyes often are, just after the Passenger has gone. She purses her lips and appraises me in a distant way.

"Hello," she replies coolly. "I don't think I know you."

"No. You don't. But I have the feeling you don't want to be alone just now. And I know I don't." I try to persuade her with my eyes that my motives are decent. "There's snow in the air." I say. "We can find a warmer place. I'd like to talk to you."

"About what?"

"Let's go elsewhere, and I'll tell you. I'm Charles Roth."

"Helen Martin."

She gets to her feet. She still has not cast aside her cool neutrality; she is suspicious, ill at ease. But at least she is willing to go with me. A good sign.

"Is it too early in the day for a drink?"

"I'm not sure. I hardly know what time it is."

"Before noon."

"Let's have a drink anyway," she says, and we both smile.

We go to a cocktail lounge across the street. Sitting face to face in the darkness, we sip drinks, daiquiri for her, bloody mary for me. She relaxes a little. I ask myself what it is I want from her. The pleasure of her company, yes. Her company in bed? But I have already had that pleasure, three nights of it, though she does not know that. I want something more. Something more. What?

Her eyes are bloodshot. She has had little sleep these past three nights.

I say, "Was it very unpleasant for you?"

"What?"

"The Passenger."

A whiplash of reaction crosses her face. "How did you know I've had a Passenger?"

"I know."

"We aren't supposed to talk about it."

"I'm broadminded," I tell her."My Passenger left me some time during the night. I was ridden since Tuesday afternoon."

"Mine left me about two hours ago, I think." Her cheeks color. She is doing something daring, talking like this. "I was ridden since Monday night. This was my fifth time."

"Mine also."

We toy with our drinks. Rapport is growing, almost without the need of words. Our recent experiences with Passengers give us something in common, although Helen does not realize how intimately we shared those experiences.

We talk. She is a designer of display windows. She has a small apartment several blocks from here. She lives alone. She asks me what I do. "Securities analyst," I tell her. She smiles. Her teeth are flawless. We have a second round of drinks. I am positive, now, that this is the girl who was in my room while I was ridden.

A seed of hope grows in me. It was a happy chance that brought us together again so soon after we parted as dreamers. A happy chance, too, that some vestige of the dream lingered in my mind.

We have shared something, who knows what, and it must have been good to leave such a vivid imprint on me, and now I want to come to her conscious, aware, my own master, and renew that relationship, making it a real one this time. It is not proper, for I am trespassing on a privilege that is not mine except by virtue of our Passenger's brief presence in us. Yet I need her. I want her.

She seems to need me, too, without realizing who I am. But fear holds her back.

I am frightened of frightening her, and I do not try to press my advantage too quickly. Perhaps she would take me to her apartment with her now, perhaps not, but I do not ask. We finish our drinks. We arrange to meet by the library steps again tomorrow. My hand momentarily brushes hers. Then she is gone.

I fill three ashtrays that night. Over and over I debate the wisdom of what I am doing. But why not leave her alone? I have no right to follow her. In the place our world has become, we are wisest to remain apart.

And yet — there is that stab of half-memory when I think of her. The blurred lights of lost chances behind the stairs, of girlish laughter in second-floor corridors, of stolen kisses, of tea and cake. I remember the girl with the orchid in her hair, and the one in the spangled dress, and the one with the child's face and the woman's eyes, all so long ago, all lost, all gone, and I tell myself that this one I will not lose, I will not permit her to be taken from me.

Morning comes, a quiet Saturday. I return to the library, hardly expecting to find her there, but she is there, on the steps, and the sight of her is like a reprieve. She looks wary, troubled; obviously she has done much thinking, little sleeping. Together we walk along Fifth Avenue. She is quite close to me, but she does not take my arm. Her steps are brisk, short, nervous.

I want to suggest that we go to her apartment instead of the cocktail lounge. In these days we must move swiftly while we are free. But I know it would be a mistake to think of this as a matter of tactics. Coarse haste would be fatal, bringing me perhaps an ordinary victory, a numbing defeat within it. In any event her mood hardly seemed promising. I look at her, thinking of string music and new snowfalls, and she looks toward the gray sky.

She says, "I can feel them watching me all the time. Like

vultures swooping overhead, waiting, waiting. Ready to pounce."

"But there's a way of beating them. We can grab little scraps of life when they're not looking."

"They're always looking."

"No," I tell her. "There can't be enough of them for that. Sometimes they're looking the other way. And while they are, two people can come together and try to share warmth."

"But what's the use?"

"You're too pessimistic, Helen. They ignore us for months at a time. We have a chance. We have a chance."

But I cannot break through her shell of fear. She is paralyzed by the nearness of the Passengers, unwilling to begin anything for fear it will be snatched away by our tormentors. We reach the building where she lives, and I hope she will relent and invite me in. For an instant she wavers, but only for an instant: she takes my hand in both of hers, and smiles, and the smile fades, and she is gone, leaving me only with the words, "Let's meet at the library again tomorrow. Noon."

I make the long chilling walk home alone.

Some of her pessimism seeps into me that night. It seems futile for us to try to salvage anything. More than that: wicked for me to seek her out, shameful to offer a hesitant love when I am not free. In this world, I tell myself, we should keep well clear of others, so that we do not harm anyone when we are seized and ridden.

I do not go meet her in the morning.

It is best this way, I insist. I have no business trifling with her. I imagine her at the library, wondering why I am late, growing tense, impatient, then annoyed. She will be angry with me for breaking our date, but her anger will ebb, and she will forget quickly enough.

Monday comes. I return to work.

Naturally, no one discusses my absence. It is as though I have never been away. The market is strong that morning. The work is challenging; it is mid-morning before I think of Helen at all. But once I think of her, I can think of nothing else. My cowardice in standing her up. The childishness of Saturday's night's dark thoughts. Why accept fate so passively? Why give in? I want to fight, now, to carve out a pocket of security despite the odds. I feel a deep conviction that it can be done. The Passengers may never bother the two of us again, after all. And that flickering smile of hers outside her building Saturday, that momentary glow — it should have told me that behind her wall of fear she felt the same hopes. She was waiting for me to lead the way. And I stayed home instead.

At lunchtime I go to the library, convinced it is futile.

But she is there. She paces along the steps; the wind slices at her slender figure. I go to her.

She is silent a moment. "Hello," she says finally.

"I'm sorry about yesterday."

"I waited a long time for you."

I shrug. "I made up my mind that it was no use to come. But then I changed my mind again."

She tries to look angry. But I know she is pleased to see me again — else, why did she come here today? She cannot hide her inner pleasure. Nor can I. I point across the street to the cocktail lounge.

"A daiquiri?" I say. "As a peace offering?"

"All right."

Today the lounge is crowded, but we find a booth somehow. There is a brightness in her eyes that I have not seen before. I sense a barrier is crumbling within her.

"You're less afraid of me, Helen," I say.

"I've never been afraid of you. I'm afraid of what could happen if we take the risks."

"Don't be. Don't be."

"I'm trying not to be afraid. But sometimes it seems so hopeless. Since *they* came here—"

"We can still try to live our own lives."

"Maybe."

"We have to. Let's make a pact, Helen. No more gloom. No more worrying about the terrible things that might happen. All right?"

A pause. Then a cool hand against mine.

"All right."

We finish our drinks, and I present my Credit Central to pay for them, and we go outside. I want her to tell me to forget about this afternoon's work and come home with her. It is inevitable, now, that she will ask me, and better sooner than later.

We walk a block. She does not offer the invitation. I sense the struggle inside her, and I wait, letting that struggle reach its own resolution without interference from me. We walk a second block. Her arm is through mine, but she talks only of her work, of the weather, and it is a remote, arm's length conversation. At the next corner she swings around, away from her apartment, back toward the cocktail lounge. I try to be patient with her.

I have no need to rush things now, I tell myself. Her body is not a secret to me. We have begun our relationship topsy-turvy, with the physical part first; now it will take time to work backward to the more difficult part that some people call love.

But of course, she is not aware that we have known each other that way. The wind blows swirling snowflakes in our faces, and somehow the cold sting awakens honesty in me. I know what I must say. I must relinquish my unfair advantage.

I tell her, "While I was ridden last week, Helen, I had a girl in my room."

"Why talk of such things now?"

"I have to, Helen. You were the girl."

She halts. She turns to me. People hurry past us in the street. Her face is very pale, with dark red spots growing in her cheeks.

"That's not funny, Charles."

"It wasn't meant to be. You were with me from Tuesday night to early Friday morning."

"How can you possibly know that?"

"I do. I do. The memory is clear. Somehow it remains, Helen. I see your whole body."

"Stop it, Charles."

"We were very good together," I say. "We must have pleased our Passengers because we were so good. To see you again — it was like waking from a dream, and finding that the dream was real, the girl right there—"

"No!"

"Let's go to your apartment and begin again."

She says, "You're being deliberately filthy, and I don't know why, but there wasn't any reason for you to spoil things. Maybe I was with you and maybe I wasn't, but you wouldn't know it, and if you did know it you should keep your mouth shut about it, and—"

"You have a birthmark the size of a dime," I say, "about three inches below your left breast."

She sobs and hurls herself at me, there in the street. Her long silvery nails rake my cheeks. She pummels me. I seize her. Her knees assail me. No one pays attention; those who pass by assume we are ridden, and turn their heads. She is all fury, but I have my arms around her like metal bands, so that she can only stamp and snort, and her body is close against mine. She is rigid, anguished.

In a low, urgent voice I say, "We'll defeat them, Helen. We'll finish what they started. Don't fight me. There's no reason to fight me. I know, it's a fluke that I remember you, but let me go with you and I'll prove that we belong together."

"Let— go—"

"Please. Please. Why should we be enemies? I don't mean you any harm. I love you, Helen. Do you remember, when we were kids, we could play at being in love? I did; you must have done it too. Sixteen, seventeen years old. The whispers, the conspiracies — all a big game, and we knew it. But the game's over. We can't afford to tease and run. We have so little time, when we're free — we have to trust, to open ourselves—"

"It's wrong."

"No. Just because it's the stupid custom for two people brought together by Passengers to avoid one another, that doesn't mean we have to follow it. Helen — Helen—"

Something in my tone registers with her. She ceases to struggle. Her rigid body softens. She looks up at me, her tear-streaked face thawing, her eyes blurred.

"Trust me," I say. "Trust me, Helen!"

She hesitates. Then she smiles.

In that moment I feel the chill at the back of my skull, the sensation as of a steel needle driven deep through bone. I stiffen. My arms drop away from her. For an instant I lose touch, and when the mists clear all is different.

"Charles?" she says. *"Charles?"*

Her knuckles are against her teeth. I turn, ignoring her, and go back into the cocktail lounge. A young man sits in one of the front booths. His dark hair gleams with pomade; his cheeks are smooth. His eyes meet mine.

I sit down. He orders drinks. We do not talk.

My hand falls on his wrist, and remains there. The bartender, serving the drinks, scowls but says nothing. We sip our cocktails and put the drained glasses down.

"Let's go," the young man says.

I follow him out.

The Prodigal Daughter
Jessica Amanda Salmonson

Once an infant transient, then circus brat, then settled and raised in a "white trash neighborhood," Jessica Amanda Salmonson returned several years ago to the city of her birth, in search of Bohemian society, which fortunately she never did find. Instead, she found happiness sharing her life with the illustrator of many of her books, Wendy Wees, in Seattle's so-called "gay ghetto" of Capital Hill, a sort of would-be Greenwich Village. She is a devotee of Asian cinema, Latin American and surrealist authors, fairy tales, Genroku Era fiction and art, vegetarian cookery, coffeehouses, and the small press.

Salmonson's short stories have appeared in numerous anthologies and magazines, including *Dragons of Light*, *Hecate's Cauldron*, *Beyond Lands of Never*, *The Berkley Showcase*, *Fantasy Annual*, *Amazing*, *Weirdbook*, and literary magazines such as Canada's *Quarry* and *Room of One's Own*. Her poetry has graced the pages of innumerable small press magazines, the first collection of same being *The Black Crusader and Other Poems of Horror and Fantasy*, now out of print and rare.

An anthologist, Salmonson has edited two collections of

short stories about amazon adventurers for DAW Books, and what is perhaps the first collection of humanist heroic fantasy, *Heroic Visions*, for Ace. Her three-volume *Tomoe Gozen Saga* has been published by Ace and translated in Europe, and her novel *The Swordswoman* for Tor Books became a Science Fiction Book Club selection.

The heroine of "The Prodigal Daughter" was originally a composite of characteristics belonging to a friend of the author, and the author herself, but soon took on a life of her own, demanding upon occasion that further tales be told. More stories are indeed planned about Dame Unise McKensie of Morska-on-the-Tarn, given time and public interest.

Four centuries agone the Castle Green had been raised on its round stone morro overlooking Morsk Valley. It held its age well. In time of war it had proven an ideal vantage-point and fortress against siege and foe. If times were not yet wholly peaceful, quarrels at least were things to settle privately, not with the aid of mobilized forces. So the Castle Green's site, in the generation of Dame Unise of Morska-on-the-Tarn, was esteemed chiefly for its scenic quality.

Unise had not returned to the Castle Green in many years. Now she stood on an elevated stone terrace, admiring the panoramic vista spread out before her. She experienced a nostalgia of lost innocence and childhood. Had she never ridden from these comfortable confines in pursuit of adventure, she might still retain a degree of her lamented innocence — or ignorance. But never her childhood; no one is gifted the choice of retaining that. So she would sing no monodies for past decisions. Had she never left the land of her birth, she would still take it all for granted: the present sight would not seem so much a wonder, nor awaken these grand emotions — nor ease her secret fears. . . .

In all her travels surely she had seen valleys as quiet and verdantly beautiful as this; but the scent and sight and sounds, even the texture of this one stone wall and the feeling of this very terrace beneath her feet — it all came together in a fashion both remarkable and unique to her senses. She could put no name to it. She knew only that the little city of Morska far below was, to her, more charmingly dignified than the richest of great capitals the world over. The mirror-smooth lakes around it were purer and more serene than the most isolated waters in which she had bathed, far from peopled lands. The lazy river itself — winding twixt the hills like someone's lazy pet serpent — was as majestic as the vast mountain tributaries with their rushing falls. And the wilderness all around was no less magnificent than game-rich, fruit-laden jungles in the South.

She had wandered far to find this place.

Yet she should not have come. Her presence would attract danger. The thought reminded her of the desperation which drove her home.

"My Lady." The voice of a woman-child interrupted her reverie. A cousin: Miranna. She had been little more than a newborn when Unise left — they were strangers to one another, though reared beneath the same roofs.

"A message, Miranna?" The girl would never have spoken without that much permission — the rules and etiquette of a noble house had not much appealed to Unise at that age either. It would be nice even now to drop the barriers of propriety and embrace this beautiful child for no reason beyond her being kin.

"Grandpapa is informed of your arrival," she said formally. "He will see you in his chamber."

Miranna led the way (as if Unise did not know it already!) up small steps and through narrow, dark corridors lit intermittently by misty whiteness through thick, translucent, quartz windows. Unise felt Miranna's tension as her own; no one ascended to the patriarch's chamber without vacillation. Unise felt small as the child before her, again in awe of a gnarled codger who had seemed, not so long ago, the supreme vessel of wisdom and power.

"Was he angry to hear I have come?" Unise asked softly. Wide eyes peered back at her, betraying awe here too; what had people told her of this woman knight-errant? How overbearing must seem a child's world, impinged upon by cantankerous venerables and women clad in chainmail and breeches.

Miranna obviously did not know a proper way to answer the question. She said carefully, "He said bring you at once. He did not smile."

Of course. He would not.

They continued up the winding, stepped corridor at the child's pace — a pace made slow by reluctance. To change the unsettling mood, Unise asked, "You would do a weary knight a favor, Miranna?"

She did not look back again, but answered quietly, with reverence, "Anything, Lady."

"First, call me Unise. For my name is not Lady."

Miranna swallowed, replied, "I will try, Lady."

Unise chuckled. Then she said, "The favor is this: the stablemistress was absent when I left my horse. Could you find her and tell her that the Lady of the Castle Green has returned a knight?"

"Oh, yes, Lady! I like her!"

"'Unise,' Miranna. Try it."

"U-Unise."

"Is it easy?"

"It is easy," she said. "But not before company. I would be scolded."

"All right. Shh!"

They came to the familiar door.

Inside the patriarch's study, Miranna waited nervously for permission, or command, to go. Receiving it, she darted back into the dark hallway like a tadpole into murky water: pleased to be on her errand, and happier to return to the courtyard to play or study or await the midday meal than to stand under the hard glare of the man none called gentle.

Lord Arlburrow was a man of morbid tastes. His study was a musty, fearful place lit by a few thick candles and sometimes by sun or moonlight through a paneless window. It was presently shuttered from within. The walls were lined with rows of ancient leather and iron-bound books, arcane yellowed scrolls, and stacks of clay tablets of a tongue older than the Castle Green by far, older than civilization; and no one but Arlburrow had deciphered their secret knowledge.

What portions of the wall were not hidden by books were disguised instead with astrological charts and cryptic diagrams. In one corner, on a pedestal, stood a blue globe of the heavens; in the opposite corner sat a slender one-eyed deity, patron of star-gazers, its head cocked back.

The old man's furniture was squat, ordinary, sturdy, made of unpadded hardwood. Upon his desk were strewn various minor implements: quill, inkwell, compass, blotter, rule; and stretched across the length of it lay a grey lynx with tufted ears and no hint of a tail. From its lazy repose, the cat transfixed the woman with a cautious yellow gaze.

The lynx had been Unise's parting gift — a kitten then; it had grown tremendously. She had wondered at the time if he would keep it.

Her grandfather ceased stroking his pet, rose from a chair behind the desk, and approached Unise. He leaned heavily on a short oak staff; he had not carried one before, Unise remembered. His lips were a hard line barely distinguishable from other lines on his face. His eyes were unreadable, and grey as the cat's fur. Unise knelt before the patriarch and presented her sword.

"I am in your service, Lord Arlburrow."

Her eyes watched the floor, and she spied a cricket moving along at the base of the desk; the lynx dropped silently at the corner and waited patiently. Unise swallowed hard and felt herself beneath her grandfather's cold, silent scrutiny. She dared not rise without permission — a paw reached out and caught the cricket, teasing it, undamaged.

Unise knew her discomfort was no greater than her grandfather's. For all his aloofness and mystery, he was a kind man deep inside, the living cornerstone of an ancient clan. His was a terrible responsibility, and traditions more than wisdom helped him cope at hardest moments. Before him now bowed an insult to traditions he valued more than blood.

That emotionless visage began to harden into something more clearly definable. He knocked the sword from the woman's outstretched hands, marring his carved cane on the weapon's keen edge. The lynx hissed and backed beneath the star-globe, its hackles raised.

"Damn you, woman!" he cursed. "To kneel before me like a man! Stand, damn, I say! Stand and curtsy as all proper women must!"

It was said this man once shared laughter that shook rafters. If so, that deep and throaty merriment had passed into legend. Unise remembered him as an omniscient extension of the Castle Green, perhaps the personification of the Castle itself, made of the same hard stone and grey throughout. But in his private way, she knew, he had always loved her, as he had all the children his long life had witnessed come into the family; and he had never hurt her.

How cruel her presence must be to him now — he who had lost a frail and lovely wife with his own life not half done, and by the portraits in the mainroom Unise shared her features in a weathered fashion. Her grandfather had endured so many hardships through the years, borne so many burdens. His wife had left a rebellious, brazen, and somewhat selfish daughter, who in turn raised a daughter with twice the courage. That alone made Unise black sheep enough — daughter of a woman who laughed at authority. But worse, now, she was knighted, and was known to have fought in battle. When she had left, they had called her hussy; what could they call her now? Their clan had contended with whores by making them outcast, speaking of them never. But a woman lean and muscled, with reddish blond hair cut scandalously close and sword at hip — *who* was she now?

She stood from her kneeling posture, biting her tongue, her face flushed and angry. She had hurt him; he was old; anger often covered other feelings — his, and hers. His wounds were the more bitter to know she was as much like him as his own once-despised daughter. Unise understood that she was, after all, a symbol of his guilt, and he knew this, and he fought.

"My Lord and grandfather," she addressed, cordial between mutual hostility. "I am knighted Dame Unise of Morska-on-the-Tarn, by my king and yours, for whom I led a battle. Yet if you command me twice, I will curtsy for your favor — though in all my travels I have seen it done but once, and that before a Lord who was later proved a bastard and usurped by the knight who was true Lord."

Arlburrow glowered. By his own breach of etiquette he had earned return insult. And hers was the more grievous blow. Already Unise regretted her words. She was demanding respect by denying it to another — the while hiding behind figurative skirts. No man would dare challenge Lord Arlburrow in this manner, be he kin or Mountain Lord. She had seen the wizened patriarch bring Mountain Lords to their knees for smaller crimes. But it was not for fear of him, but for love of him, that Unise quaked.

Possibly because it was a private affair, a family dispute, the old man relented; and he would never give in if he truly believed himself right. He stepped backward, lowering himself into a broad, hard seat.

"I will not dishonor the knighted," he said. "But if you would serve me, it must be as granddaughter and not as soldier." He looked very tired.

Unise unbuckled her sheath and, placing the sword within it, set it out of sight. Then she bent to her grandfather's cheek and left a kiss.

"Did your stars tell you I would come?" she queried.

His eyes turned up to her suddenly. "They did not," he admitted sharply. She did not understand his tone.

"But they have told you something," she said wisely. "Of a coming danger. You must look at my chart, grandfather. That danger, and I, do come together. Something stalks me — something I chanced to release from a tomb sealed in a far, past millenium. I have not yet seen it, but I know when it is near; for it instills so great an instinctual dread that there is no mistaking it. I cannot begin to describe! I am haunted, grandfather. Already others have died for it."

The tailless cat leapt silently into Arlburrow's lap and beneath his fingers. The oldster seemed to be watching the flame of a candle which reflected in those cold, grey eyes.

"I have known, since before you were born, that the Castle Green would one day come to peril. I have outlived my time awaiting it. I did not know the nature of that foe, or the outcome of the battle. I had supposed a plague, an earthquake, a return to arms. Never did I suspect a granddaughter."

He meant no belittlement, but guilt was in her mind and she replied softly, "I will go. The danger will go with me."

"It will not!" He pulled himself out of the chair, spilling the rumbling cat. "You will not! I have prepared. I have been preparing for a long time. You came to me for help; you will have it."

"I came home," she corrected, "I think to die."

Returning to the livery, Unise saw that her steed had been unbridled and washed down. Boys scurried around, hard at their labors — but the woman called Jonathon was not to be seen. Unise was severely disappointed. If Miranna had gotten the message to her, the stablemistress ought to be waiting with open arms — unless, as Unise feared, even Jonathon would be unpleased to see her.

From the loft above, Jonathon leapt, startling the knight and scaring off insecurities. "Ho!" laughed Jonathon, "and Ho! What a strapping strong thing you are!" The livery woman had landed with feline grace, and stood with fists on hip, looking her old friend up and down. "Devils but you are good to see!"

Unise's heart raced at the sight of the physically powerful woman. Jonathon's hair was a good deal longer than Unise's, cropped straight along the shoulders and giving the impression of a horse's great shaggy mane. Unise said, "Embrace me, my droll friend."

They hugged. "Droll is it? Droll?"

"Aye." They held each other at arms' length and looked far into one another's soul. "If not you would have come with me. Look at you, Jonathon. You were a swashbuckler born, more than I. Why do you choose to clean stables?"

"*I* do not clean them!" she protested. "I am *master* here!" She reached over a stall and pulled a peeping stableboy up by the ear. "Scat!" she told him, and he scurried off to more useful industry. "Adventures are for the discontent, my darling. I am comfortable; no *man* could want for more. Nor offer it. I am good at what I do — as you are at what you do, I surmise from stories told 'round supper tables. And horses do make better friends than people. With rare exception."

"You were content in my absence?" The idea hurt Unise, who had never been content. Never. She stood by as Jonathon took up curry and began to brush a mare.

"I missed you every night, if you mean that," she said. "But I was no less content. To be without you was no more painful than to wait in my loft at the call of my mistress, like some king's poor catamite. You are of noble blood — I, a common worker. And that, my love, kept us further apart than shame." She grinned at that jest.

Unise was unamused. "My love for you is no burden, Jonathon. But my responsibilities were."

"My love for you, and yours for me, Unise, would have dishonored your clan. Well I know that."

The knight fell to one knee before the stablemistress, and took one hand to hold near her cheek. And she said, "Never dishonor, Jony. No greater honor was ever mine."

Jonathon pulled Unise to her feet, then turned away, to place the mare in her stall and set the brush aside. Her humor was only for the moment broken, and she said, "I have caused you hurt! Forgive? Now that I see you I say, 'Jonathon-girl! You erred in staying here!' Come, let me show you a sight familiar!"

Jonathon patted the mare's rump and leapt out of the stall, taking Unise by the hand and tugging her along. Unise followed, up a ladder, to a loft, to a small room at the far side. It was a retreat, Jonathon's retreat from a house of many kin — a house unlike a castle, where the numbers of residents could manage not to see each other at all. It had also been a retreat for Unise, for a while, and not so long ago as it seemed.

There, on a shelf, among many odds and ends, sat a blown-glass bear with its arms held out. It was so fragile a thing, Unise was surprised it had not been broken these past years. There were other remembrances about... The room looked still-used, and Unise felt a pang of jealousy. The mattress covering the big wooden box was thick with straw; she remembered being poked by the stuffing, laughing and rolling and touching and sharing the sounds of one another's sighs. The place was unchanged. The smell of it, the sight of it — it was like the feeling she had found upon the terrace looking over all the majesty of Morsk Valley... all that majesty compressed into a room no bigger than a stall: no bigger than the warmest, happiest corner of her best memories.

"Have you had other lovers?" Jonathon asked, with a gleeful curiosity.

"Many. Men as well. You?"

"Not many. Never so good. My duties suffice." Her eyes glistened. "I cannot abide men, I fear; and the hunting ladies who come here are not like you — prim, with their riding sticks and caps. They rarely notice me, except in snide fashion. Men make better friends, I will give them that. And regret it. I have few opportunities — but I carry no torch, Unise. Good will come."

Unise could scarcely comprehend a human being so devoid of bitterness. Jonathon was a jewel — a beautiful, unbreakable gem. She took Unise firmly by the arm, and drew her toward the bed.

"No, Jon-girl; not now!" They shared laughter. "By broad of day? With urchins underneath?"

"Ho! And is that new?"

Unise looked dour and spoiled the mood. "I do not feel it. My mind is preoccupied. I am afraid, Jonathon. Afraid to die."

"We all will die, beloved Unise. What is upon you that leaves your mind so drear?"

Their eyes matched for a long time of silence. Unise saw concern, love — what did Jonathon see? Not rejection, certainly not that. A fearful reluctance to be bound, perhaps — or unrelated preoccupations. The scent of straw and horses was all around, and the musk of two women. Unise said at last, "It is nothing. Comfort me, Jonathon. I need it."

They sat upon the straw mattress, Jonathon unbuckling the leather straps of the chainmail. Beneath this, a blouse, which Unise pulled over her head — the muscles of her back rippling soft and mighty. Unise put long fingers through Jonathon's shaggy mane.

Yellow sun struck the floor, the floor covered with yellower straw. The wind was cool through the uncovered windows above; it kept them from overheating in their passions. It took her back, this lovemaking; it gave her the illusion of safety and satisfaction. It made her wonder why she ever left this, only to bring danger upon herself and all she loved. Remembering this, she could not climax — but Jonathon would forgive her that.

After a long while of careful play, Jonathon arched her back as Unise moved her hand steadily, skillfully, between the kiss of the stable woman's mons. Jonathon crooned, almost rolled to one side, gripped Unise's ankle almost too hard and said, Ah, my love, Ah. Ah.

Time had passed quickly; clouds had closed over the sun,

and as they lay together in each other's arms, their bodies cooled, and they hugged closer, after a while speaking:

"When I first saw you," Unise said, "I knew this would happen."

"We were children. You knew nothing of nothing."

"Well, I suspected. Your pa the stablemaster then, and you his best hand."

Jonathon smiled, remembering her father in the best way. He was a flawed man, but the years since his death had smoothed the corners of him in Jonathon's mind. She and Unise had shared death then — for Unise's mother died the same month of the same contagion. "When I was born," Jonathon said, "he was almost disappointed. He had wanted a son — and I did not disappoint him after all. My, but I was a rough-and-tumble. Pa had three more sons, and more daughters, but I was eldest, and his pride. Mother looks at me sometimes now, and I suspect she sees him. She is proud of me. I had more support for my strength than you."

They clung in the growing chill, and Unise remembered running naked through meadows and flinging themselves in brooks or clear lakes. They were children — swiftly knowledgeable children. They had pleased each other well. If anyone noticed, they may have thought it was something that would pass. They were never forced apart.

"You told me," Unise said, "or you boasted — that you were your pa's oldest son and strongest fighter."

"And you told me, 'You're a woman-child like me — and someday I'll make you glad of that.' I had no idea what you meant."

"See. I *did* know!"

"Ho! You did not know what you meant yourself! But I remembered the promise, and it was not long — it was not long. I lay at your side, still babes were we, and I said, 'I am glad. I am glad.' For you were right. No longer my father's son — I was your woman then. And there was sorrow in that. I wished to be neither boy, nor another's woman; not even yours. I wished to be my *own* woman, and that, dearest Unise, is why I did not go with you. I was your slave! I was glad to be free, for all the pain of it."

Unise pushed away, took up her blouse from the floor. "And now I have come back."

Jonathon touched her carefully, and they were unmoving for the moment. "You are too sensitive. I would not tell you that, if it were still true. I am stronger now. That, or I know my limitation. You were no less slave to the Castle. You were no more free than I. Did you cry on leaving?"

"No."

"There, then. It did not lessen our love."

"It will be different now," Unise said, but then stopped herself from promises. She might not live to ease old burdens, and the clouds gathering outside reminded her of that. They had appeared too swiftly, each curling nimbus. They were not entirely natural.

She recognized the signs. Now was the time to run. Flee! Upon her horse, to the next town or country. But this time she would face it, whatever it was that followed her.

"Unise!" Jonathon shook her. "What is that look on you?"

Unise whispered. "Terror, Jonathon. Terror."

Fire roared in the hearth of the big mainroom. Servants busied themselves at the Castle's multitude of shutters, and stoked fire into the myriad smaller hearths in various rooms, arming against the ensuing storm. The evening repast was done; the day had been more hectic than average. Children wrastled, shouting beneath the scrutiny of old, old portraits, tumbling about the center of the vast tiled floor. The mainroom was the evening gathering place, the warmest place on a day that grows unexpectedly cold. Aunts and nannies and cousins and middle-sons and daughters and what few guests currently resided at the Castle Green broke into factions and groups, dividing themselves among the sets of ornate furniture scattered against the high, tapestried walls. Idle talk commenced, and whisperings — largely about the tall woman in their midst, rightful Lady of the Castle, a stranger in her own home.

She stood before the fire, the hearth's maw gaping higher than her head. With hands locked behind her back, she peered into the reds and oranges and blues which danced and coruscated over the burning logs. She was clad now, after bath, in a blouse with fluffed sleeves, lace at wrists, a tightly buttoned velvet vestcoat over this. Her figure, her womanhood, was less in doubt thus clad — but even without sword and mail, she remained an anomaly in the mainroom, the only woman with breeches tucked in leather boots.

. Older men were still absent from the gathering. Some might be gone on long missions, a few to the King's navy, some to employment or businesses in nearby Morska, or to the dens of a further City that catered to those rich who gambled and drank, an equal number merely at their various duties outside the Castle itself — not to be driven indoors until the broiling weather could no longer be ignored.

Among the other fracasing children, Miranna played. She had made a sword, binding twig to limb to form hilt and blade, tacking a blouse-button to the hilt as pommel. It was poor match, the boys thought, for their own wooden swords, exquisitely carved by toymakers for the express purpose. Miranna challenged them both, then stood in a swordstance so threatening that the two boys agreed among themselves to teach her a lesson. But she was good. Her limber branch went swishing among them like a foil. They and their stiff, overlight balsas were no match for the agility of the mock weapon or its maker. The two boys were hard pressed in the game.

Unise turned from the fire and her own unspirited musings to watch the lithe youngster; it was pleasing to see. Knight strode to children, and coached the girl.

"Yes, parry my darling — that's it: thrust. Ha. Watch! They are wiser now; they're splitting up. Do not let one behind you. Again! Again! Guard the left! Thrust! Aha: Good!"

Both boys sweated under Miranna's zealous assault. When she broke the guard of the tallest — pressing her harmless creation to his chest so that the leaf at its end bent — the boy began to cry. He cried for the sake of lost face, which grown men call honor. Defeated by a girl! The other boy refused to continue, not wishing to risk the same fate; he defended his companion saying it was unfair sport. "You cheated," he said to Miranna. "You were aided!" Then he glowered at the knight as though his small manliness more than weighted his favor against her height.

The other boy continued to wail, deeming a show of genuine injury less effacing than honestly admitted defeat. Aunts and elder sisters gathered around, coddling the boy, comforting him with reinforcements until he ceased to whimper. At the same time, they railed against Miranna: you've hurt him, you naughty thing; what sort of game is this for a girl; come now, apologize to Edor; that's a good girl — now, throw that nasty stick into the fire!

The scolding levied against her strength, the forgiveness that came with cowering — Unise watched Miranna caught up in the mesmeric insistencies of wives and spinsters, until even the knight felt the dizzying effect: dance for them right, dance for them left. She remembered her own girlhood, which within these many walls had upon occasion seemed hideous after her mother's death. She remembered the powerlessness she felt in frills and petticoats while boys leapt in tights. Miranna would not cry, but Unise almost cried for her. The squealing jabber of these... these *hens* roiled in her system until she could not hold back the shout, "No! She will *not* throw her sword into the fire!"

The room was suddenly and remarkably quiet, with only the crackle of the fire and the thump of a half-burnt log to break the still. Miranna's eyes looked out from the hems of giants, as if to say, Unise, Lady, No: It will do no good.

A puffy old woman who was Unise's great-aunt and her nemesis since childhood came forward with strides as long as the knight's; and Unise wondered for a moment: what kind of human being *might* you have been? The old woman said sharply, as though Unise were still a girl to be scolded and sent off to her room: "And what kind of example do you think you are for little girls? This is your doing, with your swagger and your pants!" She turned from Unise in a swirl of long cloth, and said, "Come, Miranna. Show the Lady of the Castle Green" — did she recite the title vindictively? — "that you are not a horrible little girl."

Miranna allowed herself to be led by the puffy woman to the hearth. The child stood as before the gate of hell, and threw her makeshift toy within.

So many eyes were upon Unise, with too many accusations. Children were scudded away, lest they share Miranna's admiration. The knight stormed within herself, frustrated deep inside with an intensity that drove her thoughts to madness: she envisioned herself with sword to hand, hacking down old foes — old ladies and their smug daughters — until the mainroom was astrew with piles of fancy clothes bloodied by the folded corpses within. And after that, by God, she would await the husbands and old uncles and slay *them* one by twos by threes as they came home; for they, somehow, were the true cause of all this, though Unise could not fathom how, in their eager absence!

All this madness passed like a cloud, leaving in its wake a dampness and depression. There was a certain hopelessness in her now, but perhaps it was the doing of the restless dark outside the Castle Green — the storm rising fast, and no one but Unise and the codger in the tower aware that it was of supernatural source.

Her great-aunt approached anew, and said with a haughty fine grace which hypocritically belied hostility: "The servants have battened the Castle, and been otherwise preoccupied so that your room has not been readied. I shall see to it personally then." She started off toward a stair that led to master quarters, a room of which had once been Unise's.

Unise stopped her, saying, "Please. Do not trouble yourself. I have a place in the livery." Jonathon would applaud this statement, for the honesty of it if not the discourtesy. The face of the clucking hen before her grew puffier in wrath, revealing in this manner her knowing and disgust. But the old nemesis minded her tongue lest *others* understand so fully.

The great-aunt had little power and no authority beyond her reign over house-servants and kin. She might wish it, but she could not make it go hard for Jonathon once Unise were gone, or dead. Unise did not mean to flout; but neither could she find cause to respect the sensibilities of those who made no concern of *her* feelings. She took a mild delight in her great-aunt's deduction and disapproval.

None else understood the full meaning of Unise's stated intent; still, all remained silent, and they were yet appalled.

They had other reasons: little as they understood her, much as they feared her, she was nonetheless Lady of the Castle Green. To sleep with horses! It was unthinkable — as unthinkable as the Lady's knighthood; as unthinkable as, as, well: what if Lord Arlburrow slept in stables? It would be the same thing. No one liked him either; but they knew his place, and they knew theirs.

Unise turned from hen to gaping others, with a flourish of her arm. She addressed them:

"If I am not fit company for these children, then I am not fit beneath these roofs! No matter that I am Arlburrow's heir — so long as he or I live, *your* stations are secure. You need not fear my vengeance, whether or not I ever rule this estate. But consider: you are too small before my eyes to merit my dying anger and my welling sorrow. I pity you more greatly than you do me, and for better cause. You would beat the heart out of your bravest girls and shame them for being bold. You would tear the spirit of the mightiest, to make all women like yourselves. But fear you this: some of us survive!"

By their eyes she saw that it had all passed by their heads. They could not count her hero, or wise — for some of them had known her as a helpless babe, then mischief-maker demanding a constance of scolds. It is said, a hero will always be unheralded in her home. Nonetheless, for all their lacked respect or understanding, they held her in awe. Any eloquence she might spare for them could not help but be lost on the small minds of nobility. Whatever she said, they would discount it as proof and parcel of her awesome, perverse, and begrudgingly admirable nature. With sinking despair, Unise left them, taking the narrow stair to the Lord's loft. Miranna ran to the foot of that passage and called up the gloomy well in proud rebellion: "I love you Unise."

Behind, pointless chatter had resumed.

Big as it was, Arlburrow's cat stepped with dainty purpose, along the narrow ledge of a bookshelf, halting stone-still whenever the shelf creaked beneath the weight. Not a book or a an artifact was upset by the stalking animal. At length it was positioned above Unise's head, for she sat in the hard chair in front of Arlburrow's desk — and the lynx counted that seat its own.

Arlburrow peered through a glass at the tiny script of an old, clay tablet he had placed upon the scatter of star-charts and measures. He had queried Unise until her head was sore; and he had quested the day long through his mystic library. From what she was able to remember about the tomb — location, design within and without, precise nature of the contents, glyphs on the sarcophagus — Arlburrow had been able to date its mil- lenium, and, eventually, find the occupant's name. He had not yet said the name aloud; no doubt he would tell her in his own time, though Unise did not truly care to know whose ghost she had released. She had no need of a name for it, but, rather, its poultice. Whoever it had been, man or woman, it was an evil thing — and mighty, to have survived imprisoned aeons. She regretted her soul to hell that it was her hand which broke the ancient seals of sorcery against the fiend. Let Arlburrow keep its name — forever if he wished, for the sake of his beloved secrecies. Only, tell her of its bane.

Storm battered at Arlburrow's window, behind him and his desk, as though aware that within sat potential foe.

Unise felt old as Arlburrow, heavy and shrunken in her seat; and like Arlburrow, she found, oddly, a degree of comfort among the tomes and arcana of a library others perceived as foreboding. The dimness of light nurtured her mood. The smell of antiquity — leather, clay, papyrus, char — eased her own sense of fleeting mortality and pending doom.

The lynx hissed and set its ears far back, tensed to leap upon the head of the usurper of its seat. It was a wild beast after all, for all its gentleness with Arlburrow — and a territorial beast. Unise said with impatience and not much voice, "You cannot frighten me, Mite. You are big. But I have wrastled cats twice your size and bigger."

The lynx leapt — into the lap of the uncowed woman. She patted the animal, static tickling her fingers as lightning cracked outside.

"It follows you," Arlburrow said, looking up from studious

concentration, "because it is bound to your service. You freed it: it is yours."

Unise considered the point. "If this is so," she said, "I could command it back to its grave."

As she feared, the answer was too simple to be useful. Arlburrow said, "It is your servant as much out of gratitude as by the magic of its long-dust captors. That gratitude should not last beyond such a command. In one manner, it is fortunate the monster tracks you, granddaughter; for there was reason and intent behind each aspect of the sorceries which bound it before, and bind it yet. I shudder to consider what havoc it would bring upon the land were it free to go its way. It cannot be free until it has served its liberator — and its only service is murder."

The lynx rumbled in her lap, and kneaded her with its large, furry feet, never quite breaking flesh with its retracting, razored claws. Arlburrow had broken it of that.

What Arlburrow had told her did not relieve Unise's intense dread. Indeed, if everything he said were irrevocably true, the very act of freeing herself from the devil would endanger all of humanity the more.

"What am I to do," she said, and again, "What am I to do?" It seemed she spoke only to herself, or to the lynx who raised its tailless rear to her.

"By the stars I have calculated, the beast will not fully enclose the Castle Green until midday tomorrow — though by then, midday will be as dark as night, in the shadow of the thing! It will crush the mortar from these walls to get to you, its master, unless we prepare through the night. I have already sent riders to gather in all who reside around the Castle Green. They will wonder at that, for it has been many years since siege — but by the time all realize the true danger, I will have seen to the Castle's defense. Fetch me that case!"

He pointed to what might have been a shipping crate for a company of swords — that, or a child's coffin. It was plane, and pegged shut. Unise unsettled the cat, and took up the container. It was heavier than she had thought it would be. With barely a sound and leaving nary a scratch, she set it upon the desk. Arlburrow watched her with an odd compassion, and might have been disguising a reluctant pride over the ease with which she hefted the heavy box. He worked at the pegs; she helped. Within, five elongate objects were wrapped in oiled cloth. Arlburrow slowly unwrapped all but one: four thick rods of argent material, like silver, shone in the chamber's candle-light.

Behind Arlburrow, the window shutters rattled with a kind of desperation, as though an imp clung to the tower wall and strove for entry. Then the wind screamed. . . what? an obscen-ity? Trick of the mind and ear. . . Unise, like Arlburrow, pretended not to hear.

"What can these do?" she asked.

"Protect the Castle, I believe. You will take one to each of the high, corner watchtowers. Set them carefully facing respec-tively: north, east, south, west." He pointed to specific ones. "Do not confuse them! Like magnets, set wrong end together, they will fight one another rather than unite to form a covering matrix over all the Castle Green. No one and nothing, save the supernatural being that fills the nighted sky, will see or feel that barrier. The monster's wrath will no doubt increase — and it will be only penned out, not defeated. For victory against it, I fear you will have to prove yourself a knight to me after all." It was a hard thing for him to say. "The old magicks still upon it have provided many safeguards. If I understand the spells defined in the ancient scripts, the monster can be reduced to a semblance of its living form, and may then be defeated. But not at leisure. I confess I think it beyond you, granddaughter; but there is no other tested warrior in this county, and in any event, only its master can call it down to size. How good a fighter are you, Dame Unise?"

It was the first time he had used her title. The acknowledg-ment made her shoulders square, her back straighten, and she said, "How good need I be?"

"Better, I fear, than any warrior known to those antique sorcery-makers, or they would have this demon slain rather than imprisoned. Yet it must be tried. It will face, in mortal combat, none but the woman who unleashed it, the one to whom it is bound. For no other would it make itself vulnerable."

Without further statement, Unise took up the four rods, not querying about the fifth, and went after her task. The lynx, Mite, followed her, running up and down staircases and spatting at any servant they chanced to pass. The cat was a terror to all.

Unise's task was not swiftly completed. The Castle was huge, and it felt as though she had gone up and down every staircase within those vast confines. There were shorter routes, but mostly leading through the central mainroom. The women might be off to their varied chambers at this hour, but the men of the Castle would be in now, telling stories and imbiding small sports. And soon, the cotters and families and even the squatters on the estate would be gathering below — including Jonathon's clan — and the half-sleeping Castle would buzz with life and curiosity. Unise did not feel up to confrontations with all those puzzled folk, who soon enough would learn the danger.

She took the longer ways, the first of which brought her out into the storm. With her weighty bundle, she walked alongside the battlements of the Castle's wall, and felt the gloom pressing down from above. There was an almost beckoning sweetness to the icy terror that flooded through her veins. Sanguine promises of greatness and power impinged upon her brain: *we can rule the world as one* . . . . She ignored the seductions of the dark and came to the first of four high towers.

The crenelated lookout was rarely visited in these times of comparative peace. She ascended the spiral stair. In the circular room above, she leaned over a sill to mount the first argent rod in a setting intended for the Banner of the Castle Green, facing its proper end North. As she did this, Mite licked at wetted fur and paws. Sudden pellets of hail struck the back of her neck — vindictive stingings which she ignored until the job was done. The verse of a warrior bard passed through her thoughts unbidden:

Death by hammer, death by spear
these things would I face
One thing only do I fear
mere courage can't erase.
And that? The specter at my back
That unseen, unknown wraith's attack.

Death by tulwar, death by lance
no dirk frightens me
Only ghostly circumstance
incites my plaintive plea.
Nameless fear creeps up my spine—
That beating heart! Is it mine?

Death in battle, by the axe
near to Death I fell
But the Scythe again grew lax
and Fortune bore me well.
But what would mortal weapons do
to stay a foe the wind blows through?

Descending to an interior floor, she proceeded to the next tower, and the next, and lastly the westernmost keep. When the final rod was in position, the gloom did seem pressed back, though for the moment Unise detected no other difference.

When she turned from the uncovered window through which she had attended the banner-mount, she saw Mite with back arched and fur standing — the cat saw something human eyes could not, and was terrorized beyond recount. A moment later, lightning webbed the whole of heaven, branching from horizon to horizon as though the dome of the universe were cracking into flaming bits. Almost immediately there followed a clangor so incredible in pitch that it nearly knocked Unise to the flagstone floor.

Mite vanished down the stairwell, and would be beneath the starry globe of Arlburrow's lair long before Unise's feet had carried her there.

The terrible rage of the storm would alert all the Castle now. None would mistake that hateful roar for a natural torrent. As Unise strode quietly through halls, she heard whisperings of fear and wakening comprehension, filtering from the various private and family cells. She heard also the complaints regarding the number of rabble invited into the lower floors. Some of Unise's kin would rather huddle with small, frightened groups in dark quarters than contend the presence of serfs in larger, supportive gatherings. Hearing their talk, she regretted less that she brought them all to danger.

Servants were all about the place, lighting candles in the corridors and chandeliers in the rooms. Their faces were ashen and troubled; Arlburrow must have told them much earlier in the day to be prepared for an arduous night.

But as Arlburrow promised, they would be safe. The preternatural deluge could only fall as rain upon the Castle Green; the thing that haunted the firmament was, itself, held at bay.

By her grandfather's earlier command, Unise went briefly to the room which had not been readied for her. There, she took up her chainmail, sword and leather armor from the closet in which she had stored them against Arlburrow's sight.

She regretted that she could not attend Jonathon, who would be downstairs with the rest by now. At least her dear stablemistress would not be waiting in her loft for someone who unexpectedly did not come, reminding her of those other times of similarly unfilled expectations.

Glum of spirit, Unise took her armor to Arlburrow's chamber, where on the morrow he would, remarkably, serve as her squire. There, she piled the armor and weaponry in a corner, and fell back into the chair near Arlburrow, who seemed not to have moved in her absence. His attention did not raise from the compassing of his charts. Mite, dignity regained, lay on a small, worn carpet of intricate design, a few feet from the globe.

Unise, hair and breeches still damp, felt the ache of a long battle, though the battle was yet to begin. Weariness enfolded her limbs, her neck, her body. She longed for Jonathon's strong hands to loosen the muscles along her spine. Heavily, her head fell back, her eyes closed. Slumped uncomfortably, she slept out that horrible night.

Horses screaming in the distance awoke the knight.

She was instantly on her feet, looking left and right to regain her bearings. Kneading the crick in her neck with her palm, she strode from the chair that had served as unlikely bed to Arlburrow's single window. She unlatched it, pulled it open. The storm was gone. It ought to be well into day, but only crimson night greeted her. The horror which haunted the sky filtered the morning's sun, blocking all but a faint red from the spectrum, giving the world not the look of morning, but of bloody dark. By the grim light, she could tell the heavy clouds still hung above the castle in a gigantic sworl — yet they seemed to have played themselves dry during the long, torrential night. She could also see the whole of the countryside, showing like a faded painting in carmine and grays.

Unise's face warmed with momentary embarrassed surprise: she had never realized her grandfather had so perfect a view of the livery. She reminded herself it no longer mattered who suspected or knew about her and Jonathon. Let it be an open secret, at least! Still, it was disconcerting to think Arlburrow might have known for as long as she knew herself.

Below, Jonathon moved with swift grace, cracking a long bow whip. She never allowed it to actually lick a horse's flesh; it was used merely to herd them by its noise, back toward the stables. Something was astir, and the horses knew it. Perhaps only the red dark frightened them, as would fire, urging them to break from their enclosures. Or they may have sensed things people could not, as Mite had done. In either case, nothing could confine a horse confirmed to escape.

Donning chainmail, Unise intended to hurry to Jonathon's aid. No one person, not even Jonathon, could handle all those horses at once. But the chamber door opened, and Arlburrow entered. He was returning from some errand. His boots and the point of his walking stick were muddy. Unise wondered if he ever slept. She had wondered that when she was little, too; for even then he seemed to retire long after everyone else, and rise before.

"Not yet," he said simply.

"Jonathon is outside the protection of the Castle," she protested.

"She is in no danger. Trust me that."

"Even so. She needs help gathering the frightened horses."

"Better that she struggle with them alone," Arlburrow said, no hint of antipathy in his tone. "You have a more important task." He bent to pick up a leather breastplate. "This piece first?" he asked.

She directed him in binding her armor, piece by piece, to her tall, powerful body.

"If it kills you," Arlburrow said, "it will be free of its geas. It will still be unable to penetrate the Castle's shield, but certainly it will lower itself into the valley and level Morska-on-the-Tarn. From then, it will be a free agent, to torment all the world."

Unise's armor seemed heavier than ever before. "A terrible burden," she whispered, and he looked up into her face sharply to say, "The greatest you will ever bear, granddaughter."

He turned to his desk, where the case still sat with one rod left in its oilcloth. Arlburrow unwrapped the object... it was no mere rod after all. It was a sword made of the same argent material. She took it from him by the hilt, asking nothing of its strength.

She descended to the mainroom with Arlburrow at her side. The folk gathered there looked up from the beds made on floors and couches; children peered from their curled positions in large chairs. They were a weary, frightened lot. Servants had already begun to divide morning-cakes among them, and those awake enough ate without tasting. The few whisperings left after the long night died quickly when Arlburrow and the knight appeared. There were a hundred questions in each mind, but the sight of this formidable pair silenced them all. Arlburrow, who was rarely seen by folk outside the Castle itself, and Unise McKensie, his heir, the most notorious and unlikely soldier ever to hail from Morsk Valley... they watched these two pass through their midst, and Unise felt their stares.

At the farther entrance, Arlburrow turned and said, "It will be safe to watch from the battlements. Go!"

They did not move for a moment.

"Go!" he barked, shooing them with a gesture from his cane.

Parents snatched up babes, and they scurried with undisguised curiosity and bared excitement up the stairways toward the upper walls of the Castle Green. When the mainroom was empty, Arlburrow said, "You go on from here alone. It will meet you in Danden's Field" — the meadow was named after a ferocious battle eight generations before — "when you call it down from heaven."

"Its name, grandfather." The servants had opened the gates; her eyes looked out into gloom.

"Hophaetus."

The woman breathed deeply. Tears welled but did not fall.

"God of Iron," she said, softly, to herself.

"He was that, yes, to pagans. To us, granddaughter, he is only the ghost of a man turned devil."

She stood now at the gate and turned to face her grandfather, left behind. Red sky outlined her. She said, "Why not call him god, my Lord Arlburrow? If he slays me — and you think he will — his angry spirit will haunt the lands with a more horrendous appetite that any mortal tyrant."

"I did not say I thought he would slay you, granddaughter. He may. But the stars bode your favor, though one great tragedy is outlined by the charts. I do not know what; only, no battle is won at no cost. Remember this: Hophaetus favored his left leg in life—"

"Hurt, it is said, in his fall from paradise..."

"Or twisted in a common fashion!" he responded hotly. "His supernatural spirit was born of earth, Unise. It will die of earth, at long, long last. He may even be grateful for that. Remember the leg, that is all. He was mighty in the bronze age, when he alone wielded iron. But your sword is stronger than the bronze knives he faced before."

"He may not take the form of a man," Unise said lowly. She was afraid. Afraid. "You said a semblance. Only a semblance of his former self..."

"It is time, granddaughter."

A man stood outside with Unise's horse, bridled and shielded with its own leather garb. When Unise saw that her grandfather had seen to this, she realized also how the horses had escaped: he knew Jonathon would never watch safely from the battlements. She had to be gotten out of the way, for her own sake as well as Unise's. Unise turned back once more, and raised a gauntleted hand to him.

"Farewell, grandfather."

"Fare thee well, Dame Unise of the Castle Green."

She rode to Danden's Field.

The grass was high about her mount's legs. Unise reined the beast up short. Looking skyward, she saw the eye of the

of blue amidst the slowly sworling
ugh the opening in the sky, and lit
v magnificent the scene must look
lements!

ler horse reeled around and around at
cried, "Hophaetus! Come to me
the dance of death! We will embrace
is broken!"

rowed with malevolence. The sworls
ed, turning like a celestial whirlpool
eaven. Unise laughed, hysterical or
began to funnel down, down, until it
nt of knight and steed. The circle of
er stood a transparent column of red
The funnel circled her like a weird,
its object before smashing her.

haetus! Let me see your myth-praised

of the sky above, shrank downward
into a ball of thick, soupy mist. It
robbed with light. It grew more and
loosely the form of a man. For a
verse its progress, to lose substance
eamed its name, over and over,
materialize, until... almost in anger,
nd a blast of hot, lake-hued light:
er.

ted. She had that advantage.
she had expected him to be ugly. He
en a man with a more beautiful face.
His perfection was marred only by the redness of his skin, hair, armor, sword. He was a demon out of hell, she could not doubt that, made of fire or molten iron. But he was lovely to behold.

And there was no malice on his face. Rather, she saw in him a kind of compassion, agony, sorrow. She knew these things were feigned.

She spurred her steed to charge. The demon raised his shield against the argent sword Unise bore. The horse carried her past him; she reined about to see what affect she had had.

He had not even staggered under the blow.

His shield began to spin in his outstretched hand. It became a ball of fire and he unleashed it. The horse reared and took the fire ball full in the chest, then dropped in a heap, killed. Unise had rolled away and came to her feet prepared — prepared to die. It was clear that she could not hope to defeat this being.

There was distance between them for the moment. Hophaetus approached her slowly, the grasses shriveling into ash with every step he made. He opened his mouth. A tongue licked out like flame. Now his eyes burned her with hatred, all pain and sorrow gone. Unise raised her sword, though it now seemed a feeble gesture. He raised his sword in kind — and between these swords danced lightning.

Unise felt electricity course through her body. She felt herself glowing with some terrible power. She saw her arms, her hands, her entire body, her sword, turning a brilliant, glimmering blue. She thought: *I am a demon too.* As he was red throughout, so had she become as purely blue as sapphire. She no longer waited for Hophaetus to close the distance: she leapt for him, her lips peeled back in a gargoyle's grimace, showing him her cobalt teeth.

The battle was engaged. Unise felt herself a supernatural force. Whether the power was invested in her by her foe, to even the match, or wrought by the magic of a charmed sword... she never knew, did not care. She lived only for the fight. Broadsword struck broadsword, and the sound was not like the clash of steel. It was like the roaring of a forest fire covering half the wooded earth; or glacier ice rushing from the poles with tremulous power.

Weariness did not invade her limbs. She beat Hophaetus back. Then he beat her back. Back and forth this went until it was clear that they were evenly matched. Eternity might have passed. Unise was free of all terror, except for a moment when she envisioned herself locked in ceaseless combat on Danden's Field, to the end of time, neither warrior able to defeat the other. At least then the world she had endangered would be safe. And her aunty could charge tokens for townfolk to watch from the battlements of Castle Green.

So enrapt had she become in her battle, Unise did not see the mounted woman charge across the dell. Jonathon's whip lashed out, caught Hophaetus about the neck. The whip instantly burst into flame, and Jonathon's horse stumbled, in terror of the flame or in a pot hole, it hardly mattered. Unise remembered Arlburrow's prognostication: the battle would not be won at no cost. Was Jonathon to die?

Unise could not help the dazed woman to rise: she knew that to touch Jonathon would freeze her to the spot, just as the touch of Hophaetus would burn her to charcoal. Jonathon, raging and foolish with courage, staggered to her feet, scrambled blindly toward the fray. Unise could not speak; like Hophaetus, she no longer had a voice. She could not warn Jonathon off.

Over the dell, as from a dream, an old man came slowly, cane in hand, cat lumbering beside. He was shouting: "Get back, Jon-girl! Can you not see you are making it worse?"

The battle went unabated. But Unise had lost much ground fretting for Jonathon and now Arlburrow. Hophaetus pressed the attack. Unise stumbled backward, fell, and Hophaetus' most powerful blow knocked sword from hand. The demon stood with all his malice revealed, but he did not deliver the killing blow. He turned instead on Jonathon, knowing in his devil's manner that this would be a more painful death to Unise. And Unise remembered those sweet, dark promises Hophaetus had made to her before they had even met, haunting her dreams from the very night she chanced to free him from a tomb. She knew, now, that jealousy turned Hophaetus' wrath upon the other woman.

Mite had leapt between Jonathon and Hophaetus. The cat's hackles raised from neck to haunches, back arched high: he spat and snarled at the evil killer. Hophaetus slowed for one moment only, perhaps pondering the import of other cats he had seen — an old warlock's familiar.

Arlburrow was at the devil's back. Unise saw that the old man did not have his cane with him after all. He had removed one of the argent rods from the tower keep, no doubt weakening the defenses of the Castle itself in favor of one last and chancy gambit. It would be like Arlburrow, Unise reasoned, to sacrifice himself, to make sure he, and not Jonathon, was the price read in the stars. It was not purely heroic kindness: it was manipulative in its way. He was old. He would die soon anyway. Unise might pine unto death without Jonathon; and then the Castle Green would have no capable overseer. With Arlburrow's death, Unise knew she would be bound to the Castle, all adventure past.

The oldster raised the argent rod and, before the demon could strike either Jonathon or Mite, Arlburrow had stricken the demon's spine. A flash of white light sent Arlburrow reeling backward, to fall, unmoving. Mite meowed monstrously, and even Unise freed her voice from some icy prison to wail a terrible lament. The cry carried its horrid message of agony and loss throughout the boundaries of Morsk Valley, and beyond — unto paradise itself.

A black stripe had appeared along the spine of the otherwise uniformly scarlet being. Before Unise' own cry had faded from the valley and hills, she had reclaimed her sword, lunged toward the demon, swung the weapon not overhand, but under. She raked upward along the inside of Hophaetus' left leg. He fell to one knee, hurt, and looked up with his nefarious nature again disguised. His eyes begged mercy. But she did not hesitate. Her own sorrow had become an addition to her strength. It tipped the balance. She thrust the icy blade into the fiery heart of Hophaetus. She left the weapon there and lurched back.

Hophaetus made no sound even then. He did not move. He did not fall from foot and knee. He began to cool, his redness fading into black. He had become an iron statue of fey, masculine beauty, bent to one knee, looking up pitiably. The blue sword had returned to argent white, protruding from the devil's bloodless heart.

Red sky faded too. Sunlight flooded the site with a cheeriness that mocked. There should be rain. Tears should fall in mourning. Unise stood tall, her flesh and garb still blue, and she wondered: Am I forever like this? Mite pawed at

Arlburrow's body until — god witness — the old man moved! Unise felt drained of all power. She tried to shout again, for Jonathon to keep away: Don't touch me, I will kill you. But she could not speak, and as Jonathon reached for her, Unise fell into darkness.

Arlburrow was blind. It seemed a terrible price indeed, as the stars forewarned, for the codger's life revolved around his library. Yet he seemed to think it small enough price. He tapped the floor with his cane as he neared Unise's sick bed. She gazed out of her weariness, saw his eyes, burnt black by the light that streaked Hophaetus' spine. "I had read all those old books anyway," he said, reaching out a hand that Unise took, to draw him near her bed. "The only things left are some old clay tablets even I had not yet been able to decipher. I can feel that writing with my fingers!"

His spirits were high enough for both of them. She had heard him laugh, as folk said he had done when he was a young man. Unise, then, could repose in continued despair, leaving her portion of gladness to Arlburrow. The horror he had lived these years to defeat was gone — and whatever days were left him, he could live them at leisure, though in darkness. Unise's future was equally certain: the day would yet come when she would be bound to Castle Green. Arlburrow had survived the battle well, giving her respite from responsibility. But how much longer could he live? Perhaps he never slept — but eventually, the longer sleep would catch him.

These were selfish thoughts Unise had, to begrudge an old man a peaceful death. She did not want to master a castle. She was not sure *what* she wanted. At present, she felt she had had her fill of adventure.

Miranna brought tea to Unise's room. The girl seemed distraught less by what had transpired on Danden's Field than by the fact that Unise lay now in bed like a sick old nanny. Most of the women Miranna had known had fallen ill at one time or another, without visible cause; she had thought Unise above this.

There was a disturbance in the hall. Arlburrow stepped aside, cocked an ear. Unise's great-aunt's voice was complaining of horse smells and rabble. She sounded shrill and angry. Jonathon's unperturbable nature was for once perturbed: "Put it up your arse, biddy!" She burst into Unise's room, the puffy woman storming behind, insisting stable workers did not belong in the master quarter of the Castle, or in any other part. Seeing Arlburrow silenced the old aunt, but Jonathon swept by the blind man and the child without explanation or apology. She tore the covers off Unise's bed, and demanded. "Up with you, lazy wench. Beds never cured melancholy! You need sun!" She forced Unise up, helped her to dress, slapped her behind. She even drank Unise's tea. The great-aunt stewed in her place, but Arlburrow laughed encouragement. Miranna went with the women into the gardens while, at Arlburrow's request, one puffier and puffier aunt saw that the Castle coffers were deeply plumbed so that a royal feast might be prepared for all the silly rabble who had spent the night in Castle Green.

But one serious matter remained. Before nightfall, Arlburrow told Unise to be certain the iron god was carted to the long unused, deepest dungeons of Castle Green. There, Hophaetus was locked away, a hauntingly lifelike statue of fey and sorrowful beauty, to await some other hapless hero who might draw the argent sword from his chest.

Broken Tool
Theodore L. Thomas

Theodore L. Thomas is a graduate of the Massachusetts Institute of Technology and a former practicing chemical engineer. He later attended and graduated from Georgetown University Law School and was admitted to the Bar of the District of Columbia and the State of Connecticut. He has been a practicing patent lawyer for the past twenty-eight years.

Starting in 1949 and continuing for thirty years, Thomas wrote a newspaper column entitled, "Science for Everybody," which appeared twice a week in a Connecticut daily newspaper. The subject matter of this column ranged from astronomy through psychology to zoology. He has free-lanced such science articles as "The Twenty Lost Years of Solid State Physics," and "The Chemistry of a Coral Reef," the latter illustrated with his own underwater photographs. Additionally, Thomas has appeared on a weekly radio program in Washington, DC, as "The Science Story Teller," and has given talks before numerous groups on a variety of subjects. For two years he wrote a monthly magazine column called "The Science Springboard."

Thomas has long been active in the science fiction field. To date he has published about seventy short stories in a number of magazines, many of which have later appeared in anthologies. With Kate Wilhelm he has published two science fiction novels, *The Clone*, Berkeley, 1966, for which a motion picture version has been optioned, and *The Year of the Cloud*, Doubleday, 1969. A motion picture option is also out on his Weatherman Trilogy, a series of three novelettes.

The slide rule broke in half in Carter's fingers. He dropped the pieces onto the folder, and looked up to meet the gaze of Cecil Hardy. Carter said, "I want this one, Cecil. I want this one badly." His lips moved, but his teeth remained clenched.

Hardy nodded slowly. "I know you do, Walter. I know how you feel."

"Do you?" Carter stood up and stepped over to face a bank of instruments. His back was toward Hardy. "Do you? I raised that boy from a pup. I took what they sent me and out of it I made a man. I made the best man the Academy has ever seen. I saw the raw material was there so I gave him the best I've got, and he soaked it all up like a sponge. He's got deep space in his marrow, that boy. He's got—" Carter broke off, and then added, "If young Walt had lived, he'd be just like Lightner. You see how it is?"

Hardy rose from his chair and placed a hand on Carter's shoulder. He turned Carter around so he could see his face, then he said, "I've known how it was for years, Walter. I've watched it."

Some of the steel went out of Carter's back. "You mean it was noticeable?"

Hardy smiled and shook his head. "No. Not noticeable in the sense you mean. I noticed it because it is my business to notice such things, and because you and I have been friends for a long time. I've seen what happens to your eyes when you look at Lightner. But nobody else would notice."

Carter blew out his breath, ran a hand through his short iron-gray hair, and nodded. "I tried not to let it show."

"You didn't. You kept it concealed pretty well, I thought. Maybe too well. Lightner does not think of you the way you do of him."

"I know. I couldn't possibly let him suspect the way I felt;

that would have been intolerable. That's all the more reason why I've got to see him in deep space — to make it up to him. That boy will take over the Deep Space Command some day. When he does he'll be a better man than I am. He's got to make it — for me, for himself, and for Earth itself. Men like that are rare. We need them."

Hardy looked at the chronometer and said, "Well, we'll soon know. He's putting his flier down just outside the town now. He'll be home in a few minutes. I'd better see to my instruments." He turned and began snapping switches and adjusting dials.

Carter stepped to his side and said, "Cecil."

Hardy looked at him questioningly.

"Why is it necessary to do this in Lightner's case? He's been superlative in everything for years. We can safely skip this and pass him anyway."

Hardy's eyes widened. "Walter, you don't really mean that. This final test is the only means we have of getting down to the core of the man. His emotions on going home will tell us whether he really is a deep-space man or just another very skillful space pilot. We have no other way of knowing. You know we must do this." He paused, and said, "Why are you so afraid of this test, Walter? Do you know something I don't? Are you afraid Lightner won't pass it?"

Carter's back stiffened. "Of course not. Go ahead, run your test. The boy will come through."

A thousand miles away Lightner dropped his flier onto a small field. The ship had not stopped before he bounded from the cockpit and looked around. It was late afternoon. The breeze had waned and the air lay still over the land. Lightner bent his head back and breathed in the smell of the sun-drenched grass. He looked to the southwest, into the setting sun, and saw there the tall pin-oak standing unchanged. What branch had it been? The third from the top? Shading his eyes from the sun he carefully inspected the branch, but there were no traces of the kite that had flopped there for years. Even now, looking at the branch, Lightner could feel the time-washed agonies of that young boy who watched the destruction of his first-built kite on that branch. He smiled, remembering the gentle voice of his father, arm around shoulders, explaining that this was the stuff of life, and how the two of them built an even better kite that flew high and steady for days on end.

Lightner turned and walked down the road that led to town. He walked fast at first, but then he slowed his pace as memories pushed into his mind. Here was the fence, no longer suitable for that game of long ago, the gaps in it rendering impossible the requirement that a boy travel a quarter mile without touching the ground. Was it here? No, there, where stood the thorny bush in which he and Joey Knobb had thrashed around with gory murder the momentary object; finally they had gone home together covered with lacerations and punctures not one of which was caused by anything done by the other boy. Lightner grunted; Old Man Carter would not have thought much of his prowess in that fight.

Ahead was the final bend in the road, and the great willow tree stood as always, mushrooming above the other trees, looming out over the road. Lightner walked under it, into the tree-tunnel where the branches had been cut away to allow the passage of vehicles on the road. Under the tree was the usual tree litter, and through it, over on the other side was the cemetery. Lightner could see the headstones through the low-sweeping branches of the willow, glowing stone-white against the green background. He looked toward the part where his mother and father lay buried, and almost, he turned off the road, but he did not. The road completed its turn and widened into the straight run of concrete that was Main Street. Lightner stood still and looked down.

The setting sun was at his back, and the slanting rays cast a reddish glow down the street. A few people sauntered along the sidewalks, and an occasional car moved down the street and turned off. The soft sound of voices and the purr of motors came to him through the still warm air. Lightner shook his head. It had not changed. Here and now, in a time when men fought toward the stars, was a town — his town — standing as it had stood for a hundred years. Would another hundred years see any change? Lightner shook his head again, and walked to the sidewalk.

He passed Murphy's Garage, backed in against the trees at the edge of town. Soon he passed some people, one of whom he knew, but he did not stop. They looked questioningly at the tall lithe figure in the uniform of a Senior Space Cadet that glided silently by. But it was not until he walked past Martin's Drug Store that anyone spoke.

Mr. Martin detached himself from the group that loitered in front, stepped up to him, and said, "Aren't you John Lightner's boy?"

Lightner smiled, thrust out his hand, and said, "Hello, Mr. Martin."

Mr. Martin took it, and while shaking it he turned to the group and called, "Look who's here. John Lightner's boy, Billy, come to pay us a visit."

The group resolved itself into individuals, and they all gathered around. Many of them Lightner knew and he was busy shaking hands and telling them he was well.

There came a time when the invitations for a visit had all been extended, the latest news discussed. A half-silence fell, and they stood smiling at him and looking self-consciously down the street. Lightner saw they understood; he wanted to move on and see his home, and they did not want to bar his way. He waved good-by, and walked.

Past the Feed Store he went, where a farmer loaded his truck with bags of feed concentrate. Lightner could smell the dry haylike aroma of the feed wafted to him by the breeze that began to stir in the gathering dusk. He turned the corner on his street, walked two blocks, and then realized that he was in front of Agnes Moore's house. He looked at the dark front porch and he remembered another time, long ago, when the porch had been dark.

The porch swing was still there, the one he and Agnes had been sitting on, quiet and tense, with the feeling of thunder in the blood. There was a round shoulder nestled close up under his arm, and the moment came when their breathing seemed to stop, and then begin again, quick and short. At that instant her father unexpectedly swung up the front walk and found them sitting rigid and quite far apart on the porch swing. If he had suspected anything he gave no sign, for he nodded pleasantly and walked into the house.

Lightner smiled as he remembered the episode. He felt no trace of embarrassment, only a kind of mild surprise that he should once have considered such things important. There were lights coming on in the Moore house, but he did not go up to the door.

He turned and went on, and in the next block he stopped before his house. It was dark; the present owners were apparently not at home. There was little change. The privet hedge had been cut way back, and there were new bushes where the front walk joined the side walk, and there was a new coat of paint. But it was his home, and he stood on the side walk in the gathering darkness and looked at it. A host of memories filled his heart and flooded his mind.

And a thousand miles away two men watched with desperate intensity as the pens drew their inky traces across the creeping ribbons of paper.

Lightner looked at his home, and then he looked up through the trees that shrouded it. Gleaming faintly through the leafy branches were the stars. Lightner stepped out into the street where he could get an open view of the evening sky. He stood with feet wide apart and head tipped back, staring at the stars. And the stars seemed to stare back at him.

The distant suns smiled on him, and winked beckoningly. Like a woman, he thought, aloof, distant, cool, yet inviting — so inviting to come and taste the things unseen, the hot wash of half hidden fires. Lightner's breath came quick, and his mouth opened.

There was his life. There was what he was for. All the training, the pounding years, the operations, the grueling study and toil, the deprivation, all of it was, after all, for the single purpose of fitting him to be a creature of those suns. Many had tried to turn him aside, but he had won through. Carter, Old Man Carter himself, had taken up the task of punishing him as no other man in the Academy had been punished, harsh long hours of work when the others rested, constant practice toward a perfection no other approached. But he had showed them. He had taken the worst they had to offer and soaked it up like a sponge. They could not stop him now; now he was ready. Now, despite everything they had done to stop him, he was ready for deep space.

Lightner's arms raised slowly from his sides, raised until they stretched overhead. He stood with feet wide apart, head tipped back, arms reaching up toward the stars. Thus he stood.

His breath rattled in his throat. The sound of it jarred him and brought him back to where he was. He dropped his arms and looked wildly around, and half staggered to the side walk. His home loomed in front of him in the darkness and he smiled at it, a tight, grinning sort of smile. It was pleasant to see it again, but what was he doing here? This was not where he belonged. He glanced up. Out there, that was his destiny, in deep space. He laughed aloud and felt contentment well through him. And with singing heart he turned to go back to the flier. He walked swiftly now, looking neither to the right or the left.

Hardy sat back after a lengthy and detailed study of the charts. Before he could speak Carter saw the answer in his face, and Hardy saw that he knew. Reaching across the table Hardy placed a hand on top of Carter's hands and said, "Walter, I am sorry. I am so very very sorry."

Carter made no answer.

"This boy has nothing to come back to, no fundamental ties with Earth. Deep in his heart he is not interested in us or our planet. He wants nothing but deep space; he puts it ahead of everything."

Carter said nothing.

Hardy grabbed both of Carter's hands and shook them. "Walter, that boy is a fanatic. You can't have that kind of man in deep space. He's no good for you, or the Command, or Earth. Don't you see that?"

Carter looked up, and Hardy saw his eyes. There was a strange wildness in them unlike anything Hardy had seen before.

Carter took a breath to speak, but Hardy spoke first. "Don't say it, Walter. Look, when that boy is under stress his decisions might be those of a madman. He might react normally, but the chances are he won't. He loves space so much he's not stable; a man has to love something else more than the thing he devotes his life to, otherwise he's a fanatic and you can't trust him. Same way with you right now. You love this boy, but — How do those lines go?

'I could not love thee half so much
Loved I not honor more.'

There's the answer to your problem."

Carter bent his head forward and rested his forehead on his clasped hands. He sat motionless, and then his forearms quivered and his hands grew white from the pressure of the clenched fingers. He slammed his hands on the table top, and reached over and picked up the broken pieces of the slide rule. He jostled them in the palm of one hand, staring at them, and then he looked up at Hardy. The wildness was gone. He said, "It's all right, Cecil. Thank you, thank you very much." And he tossed the broken slide rule into the wastebasket.

How We Saved the Human Race
David Gerrold

David Gerrold began his science fiction career in 1967, as a writer for "Star Trek." His first sale was the episode entitled "The Trouble With Tribbles," one of the most popular episodes in the show's history. Gerrold later wrote two non-fiction books about "Star Trek": *The World of Star Trek*, the first in-depth analysis of the show, and *The Trouble with Tribbles*, in which he related his personal experiences with the series. Gerrold has since written many other television scripts, including episodes of "Logan's Run," "Land of the Lost," and the "Star Trek Animated TV Series." He has served as story-editor for "Land of the Lost" and "Buck Rogers."

Gerrold is also a well established science fiction novelist. His best known works are *When Harlie Was One* and *The Man Who Folded Himself*, both of which were nominated for the Hugo and Nebula awards. Gerrold has been nominated for the Hugo three times and the Nebula four. He has published seven other novels, five anthologies, and a short story collection. In 1979, he won the Skylark award for imaginative fiction.

Gerrold is thirty-nine years old and lives in Los Angeles with three peculiar dogs, two and a half cats, a computer with delusions of sentience, and a butterscotch convertible. He is a skilled programmer and contributes occasionally to *Creative Computing*, *Infoworld*, and other home computing periodicals. He also writes a monthly column on science fiction for *Starlog* magazine. Gerrold is currently working on Book Three of *The War Against the Chtorr: A Rage For Revenge*. It will be his twenty-second book.

TEST TRANS CODE ALPHA ALPHA TAU
1234567890 − =
QWERTYUIOP
ASDFGHJKL +
ZXCVBNM,./
THE QUICK BROWN FOX JUMPED OVER THE LAZY DOGS.
      END TEST
      MESSAGE BEGINS HERE
DATE/MAY-14-2037
FROM/THE UNITED STATES AMBASSADOR TO BRAZIL
TO/THE PRESIDENT OF THE UNITED STATES
FILE/BRZ-9076-THX
CODE/ALPHA-ALPHA-TAU/475FGH5142037
STATUS OF DOCUMENT/CLASSIFIED/TELEPRINTER
CODE-   FGH.
MR. PRESIDENT, IN PLAIN TERMS THE ANSWER IS NO.
THE GOVERNMENT OF BRAZIL ABSOLUTELY REFUSES
TO RELEASE THE BODY. THERE CAN BE NO POSSIBLE
NEGOTIATION ON THIS. THIS IS AN INTERNAL MAT-
TER—THEY CLAIM—AND NO OTHER POLITICAL BODY
WILL BE ALLOWED TO INTERVENE. OF COURSE, THIS IS A
BLATANT GRAB ON THEIR PART, BUT THERE IS
NOTHING WE CAN DO ABOUT IT. I + M AGAINST MAK-
ING ANY KIND OF FLAP.
FIRST OF ALL, WORLD-WIDE OPINION GENERALLY
FAVORS THE BRAZILIANS. ANY ATTEMPT BY US TO
PRESSURE THEM WOULD ONLY PRODUCE HOSTILE
REACTIONS—AND THAT + S THE LAST THING WE WANT
NOW.
SECONDLY, THEY WANT TO TAKE CREDIT FOR LEDGER-
TON + S CAPTURE. THEY FOUND HIM AND THEY EXE-
CUTED HIM. OR RATHER, THEY ATTEMPTED TO. IT WAS
MOST UNFORTUNATE THAT THE CROWD BEAT THEM

TO IT. THERE ARE THOSE WHO SUGGEST THAT THE POLICE DELIBERATELY LET THE LYNCH MOB IN, BUT I WOULD DISCREDIT THAT STORY. THEY LOST TWELVE OF THEIR OWN MEN IN THE DISORDER.

ANYWAY, THEY WANT TO TAKE THE CREDIT, AND FRANKLY I THINK WE OUGHT TO LET THEM. THIS IS NOT TO SUGGEST APPEASEMENT, BUT THIS GOVERN-MENT IS THE FRIENDLIEST ONE BRAZIL HAS HAD IN TWELVE YEARS AND I WOULD LIKE TO KEEP IT THAT WAY. ANY PRESSURING ON OUR PART WOULD DEF-INITELY COOL RELATIONS. — AND PRESIDENT GARCIA WON + T BEND TO PRESSURE ANYWAY. POLITICAL REASONS. THE MILITANT RIGHTISTS WOULD USE SUCH ACQUIESCENCE AS A LEVER AGAINST HIM. — SO . . . I THINK WE + D BETTER JUST MAKE INEFFECTUAL NOISES FOR NOW, LOUD ENOUGH TO PLACATE OUR OWN PEO-PLE, BUT NOT LOUD ENOUGH TO ANNOY JUAN PABLO GARCIA.

BY THE WAY, THE BODY WILL REMAIN ON PUBLIC DISPLAY FOR ANOTHER DAY AND A HALF. — YES, STILL HANGING FROM THE GALLOWS, BULLET HOLES AND ALL — I + VE SEEN IT AND IT + S A GHASTLY SIGHT. NOT EVEN LEDGERTON DESERVED WHAT THEY DID TO HIM. YOU KNOW OF COURSE THAT THEY CASTRATED HIM TOO.

IN ANY CASE, I HAVE IT FROM GARCIA HIMSELF THAT IT WILL BE TAKEN DOWN TUESDAY AND CREMATED. THE ASHES ARE GOING TO BE SCATTERED AT SEA. NO, WE CAN + T STOP THAT EITHER.

I WISH I COULD BE MORE ENCOURAGING AT THIS TIME, BUT ALL I CAN DO IS SAY THAT IT + S A ROTTEN SITUA-TION ALL AROUND. I + LL HAVE A MORE DETAILED REPORT LATER. DESPITE OUR CLAIMS TO THE CON-TRARY, THERE ARE STILL TOO MANY PEOPLE DOWN HERE WHO BELIEVE THE WHOLE THING WAS A C.I.A. PLOT.

FOR GOD + S SAKE, THIS IS ONE TIME WHEN I HOPE OUR OFFICIAL POSITION COINCIDES WITH THE TRUTH.

SINCERELY,

5-14-2057/DATELINE:BRAZIL.
CARDINAL SILENTE TODAY DEDICATED THE MONU-
MENT AND ETERNAL FLAME COMMEMORATING THE
MARTYR DANA LEDGERTON. THAT SUCH A HIGH-
RANKING MEMBER OF THE CATHOLIC CHURCH
SHOULD TRAVEL TO BRAZIL FOR THE CEREMONIES SUG-
GESTS IMMINENT BEATIFICATION OF THE MARTYR. THE
CARDINAL HIMSELF SAID. . . .

PSYCHIATRIC INDEX REPORT
COMSKOOL TWELVE, MANWEATHER COMPLEX, CALIF.
May 1, 2003
Dana Ledgerton, DL 571-60-5683, age nine.

Child is unfortunately too smart and too pretty for his own
good. Male, age nine, fair skin, pale hair, thin, under-sized for
age (poor nutrition again, damn these comskool minimums),
lives in Comskool Creche. Unfortunately, subject also has
advanced intelligence. (Tests enclosed.) Presently enrolled two
grades above average for his age level. This physical discrepancy between him and his classmates generates extreme
feelings of inferiority, coupled with strong motivation to
succeed. Success on mental level increases antagonism
between himself and peers, but it is the only arena in which he
is fairly matched with his classmates. The kid takes a lot of
teasing about being a sissy, and his sense of masculine
identification is weak. I'll give odds of ten to one that he's a fag
by the time he's twenty.
RECOMMENDATIONS: None. There's nothing we can do.
Tough.

SUPERVISOR'S REMARKS: *Dammit, Pete! Can't you be a little
more clinical than this!* (signed) H.B.

MAY 9, 2011
LABOR POOL STATUS BOARD, CALIF. 99-5674
UNIT MONITOR FORM JHX-908
DANA LEDGERTON, DL 571-60-5683

Subject is thin, very fair, blond hair. Small for his age.
Required to perform eighteen hours of Class IV labor per week

in order to support education demands. Assigned to manual labor in University Caf-Com. Designation: busboy.

REMARKS:

Subject discovered in Comskool Personal committing homosexual act with fellow student at age twelve. Referred to Psych-Stat who confirmed unit's sexual outlook. No recommendation made. Subject's sexual preference has no bearing on his ability to perform Class IV labor.

RECOMMENDATION:

Leave to discretion of local supervisors.

MAY 45, 2035

FROM: FIELD OPERATIVE JASON PETER GRIGG

TO: F.B.I. DIRECTOR WARREN J. HINDLER, HOOVER CENTER, WASHINGTON, D.C.

FILE: LEDGERTON, YTR 5683

Chief,

Sorry for the sketchiness of this report; I'll have to do a complete rundown when I get back. This thing is a mess to the nth power. The Manweather records only go back twelve years. Before that, it's incomplete and often sketchy. Yes, I know that's hard to believe, but Manweather was one of the hardest hit during the sex and protein riots, and a lot of their records were wiped clean by the activists.

I'll be sending along telefaxes of the working papers, but until they arrive, here's a rough summary.

Ledgerton's birth was an accident. He wasn't wanted, not by his parents, not by the local board. When he came along, unannounced and unwelcome, the parents were sterilized and sent to Labor-Module 14, Manweather. The child was transferred to the Comskool Creche, which had only been open two years at that time and still had elbow room. However, due to shifting population pressures, Manweather became one of the densest concentrations in Calif. Within five years, it was a behavioral sink.

Competition wasn't Ledgerton's big thing. He preferred to withdraw into himself. Because his teachers and psych-stats kept telling him how smart he was and how he should be proud of himself, he became narcissistic and introverted. He took a lot of fag-baiting from his classmates, too.

There's a full psych-profile in here somewhere. I was lucky to find that. According to the shrink, "Little Dana" wasn't as self-assertive as he should have been and too many of his life-choices were made because population pressures forced him into them and he didn't feel like fighting back.

His college career tends to bear this out. He went into bio-chem strictly by accident. It was the only classification still open that he was qualified for. And it was either that or the unskilled labor pool. Nuff said about that.

MAY 24, 2014
UNIVERSITY OF CALIFORNIA AT INDIO
REAGAN HALL
FLOOR MANAGER'S MEMO
SUBJECT: REASSIGNMENT OF ROOMS
Dana Ledgerton DL 571-60-5683 and Paul-John Murdock PJM 673-65-4532 have been reassigned (at their request) to room 12-32, the "lavender hills" section. This leaves rooms 6-87 and 7-54 with only one person in them. Immediate reassignments available for each.

MAY 3, 2015
UNIVERSITY OF CALIFORNIA AT INDIO
PSYCH-STAT REPORT, CONFIDENTIAL
SUBJECT: PAUL-JOHN MURDOCK PJM 673-65-4532
Subject is tall and husky. (6'1" and 161 lbs.) Fairly well built. Dark hair, curly. Thin face. "Penetrating" eyes — an illusion produced by deepset sockets and heaviness of eyebrows. Prone to long periods of moodiness and introspection. Theatre arts major.

He has been living for the past year with another male student and the relationship is apparently sexual. However, subject's emotional involvement tends to be shallow. He has a long history of casual sexual encounters with his fellow students, both male and female, and probably would not grieve if this relationship were to end abruptly.

I suspect the continued use of mildly narcotic drugs, including such illegal agents as "Spice," "Pink," and "Harrolin."

(No definite proof here.) Subject's manner is lackadaisical and uncaring. Selfish, introverted, narcissistic. Typical T.A. major: more concerned with things on a "higher plane" than with the exigencies of everyday life.

Subject's strongest motivation for continuation of education is the avoidance of the labor-draft.

RECOMMENDATION: 1-A status.

STATE OF CALIFORNIA, INFORMATION DUP-OUT.
APPLICATION FOR CONTRACT TO ENTER STATE OF LEGAL MARRIAGE
DATE: MAY 12, 2015
APPLICANTS:
DANA LEDGERTON DL 571-60-5683
PAUL-JOHN MURDOCK PJM 673-65-4532
LENGTH OF CONTRACT: THREE YEARS
PURPOSE: MUTUAL INTERDEPENDENCE
CONDITIONS: INDIVIDUAL PROPERTY MAINTENANCE; DISSOLUTION TERMS NON–NEGOTIABLE. MUTUAL INHERITANCE.
RESIDENCE: REAGAN HALL, UNIVERSITY OF CALIFORNIA AT INDIO, ROOM 12-32
DISPOSITION OF APPLICATION: GRANTED. WILLIAM APTHEKER, COUNTY CLERK.

HARDCOPY FRAGMENT IN FILE, dislocated page, thought to be part of report by investigating agents. (Nature of agency not known.)

"...*after his marriage broke up, he remained at the University for another three years. He tried to reconcile the contract several times, but twice he couldn't get in touch with Paul-John and the third time, Paul-John was vague in his reply.*

"*After that, he concentrated heavily on his studies. He won a Ph.D. in bio-chemistry and an M.A. in medicine. They were (in the words of the department head) 'Uninspired degrees'. Meaning he was qualified, but not exceptional.*

"*Somehow he landed a teaching position and was able to hold onto it for several years. They had him giving the freshman science classes, something nobody else wanted to do.*

"What he did on his own time during those years is beyond me, though I suspect he spent a lot of time at the artshows."

MAY 32, 2027
COLORADO COLLEGE OF SCIENCE
DENVER, COLORADO
FROM: *Dr. Margaret James-Mead*
TO: *Dept. Head Harlan Sloan*
Hal,
       If I have to look at that "wispy little thing" wandering around the halls of this college one more day, I think I'll puke. You know who I mean. That man is a disgrace to the institution.
       I don't care how you do it, but you've got to get rid of him. If you can't find something on him, make something. If you don't ask him for his resignation within a week, I'll give you mine instead.
       Love, Maggie.

May 34, 2027
My dear Dr. Ledgerton,
       It is with deepest regret that I must ask you to resign your position with the Denver College of Science. Your record here has been without blemish; however, we find that there is no longer any need for your services and are forced to take this rather unfortunate step.
       I assure you that it has nothing to do with your personal life, or the incident with Dr. James-Mead. It is instead a question of...

MAY 3, 2029
INTERBEM CHEMICAL RESEARCH
PORTION OF SUPERVISOR'S REPORT
       "... the Ledgerton group seems to have come closest to a workable solution of this problem. They have generated an experimental strain, temporarily, designated NFK-98, which appears to combine the functions of both DFG-54 and DFS-09 into one continuous process, rather than the two separate steps we have today.

"Suggest further experimentation along these lines to substantiate the findings and put them into production. The Ledgerton group should be commended. Despite his unappealing appearance, Ledgerton is a tireless worker. Morale of the technicians working under him is not as good as it could be, but they do produce usable results.

"The viral research teams should be expanded as soon as possible in order to. . ."

INTERBEM CHEMICAL RESEARCH
MAY 9, 2029
TO ALL EMPLOYEES:
COMPANY FACILITIES ARE NOT TO BE USED FOR PRIVATE RESEARCH PROJECTS WITHOUT FIRST SECURING PERMISSION FROM DEPARTMENT HEADS. IT IS UNDERSTOOD THAT INTERBEM RETAINS THE RIGHT OF FIRST OPTION ON ANY COMMERCIAL APPLICATION OF PRIVATE DISCOVERIES PRODUCED BY INTERBEM EMPLOYEES. REMEMBER, THIS PRIVILEGE IS CONDITIONAL UPON FULFILLMENT OF MINIMUM QUOTAS AND WILL BE REVOKED IF THEY ARE NOT MET.

MAY 1, 2030
FIRST DORIAN CHURCH OF AMERICA, OSCAR WILDE CONGREGATION, CONFIDENTIAL MEMBERSHIP REPORT:
Dr. Dana Ledgerton, employee of InterBem Corporation, age thirty-six. Unmarried.
Dr. Ledgerton was interviewed by the membership committee whose discussion follows. J.M. commented at length that Dr. Ledgerton is thirty-six and physically unappealing. He suggested that the only reason Ledgerton wants to join is because he cannot find sexual partners anywhere else.
K.R. found J.M.'s attitude and phrasing undignified and demeaning.
L.N. said that Ledgerton's primary purpose in joining the church is probably loneliness.
J.M. agreed, but said that loneliness was just another way of saying "horniness."

L.N. insisted that the applicant was basically good intentioned. Lots of people join churches because they are lonely. Why should the Dorians be any different?

K.R. interrupted both of them to speculate on whether or not Ledgerton really did embrace the principles of Dorianism.

Ledgerton was called back into the room then and further questioned. He responded at length and the discussion continued again, while he waited outside.

A.S., visiting minister from the bay area, cast his support in favor of Ledgerton. Most people, he said, are not aware of all the precepts of Dorianism when they join, and it would be unfair to hold that against Ledgerton.

A vote was taken then, and Ledgerton was admitted to the membership by a count of 4-1. He was readmitted to the room and sworn to uphold the church and the principles upon which it was founded, that overpopulation is a sin and that all Dorians will devote their whole lives to zero population growth.

Dr. Ledgerton will be presented to the general congregation at the next open meeting.

MAY 39, 2031
INTERBEM CHEMICAL RESEARCH
SUPPLY REQUISITION
Need: Forty hours' use of electron microscope for viral research. Private project. After hours use will be okay. Would appreciate available times as soon as possible.

(signed) D. Ledgerton

MAY 14, 2032
INTERBEM CHEMICAL RESEARCH
SUPERVISOR'S MEMO
Spoke to Ledgerton today about his after-hours research. He's been working on this one project for nearly a year now, and he has spent nearly thirty-five thousand dollars on it. When questioned how much longer this line of research would continue, Ledgerton declined to say, but seemed to indicate that it would not be much longer.

I asked if he were close to a solution. He replied that he was closer to finding out that there was no solution, but would not go into any further detail. I suspect he does not want to discuss his project. A complete report on the objectives of his program and his findings has been ordered. He has until the end of the month to submit it, at which time it will be evaluated and decided whether or not he will be allowed to continue.

He was upset, but not as much as I expected. Perhaps he is nearing the end of his research after all. He mentioned something about a possible sabbatical later in the year. If he requests it, it is my recommendation that it be granted. His lapse in work has been only recent and may be due to personal problems. Ledgerton has always been a good worker, although his personal manner does leave something to be desired.

MAY 50, 2032
INTERBEM CHEMICAL RESEARCH
REQUEST FOR LEAVE OF ABSENCE
APPLICANT: DANA LEDGERTON DL 571 60 5683
REASON: VACATION, INDEFINITE LENGTH
DISPOSITION OF APPLICATION: GRANTED
REMARKS: *(Scrawled in pen.) Good. I never liked him anyway.*

MAY 50, 2032
FIRST DORIAN CHURCH OF AMERICA, OSCAR WILDE CONGREGATION CONFIDENTIAL MEMBERSHIP REPORT:
The membership committee then considered a motion to expel D.L.

J.M. wanted to go on record as being opposed to D.L.'s membership in the first place. It was duly noted.

L.N. inquired as to what the charges against D.L. were.

J.M. said that D.L. has not been faithful to the principles upon which the credo is based.

K.R. noted that D.L. has been observed almost nightly in the company of "paid female prostitutes."

L.N. requested amplification of this charge.

J.M. presented receipts made out to D.L. from the Xanadu Pleasure Corp.

L.N. wanted to know how J.M. got the receipts, but he was ruled out of order. The issue at hand is D.L.'s transgressions, not J.M.'s source of information.

L.N. disagreed, saying that we should not be "spying on our brothers." He was ruled out of order again.

The vote was taken and D.L. was expelled by a vote of 4-1. The general membership will be informed at the next open meeting.

MAY 7, 2036
FIRST DORIAN CHURCH OF AMERICA, OSCAR WILDE CONGREGATION CONFIDENTIAL MEMBERSHIP REPORT:

L.N. called the special meeting to order at 8:00 p.m. The first order of business was the reconsideration of the expulsion of D.L. four years ago. In light of recent events, it has become obvious that D.L.'s actions at that time were not in violation of the basic principles of Dorianism.

If anything, D.L., more than any other member, has done the most to further the cause of zero population growth.

K.R. noted some additional facts about the situation and a vote was taken. D.L. was unanimously readmitted to the congregation. He has not been notified because his whereabouts remain unknown.

It was decided not to apprise either the public or the general membership of this decision because of the adverse publicity this might bring to the church.

MAY 27, 2033
FILE: 639 RADZ
SUBMITTED BY: RESIDENT PHYSICIAN JAMES-TAYLOR RUGG

Mr. and Mrs. Robert D_____ came into my office on May 6 of this year. They have been trying for six months to start a baby and have had no success. I initiated the Groperson tests as well as a routine physical examination of each.

Mrs. D_____ is in excellent physical condition and well-suited for child-bearing. Mr. D_____ tests out with a normal sperm count and is in no need of semination-cloning. I'm sure that the rest of the tests will also turn out negative. I admit it, I'm stumped, and I pass this case on to the board with all the rest.

WRITTEN IN INK ACROSS THE BOTTOM: *Dammit! This is*

the twenty-third one of these I've seen in the past two months.
What the hell is going on?

(signed) B. V.

5-21-2033/TIMEFAX
...SURPRISINGLY, THE ONLY PLACE WHERE THE
POPULATION GROWTH HAS KEPT WITHIN ITS PRO-
JECTED LIMITS HAS BEEN SOUTHERN CALIFORNIA, THE
DENSEST URBAN COMPLEX IN THE COUNTRY. THE
STATE SURGEON GENERAL OFFERED NO EXPLANATION
FOR IT, BUT USED THE OCCASION TO CONDEMN THE
ARTIFICIAL ADDITIVES IN THE YEAST-CULTURES. HE
NOTED AN INCREASE IN THE NUMBER OF MARRIED
COUPLES CONSULTING DOCTORS ABOUT THEIR IN-
ABILITY TO CONCEIVE AND HINTED THAT THERE
MIGHT BE A CONNECTION.
IN CLEVELAND, DR. JOYCE FREMM DISCOUNTED THIS,
SUGGESTED INSTEAD THAT THE CALIFORNIA
SLOWDOWN WAS A RESULT OF ITS BECOMING "ONE
GIANT BEHAVIORAL STINK." WHEN ASKED IF SHE DIDN'T
MEAN "BEHAVIORAL SINK," DR. FREMM REPLIED, "I
KNOW WHAT I SAID."

5-3-2034/TIMEFAX
CONCERN OVER THE SO-CALLED "INFERTILITY PLAGUE"
HAS SPREAD EVEN TO THE EASTERN BLOC NATIONS.
THE LATEST CITIES TO REPORT DECLINING BIRTH
RATES INCLUDE MOSCOW, PEKING, HONG KONG,
TOKYO, OSAKA, HANOI, NEW DELHI AND MELBOURNE.
EARLIER IN THE WEEK, THE PARIS COUNCIL MET AGAIN
TO REPORT STILL NO SUCCESS IN FINDING THE CAUSE
OF THE DECLINE.
DR. JOYCE FREMM, WORKING OUT OF SOUTHERN
CALIFORNIA COMPLEX, UNIT HOSPITAL 43, ADMITTED
THAT HER TEAM WAS NO CLOSER TO THE CAUSE THAN
THEY HAD BEEN A YEAR AGO. "ALL WE KNOW ABOUT IT,
WHATEVER IT IS," SHE SAID, "IS THAT IT KEEPS PEOPLE
FROM STARTING BABIES."
SHE GAVE NO INDICATION WHEN A SOLUTION MIGHT

BE FOUND. WHILE SHE WAS SPEAKING, THE W.H.O. RELEASED A LIST OF AN ADDITIONAL FOURTEEN NATIONS WHOSE BIRTH RATES HAVE BEGUN TO SHOW THE INITIAL SLOWING THAT INDICATES THE PRESENCE OF THE SYNDROME.

MAY 9, 2034
MEMO TO: DR. JOYCE FREMM
FROM: DR. VICTOR-WEBB KING
Joyce,

I don't know how important this is, but it wouldn't hurt to track it down. Out of the last three hundred couples I've interviewed, nearly sixty percent of the men have met their wives and been married only in the past eighteen months. Out of this group, nearly half report occasional pre-marital visits to a joy house, and nearly a third of all men we interviewed have had some kind of professional contact.

More important however, is that *at least one partner in every couple has had at least one pre- or extramarital contact with a partner other than wife or husband.*

The former fact is way out of line with the statistical average; the latter implies a definite connection. Could the Xanadu Pleasure Corp. be an active vector of the disease?

MAY 11, 2034
MEMO TO: DR. VICTOR—WEBB KING
FROM: DR. JOYCE FREMM

(1)   We don't know yet that it's a disease.

(2)   Make no public announcement of this — especially do not suggest that Xanadu or any other company may be connected with it.

(3)   Check it out immediately.

MAY 11, 2034
MEMO TO: DR. JOYCE FREMM
FROM: DR. CARLOS WAN-LEE
Dr. Fremm,

I believe my section has come up with a clue as to the nature of the syndrome. Sperm from one hundred affected men has been compared with the sperm of one hundred unaffected men; i.e. men whose wives have been impregnated within the past two months.

There is a minor but definite difference in the enzyme output of the affected sperm cells. All of the affected men (excepting three with very low sperm counts) had this qualitative difference in their enzyme production. Ninety-three of the unaffected men had normal enzyme production.

We're exploring this further and will have a more detailed report at the end of the week.

MAY 30, 2034
REPORT TO THE WORLD HEALTH ORGANIZATION BY DR. JOYCE FREMM
TRANSCRIPTION OF REMARKS – MOST CONFIDENTIAL
Gentlemen,

We have discovered the cause of the infertility plague, and we believe that it is only a matter of time until we discover the cure.

The cause of the plague is simple: We have been hit by a new kind of venereal disease – a benevolent tyrant, so to speak. It has an incubation period of less that twenty-four hours, and its immediate effects are so mild as to be negligible; perhaps a headache or a mild sense of nausea, that's all; but after that, the victim will pass the infection on to everyone he or she has intimate contact with.

Both males and females are carriers of the disease, creating an ever-increasing reservoir of active infection, with promiscuity its vector.

The disease has no effect on females of the species. To them, it is a benevolent parasite. It lives in the female reproductive tract and minds its own business. Unfortunately, its business is to infect that woman's every male contact.

And each time it does that, if effectively castrates the man. Viability of the sperm cells is reduced to 7% of what is considered normal.

The causative agent is a virus. It is a new strain and related to nothing we have seen before. Were it not for the fact that artificial virus tailoring is still such an infant science, I would suspect a vast campaign of virological warfare is being waged against the human race.

The viral bodies live and breed in the cells lining the vaginal wall. During intercourse, the release of certain hormones cause them to become active, and the viral bodies migrate into the male organ — usually through the urethra, but occasionally through a mild, almost unnoticeable rash.

The virus then migrates to the testes, specifically to the sperm-forming cells. The viral DNA chains attack these cells, burrowing into the cell walls, throwing off their protein sheaths and becoming just another hunk of DNA within the cell. Impossible to discover.

The result is small, very small — but very noticeable. The sperm cell no longer *"cares."*

The average human male ejaculation contains three hundred million sperm cells. Ideally, each of these cells has the capability of being *the* cell to fertilize the waiting egg; but after being infected by the virus, the quality of the whole ejaculation is changed. The sperm cells still race madly up the Fallopian tubes to meet the ovum — but when they get there, they can't fertilize.

You see, each sperm cell carries a tiny amount of an enzyme called hyaluronidase. Hyaluronidase sub-one, that is. No matter what the enzyme is called, though — what does matter is that the virus changes the male so that he no longer produces that enzyme. Instead, he produces something else, some other enzyme. The virus adds a few little acids of its own to the amino chain of the enzyme, and instead of $hyaluronidase_1$ we get $hyaluronidase_2$ — a very different creature altogether.

$Hyaluronidase_2$ is not as active as $hyaluronidase_1$. It takes longer to do its work. Much longer.

Although only one sperm cell is needed for fertilization to occur, three hundred million are provided in order that one will succeed. But because only one is needed, the other two million, nine hundred ninety-nine thousand, nine hundred and ninety-nine sperm cells must be resisted. For that reason, the cell wall of the human ovum is too strong for any individual sperm cell to break down. Hyaluronidase is the enzyme that breaks down or softens the cell wall, and it takes the combined effort of all the sperm cells to provide enough of the enzyme to soften the wall enough for just one sperm cell to break through. Immediately upon fertilization, a change takes place in the cell wall to prevent other sperm cells from breaking in, a calculated resistance to their pressure.

But, if all those sperm cells are producing hyaluronidase$_2$ instead of hyaluronidase$_1$, fertilization will never take place at all. (Except in rare cases — too few to be considered.) The changed enzyme is still an enzyme, and it still works to soften the cell wall of the human egg — but it takes at least ten times longer to do it. And by that time, most of the sperm cells are already dead, dying, or too weak to complete the task of fertilization.

In addition, the ejaculation will also have introduced enough viral bodies into the woman so that if she weren't already, now she too will be infected and will pass the disease on to every subsequent male contact.

Insidious, isn't it?

Other than that, the virus has no effect at all on living human beings — only on the unborn. They stay that way. Unborn.

MAY 47, 2034
SUPPLEMENTARY REPORT, VIRT 897
W.H.O. FILE BVC 675
SUMMARY: The virus, designated VIRT 897, seems to have made its initial appearance on the western coast of the American continent in June or July of 2032, specifically in the area of the Southern California Urban Complex known as Angeles (colloq. L.A. or "Ellay.") From there it migrated along the heaviest tourist routes, traveling eastward to Denver, St. Louis, Chicago, Dallas, Miami, and scattered parts of the eastern seaboard Urban Complex.

Within six months, it had also appeared and made its effects known in Seattle, Portland, Detroit, Pittsburgh, and scattered areas surrounding. It extended the complete length of the western coast, being specifically virulent in Frisco and Diego counties, as well as in the areas already noted. It spread to Tia Juana, Mexico City, and Acapulco. The same trend occurred simultaneously on the eastern coast, with scattered pockets of sterility spreading out from Boston, York, Jersey, Philadelphia, and D.C. areas of the Urban Complex. Also affected were Toronto, Montreal and Quebec, as well as scattered areas surrounding.

At about the same time, it leapt both oceans simultaneously. Tracing the path of the falling birth rate, the disease showed up in London, Paris, Rome, Berlin, Warsaw, Munich, Belgrade, Dublin, Saigon, Seoul, Hanoi, Tokyo, Okama, Osaka, Peking, Honolulu, Hong Kong, Melbourne, Sydney, Buenos Aires, Caracas, Panama City, Havana, and scattered points on the east African Coast as well as in the Mediterranean and Mid-East areas.

It is obvious that there are too many active vectors by this time, making it increasingly difficult to trace the spreading waves of infection. Not only does the disease move too rapidly, but once the waves of infection overlap, their directions blur.

There is no way to tell at this time whether the origin of the disease was deliberate or accidental or a combination of both.

Detailed analysis charts are enclosed.

INTERBEM CHEMICAL RESEARCH
MEMO TO: DR. LEON K. HARGER
FROM: SECTION SUPERVISOR VANCE
Dr. Harger,
I've just finished reading the W.H.O. report on the sterility plague and a rather curious anomaly has caught my eye. I'm forwarding it to you to see if you catch it too. If you do, give me a buzz. If not, then forget I said anything.

MAY 50, 2034
INTERBEM CHEMICAL RESEARCH
MEMO TO: ALL DEPARTMENTS
FROM: DR. LEON K. HARGER
Urgent! I need all data pertaining to Dr. Dana Ledgerton DL 571 60 5683 and any and all research that he might have been involved in while he was employed here. Also, anyone

knowing his whereabouts or the itinerary of his sabbatical trip, please contact me immediately. I cannot overstate the importance of this information!

MAY 1, 2035
TO: SUPREME COURT JUSTICE DOUGLAS JOSEPH WARREN
FROM: UNITED STATES ATTORNEY GENERAL ALFRED G. WYLER
Dear Doug,

This is strictly *off* the record, and you might want to burn this note after reading it.

I've been talking to the President, and he and I concur that it would be extremely unwise to allow the InterBem Company to be sued merely because Ledgerton was an employee of theirs at the time he constructed the Ledgerton Virus.

Yes, I've studied the briefs in the case. I know that the appealing lawyers make a good case for the company's negligence in not keeping tighter reins on their employees' after-hours research. They also make a good case that Ledgerton would have been unable to construct his artificial venereal disease without the company's research facilities.

However, no matter how good their case is, both the President and I agree that at this time it would be best for all parties if the appeal were turned down. The InterBem Company has been most cooperative with us in *every* area of our investigation, especially in our efforts to develop the artificial enzymes. To allow them to be sued now might destroy them as a viable corporation and would cost us a valuable ally in our fight against this thing.

I don't know if you're familiar with this fact, but my office has registered more that five hundred thousand separate actions against InterBem. That corporation can't afford to be embroiled in this kind of legal piranhaism. If you allow this first appeal to be granted, we'll be setting a dangerous precedent that might cost the United States a valuable natural resource — i.e. a commercially healthy corporation.

Yes, I know this smacks of pressuring, but this case is too important to allow you to make a decision without knowing the administration's views on it. If you have any questions, don't hesitate to call me.

(signed) Alfred

MAY 7, 2035
FROM: FIELD OPERATIVE JASON PETER GRIGG
TO: F.B.I. DIRECTOR WARREN J. HINDLER, HOOVER CENTER, WASHINGTON, D.C.
FILE: DANA LEDGERTON, YTR 5683
Chief,

It's my guess that the Paul-John Murdock lead is going to be another dead end and we'll probably have to start digging backward. (I'll try to get up to Manweather Complex before the end of the month, though I don't think I'm going to find much up there.)

We located Murdock in South Frisco, where he's working as a shoe salesman. He has neither seen nor heard of Ledgerton since their post-college days. Apparently, he doesn't miss him either. I get the impression that the only reason they married was so that Murdock could avoid the labor-draft. The full interview tape is enclosed.

On the other side of it, there's some evidence that there was an emotional involvement on Ledgerton's part and that he's been trying to contact Murdock, but without success. We'll continue to monitor Murdock on the off chance that Ledgerton is still trying.

Oh, one more thing. The latest word on Ledgerton hints that he is somewhere in Africa and heading south. But I doubt it. Last week, he was in Scotland.

MAY 14, 2036
THE CONGRESSIONAL RECORD
CONGRESSMAN JOHN J. HOOKER; DEM, GEORGIA

Gentlemen, we are presented today with a unique opportunity. The development of the artificial enzyme insures that the human race will not die out — and it gives us the chance to end, once and for all, the population explosion.

We need not manufacture the enzyme indiscriminately, nor need we make it available to every member of the world's population. In fact, even if we wanted to, it would be beyond our technology to service twenty billion individuals.

We are not geared for rehabilitating the human race; we can only provide enough enzyme for a fraction of the people. Dr. Fremm has stated that even if we began a massive synthesis program right now, we would never be able to reach all of those who are infected.

According to Dr. Fremm and others, it is only a matter of time until every man, woman, and child on this planet has the disease. When that happens, the only people who will be able to procreate will be those to whom we provide the enzyme.

Gentlemen, I say to you — here is an opportunity we cannot pass up — historians will condemn us if we allow this golden moment to slip out of our grasp — the chance to optimize the human race, to remake humanity. Therefore, I wish at this time to introduce this bill which would give the government the right to withhold the enzyme from those individuals who are judged to have undesirable genes...

(The rest of Congressman Hooker's speech was drowned out.)

MAY 20, 2036
BERKELEY NEW PRESS:

> U.S. PLANS RACIAL WARFARE...
> Hooker (The Aardvark)'s plan would be only the first foot in the door. For instance, what would keep the establishment slime from declaring Negro-ness an "undesirable trait"?
>
> In cities across the nation, Freedom Now groups are planning urban disturbances to demonstrate their opposition to any form of "optimization," which would be only another word for genocide. The right to bear children is a right, not a privilege — and certainly not something that can be legislated. All right-thinking citizens are urged to come this weekend to the Free People's Plaza...

MAY 3, 2037
FROM: FIELD OPERATIVE JASON PETER GRIGG
TO: F.B.I. DIRECTOR WARREN J. HINDLER, HOOVER
CENTER, WASHINGTON, D.C.
FILE: LEDGERTON YTR 5683
Chief,

The monitor on Murdock has turned up an interesting postcard (fax herewith enclosed) postmarked Brazil. Although there's no name signed to it, the content and phrasing could be a code of some sort. Or perhaps a reference to a personal experience known only to Murdock and Ledgerton. It should be checked out by one of our Brazilian operatives as soon as possible. I would appreciate being kept informed on this lead.

5-9-2037/TIMEFAX
...THE RIOTERS FOCUSED PARTICULARLY ON THE SYMBOLS OF ESTABLISHMENT CONTROL. FOUR BIRTH CONTROL CENTERS IN HARLEMTOWN WERE SACKED AS WELL AS ALL BUT ONE OF THE AREA'S TEN ENZYME CONTROL CLINICS. THIS OUTBREAK WAS THE WORST RIOTING TO HIT THE CITY IN SEVEN MONTHS, AND ACCORDING TO MAYOR GILBERT ROCKEFELLER, "IT DOES NOT LOOK AS IF THE END IS IN SIGHT."
MEANWHILE, IN WASHINGTONTOWN, THE PRESIDENT DEPLORED THE NATION'S GROWING TREND TO VIOLENCE AND PROMISED IMMEDIATE STEPS TO HALT IT IN THE FUTURE. WITH THAT, HE SIGNED INTO LAW THE CONTROVERSIAL MANPOWER CONTROL BILL...

5-11-2037/DATELINE: BRAZIL. RIO DE JANEIRO. PRESI-DENT GARCIA TODAY ANNOUNCED THE CAPTURE OF THE NOTORIOUS RACE-CRIMINAL, DANA LEDGERTON (DL 571 50 5683) AT RIO DE JANEIRO AIRPORT. LEDGER-TON WAS ATTEMPTING TO BOARD AN AFRICAN-BOUND FLIGHT WHEN BRAZILIAN AGENTS SCOOPED HIM UP. HE IS BEING HELD IN RIO INDEFINITELY.
THE BRAZILIAN GOVERNMENT HAS ANNOUNCED IT IN-TENDS TO TRY LEDGERTON FOR THE CRIME OF GENOCIDE, AS WELL AS OTHER CRIMES AGAINST

HUMANITY. ANGRY CROWDS HAVE BEEN MILLING IN THE STREETS OF RIO EVER SINCE THE ANNOUNCEMENT OF LEDGERTON'S CAPTURE WAS MADE.

WORLDWIDE REACTION TO THE ANNOUNCEMENT WAS IMMEDIATE. IN THE UNITED STATES, THE PRESIDENT SAID . . .

MAY 5, 2040
REPORT TO THE WORLD HEALTH ORGANIZATION BY DR. JOYCE FREMM
MOST CONFIDENTIAL — TRANSCRIPTION OF REMARKS
Gentlemen,

Our recent studies on the enzyme synthesis program suggest that there is just no way to do what you ask — at least not without massive appropriations — and I, for one, am opposed to it.

(Pause)

If I may continue. . . . If I may continue. . . I'll wait. . . .

If the delegate from Nairobi will stop calling me a racist slime long enough to listen, I will explain my position. Any appropriations for the enzyme synthesis would have to be made at the expense of other programs — and the amount of money needed to do what the delegate from Nairobi wishes us to do would necessitate the closing down of almost every other United Nations Program now in existence, with the exception of the pollution board. And the pollution board is far more important than this!

If I may continue. . . . I believe that there is a way to save the human race, but enzyme synthesis is not it. In any case, a few years of minimal breeding will not hurt this planet any. There are about nineteen and a half billion too many people on Earth already.

5-11-2041/TIMEFAX
THE IRISH CIVIL WAR, WHICH HAS BEEN SMOULDERING FOR MORE THAN TWENTY YEARS, BURST INTO THE NEWS AGAIN TODAY WITH THE BURNING OF DUBLIN. THE CATHOLIC FACTION IN IRELAND CONTINUES TO CHARGE THAT THE NEO-PROTESTANT GOVERNMENT IS

WITHHOLDING THE ENZYME FROM CATHOLIC MOTHERS IN AN ATTEMPT TO REDUCE THE NUMBER OF CATHOLICS IN THE NATION. THAT CHARGE WAS ECHOED ACROSS THE GLOBE BY OTHER MINORITIES IN OTHER NATIONS. IN ISRAEL, THE ARAB AND LEBANESE NATIONALS CHARGED THE ISRAELI GOVERNMENT WITH DELIBERATE BIRTHCRIMES. THE JEWISH MINORITY IN THE SOVIET UNION LEVELED THE SAME CHARGE AGAINST THE KREMLIN. THE CHINESE MINORITIES IN MALAYSIA AND INDIA HAVE ALSO CHARGED THOSE TWO GOVERNMENTS WITH WITHHOLDING THE ENZYME.

THIS BRINGS TO A TOTAL OF FORTY-THREE, THE NUMBER OF COMPLAINTS REGISTERED WITH THE U.N. MINORITY PROCREATION CONTROL OFFICE.

MAY 19, 2041
TO: THE PRESIDENT OF THE UNITED STATES
FROM: WARREN J. HINDLER, HOOVER CENTER, WASHINGTON, D.C.

Mr. President,

The situation is becoming more and more serious every day. I have reports coming across my desk that indicate that the activists are planning to step up the number of urban disturbances within the next two months. This nation is headed for civil war unless some way is found to take the steam out of the Anti-Enzyme movement.

I would like to recommend immediate action along the following lines. . . .

MAY 20, 2041
POLICE REPORT, MANWEATHER COMPLEX

At 7:45 pm, Officers J.G. and R.F. investigated a complaint at 1456 Rafferty Avenue, Block 12, Apt 56-789. Investigating Officers found Donald Ruddigore in process of assaulting his wife, Alice. Woman had already sustained minor injuries.

Ruddigore explained that his wife had told him she was pregnent. As he had been infected with the Ledgerton Virus some years earlier, he knew that he could not be the father of the child, and he had only begun beating her when she refused to tell him who the real father was.

When questioned, Mrs. Ruddigore insisted that she has never copulated with anyone but her husband. Officer G. suggested that both Ruddigores see a County Clinician before the week was over.

Mr. Ruddigore became abusive at this and had to be forcibly restrained. He was booked at Station 12 (preventive detention) and released the following morning on his own recognizance. Mrs. Ruddigore spent the night at her sister's after being released from the Emergency Hospital, where she was treated for minor scalp injuries.

As he was being taken into custody, Mr. Ruddigore noted that he was "glad that whoever the bastard is, now he's got it too!"

MAY 38, 2041
TO: DR. JOYCE FREMM
FROM: DR. CARLOS WAN-LEE
Joyce,

I've had four physicians call me in the past two days wanting to know if someone is bootlegging enzyme or something. All of them report a number of women (with previously infected husbands) turning up unexpectedly pregnant. Yes, I know it sounds like adultery, but I suspect it is something more. I'd like to talk to you about it in detail. I think we should investigate this. Are you free for lunch?

5-14-2042/DATELINE:BRAZIL. IN RIO TODAY, A CROWD OF MORE THAN TEN THOUSAND FORMED IN FRONT OF THE LEDGERTON GALLOWS TO HOLD A MEMORIAL SERVICE FOR DANA LEDGERTON, WHO DIED FIVE YEARS AGO ON THIS SPOT. WHILE LEDGERTON'S NAME IS STILL REVILED IN MANY PARTS OF THE GLOBE, A GROWING NUMBER OF PEOPLE ARE BEGINNING TO REALIZE THAT NOT EVERY EFFECT OF THE LEDGERTON VIRUS IS NECESSARILY EVIL. THE BRAZILIAN BIRTH RATE, FOR EXAMPLE, HAS DROPPED TO A COMFORTABLE...

MAY 20, 2042
REPORT TO THE WORLD HEALTH ORGANIZATION BY
DR. JOYCE FREMM
TRANSCRIPTION OF REMARKS — FOR PUBLIC RELEASE

..what happened is this: The virus has mutated. It wasn't stable. Few viruses are.

We have, in the laboratories, taken the virus through a total of seven different mutations, each of which has a different effect on human fertility. At present, we have no way of stopping the virus completely, but if our early tests hold true, the human race will be able to stop worrying about its birth rate.

Ledgerton Virus sub-one reduces fertility to a scant 7%. Variety sub-two, which is currently sweeping the globe, raises that percentage to 53%. Certainly not what it was before, but high enough for two very determined people to start a baby, if they wish. The other varieties, which we've produced through careful bombardment of radiation (and other techniques), produce fertility levels ranging from 89% normal to 17%.

We can expect the virus to keep mutating at least once every four years. This is often enough to keep humanity from developing any kind of immunity to it. Also, it will hold the birth rate down, without keeping it dangerously depressed.

Gentlemen, without knowing it, Dr. Ledgerton seems to have stopped the population explosion.

MAY 43, 2045
TO: THE PRESIDENT OF THE UNITED STATES
FROM: THE SECRETARY OF INFORMATION
Mr. President,

Enclosed are samples of the publicity releases you requested.

You will note that we have taken great pains to minimize Ledgerton's homosexuality. As you said, "It wouldn't do to have an effeminate American hero."

Motivational Research indicates that the need for a new American hero is greater than ever now, especially since the recent Mexican defeat. For that reason, I urge that we initiate this program as soon as possible.

MAY 49, 2045
MINISTRY OF INFORMATION PAMPHLET
#354657-098
   . . . Singlehandedly, this determined little man stopped the population explosion, stopped it dead with a biological brake — then he set that same brake so that it would release gently, allowing the race to maintan itself, but to cease its cancerous growth. When the death rates level off in the next few generations to match the new birth rates, the Earth will enjoy an era of peace and prosperity such as it has never known before. . . .

MAY 4, 2046
TO: THE SECRETARY OF FINANCE
FROM: THE PRESIDENT OF THE UNITED STATES
Dear Jase,
   Sorry, but I'm going to have to ask you to quash your economic report on the primary causes of the current depression.
   You're probably correct that the economy's continued growth is a direct factor of the nation's population spiral — but we can't suggest that fact publicly without starting a minor panic. (Besides, anything which would reflect negatively on the Ledgerton Program would not be welcome in certain circles.)
   I would agree with your recommendations though, and if you will circulate copies of your report (privately) to the Vice President and to the Secretary of Commerce, and also to the Secretary of the Treasury, between us we can initiate some of the steps you recommend to keep our financial heads above water.
   And the sooner the better. This is an election year and we want to retain control of the House.

MAY 19, 2049
EXCERPT FROM *TODAY'S PSYCHOLOGY*
   . . . one of the effects is the disappearance of the term "unwanted child" from the language. There is no such thing any more as an unwanted child. All children are wanted. Just look at the crowd of adults standing by the fence at any playground today.

Of course, not all the cultural changes are so beneficent. For instance, in the past, the pregnancy of an unmarried girl could quite likely have been the result of a mistake. Today, it can only be the result of several nights of steady "mistakes."

However, now that the onus of pregnancy has been removed from intercourse, certain other moral conventions are vanishing. Women are enjoying a sexual freedom even greater than that of the late twentieth century, when use of the oral contraceptive became widespread.

In general, the population of the nation is more birth-conscious than ever before, and one of the side effects has been a reduced tolerance for social and sexual deviants. Homosexuals have been driven out of several cities, and there is some reason to believe that this trend will continue for some time. . . .

5-6-2050/TIMEFAX
. . .FOUND BEATEN TO DEATH IN AN ALLEY. THE MAN WAS LATER IDENTIFIED AS PAUL-JOHN MURDOCK, A VAGRANT. POLICE SUSPECT THE BEATING DEATH IS JUST ONE MORE IN A SERIES OF "ANTI-FAGGOT" INCIDENTS THAT HAVE RACKED URBANA IN RECENT MONTHS.

5-10-2053/TIMEFAX
. . .THE PRESIDENT ANNOUNCED TODAY A NEW STAMP COMMEMORATING THE WORK OF DR. DANA LEDGERTON, CONSTRUCTOR OF THE FERTILITY VIRUS. THE STAMP WILL GO ON SALE IN FOUR DAYS, TIMED TO COINCIDE WITH THE SIXTEENTH ANNIVERSARY OF HIS DEATH. . . .

JEFFREY M. ELLIOT is the author of over 30 books and 450 articles, reviews, and interviews. His work has appeared in more than 250 publications, both in this country and abroad, and has been nominated for several literary awards. In the science fiction-fantasy field, he is perhaps best known for his feature interviews with noted authors, editors, publishers, and artists. His articles have appeared in nearly 40 genre publications, among them: *Future Life*, *Starlog*, *Galileo*, *Starship*, *Amazing*, *Science Fiction Review*, *Foundation*, and *Whispers*. He has published numerous science fiction-fantasy works, including: *Science Fiction Voices*, *Fantasy Voices*, *Pulp Voices*, and *Science Fiction Masters*. He is presently a contributing editor of *Spectrum Stories*, a new national circulation science fiction magazine, and the *SFWA Bulletin*, the official publication of the Science Fiction Writers of America.

Also available from Alyson

Don't miss our *free* book offer at the end of this section.

☐ **ONE TEENAGER IN TEN: Writings by gay and lesbian youth,** edited by Ann Heron, $3.95. One teenager in ten is gay; here, twenty-six young people tell their stories: of coming to terms with being different, of the decision how — and whether — to tell friends and parents, and what the consequences were.

☐ **THE BUTTERSCOTCH PRINCE,** by Richard Hall, $4.95. When Cordell's best friend and ex-lover is murdered, the only clue is one that the police seem to consider too kinky to follow up on. So Cordell decides to track down the killer himself — with results far different from what he had expected.

☐ **A DIFFERENT LOVE,** by Clay Larkin, $4.95. There have been heterosexual romance novels for years; now here's a gay one. When Billy and Hal meet in a small midwestern town, they feel sure that their love for each other is meant to last. But then they move to San Francisco, and the temptations of city life create complications they haven't had to face before.

☐ **THE LAW OF RETURN,** by Alice Bloch, $7.95. The widely-praised novel of a woman who, returning to Israel, regains her Jewish heritage while also claiming her voice as a woman and as a lesbian. "Clear, warm, haunting and inspired" writes Phyllis Chesler. "I want to read everything Alice Bloch writes," adds Grace Paley.

☐ **BETWEEN FRIENDS,** by Gillian E. Hanscombe, $6.95. Frances and Meg were friends in school years ago; now Frances is a married housewife while Meg is a lesbian involved in progressive politics. Through letters written between these women and their friends, the author weaves an engrossing story while exploring many vital lesbian and feminist issues.

☐ **IRIS,** by Janine Veto, $6.95. When Iris and Dee meet in Hawaii, they both know that this is the relationship they have each been looking for; all they want is to live together on this island paradise forever. But the world has other plans, and Iris is forced to fleet to a desolate Greek island. When they are united, Iris and Dee find that their love must now face a formidable foe if it is to survive.

☐ **ROCKING THE CRADLE: Lesbian mothers, a challenge in family living,** by Gillian E. Hanscombe and Jackie Forster, $5.95. A look at both the social and personal aspects of lesbian motherhood; the implications of artificial insemination by donor; and how children feel about growing up with lesbian mothers.

☐ **ALL-AMERICAN BOYS,** by Frank Mosca, $4.95. "I've known that I was gay since I was thirteen. Does that surprise you? It didn't me...." So begins *All-American Boys,* the story of a teenage love affair that should have been simple — but wasn't.

☐ **THE MOVIE LOVER,** by Richard Friedel, $6.95. The entertaining coming-out story of Burton Raider, who is so elegant that as a child he reads *Vogue* in his playpen. "The writing is fresh and crisp, the humor often hilarious," writes the *L.A. Times.*

☐ **CHINA HOUSE,** by Vincent Lardo, $4.95. This gay gothic romance/mystery has everything: two handsome lovers, a mysterious house on the hill, sounds in the night, and a father-son relationship that's closer than most.

☐ **THE ALEXANDROS EXPEDITION,** by Patricia Sitkin, $5.95. When Evan Talbot leaves on a mission to rescue an old schoolmate who has been imprisoned by fanatics in the Middle East, he doesn't realize that the trip will also involve his own coming out and the discovery of who it is that he really loves.

☐ **DECENT PASSIONS,** by Michael Denneny, $6.95. What does it mean to be in love? Do the joys outweigh the pains? Those are some of the questions explored here as Denneny talks with a gay male couple, a lesbian couple, and a straight couple about all the little things that make up a relationship.

□ **REFLECTIONS OF A ROCK LOBSTER: A story about growing up gay,** by Aaron Fricke, $4.95. When Aaron Fricke took a male date to the senior prom, no one was surprised: he'd gone to court to be able to do so, and the case had made national news. Here Aaron tells his story, and shows what gay pride can mean in a small New England town.

□ **YOUNG, GAY AND PROUD,** edited by Sasha Alyson, $2.95. Here is the first book ever to address the needs and problems of a mostly invisible minority: gay youth. Questions about coming out to parents and friends, about gay sexuality and health care, about finding support groups, are all answered here; and several young people tell their own stories.

□ **COMING OUT RIGHT, A handbook for the gay male,** by Wes Muchmore and William Hanson, $5.95. The first steps into the gay world — whether it's a first relationship, a first trip to a gay bar, or coming out at work — can be full of unknowns. This book will make it easier. Here is advice on all aspects of gay life for both the inexperienced and the experienced.

Talk Back!

The Gay Person's Guide to Media Action

Lesbian and Gay Media Advocates

Get this book free!

When were you last outraged by prejudiced media coverage of gay people? Chances are it hasn't been long. *Talk Back!* tells how you, in surprisingly little time, can do something about it.

If you order at least three other books from us, you may request a FREE copy of this important book. (See order form on next page.)

To get these books:

Ask at your favorite bookstore for the books listed here. You may also order by mail. Just fill out the coupon below, or use your own paper if you prefer not to cut up this book.

GET A FREE BOOK! When you order any three books listed here at the regular price, you may request a *free* copy of *Talk Back!*

BOOKSTORES: Standard trade terms apply. Details and catalog available on request.

Send orders to: **Alyson Publications, Inc.**
PO Box 2783, Dept. B-42
Boston, MA 02208

— — — — — — — — — — — — — — — —

Enclosed is $_____ for the following books. (Add $1.00 postage when ordering just one book; if you order two or more, we'll pay the postage.)

_____

_____

_____

_____

_____

_____

☐ Send a free copy of *Talk Back!* as offered above. I have ordered at least three other books.

name:_____

address:_____

city:_____ state:_____ zip:_____

ALYSON PUBLICATIONS
PO Box 2783, Dept. B-42, Boston, Mass. 02208

This offer expires June 30, 1985. After that date, please write for current catalog.